IDYLLS OF THE COLLAR

MARY SHEERAN

Wingspan Press

The quotes from the Hebrew Bible textbook are from *The Hebrew Bible: A Socio-Literary Introduction* by Norman Gottwald, Fortress Press, 1987. With my thanks to the late and wondrous Professor Gottwald.

I am grateful to Kristi Duarte, Kate Henderson Kresse, and Merritt McKeon for their suggestions tactfully blended with encouragements and to Cate Perry, who edited the manuscript with keen eyes and a sensitive heart.

Published in the United States and the United Kingdom
by WingSpan Press, Livermore, CA

The WingSpan name, logo and colophon are the trademarks
of WingSpan Publishing.

ISBN 978-1-63683-067-4 (pbk.)
ISBN 978-1-63683-488-7 (hardcover.)
ISBN 978-1-63683-945-5 (ebook)

Printed in the United States of America

www.wingspanpress.com

For Hilda Regier
who simply asked if I wanted to join a church choir.

And for
Chelsea Community Church
NYC
Who took me in
No matter what.

"For we have to ask ourselves, here and now, do we
wish to join that [academic] procession, or don't we?
On what terms shall we join that procession?
Above all, where is it leading us,
the procession of educated men?"

– Virginia Woolf *(3 Guineas)*

PRELUDE

I must watch myself when I put my foot down off a curb. My right foot is usually the problem, but I wouldn't say the left is free of any responsibility.

I think this is how it started.

Back when my father was "Daddy," he took my hand and led me to the bottom of the little hill that sloped down from our house to the street. And he said, "When you cross the street, you look both ways. All the time. You look right and you look left. We're near a corner, and a car can turn that you don't see at first. You look right and left." (This was how I learned, by the way, which side was right and which side was left.)

He didn't forbid me to cross the street at all because there were too many kids who lived on the other side of the street, and he knew we'd be going back and forth. He put my older sister, Jules, in charge of me, but that was not going to work because Jules wandered around by herself, in her own world, so I had to be in charge of myself. My brother Dirk was at the stage when all he cared about was a ball, a bat, and his cronies. He wouldn't have seen or cared if I ran into the street.

Crossing the street is tricky stuff because I had to pay attention to where I was going, so I wouldn't trip. Our road hadn't been fully paved yet and it wasn't quite even. I learned to pause when facing forward to see where my feet were going.

Daddy practiced with me over and over and then watched me cross the street by myself a few times.

Stepping off the curb could mean instant death. He didn't say that, but I figured it out.

"Okay, you know how to do it," he said to me. "I'm proud of you.

You cross the street just like that no matter what any of the other kids are doing."

One day not long after, Mom and I went across the street to visit Mrs. Mayer, an elderly lady with a hefty laugh who loved to gossip. I sat politely, as usual, listening and trying to understand, and looking at the landscape paintings on the wall. Then, glancing out Mrs. Mayer's big window, I noticed a few girls playing across the street in the Inningers' yard. Grandpa Inninger didn't mind our playing in his yard and fields if we didn't damage anything. I wanted to go and play with them now, not listen to Mom and Mrs. Mayer. Mom, perhaps not thinking that I'd have to cross the street, said it was okay. Or maybe she didn't want me to hear Mrs. Mayer's stories. I hate to think that she didn't care, but that thought has crossed my mind more than once.

I hurried out the door, I waved at the girls and darted across the street. A car screeched to a stop inches from me. I looked up into the windshield. The driver looked scared to death. Her eyes and mouth were wide open, and she was really gripping the steering wheel. I waved at her and ran over to the girls, but before I reached them, one of them yelled, "Hey, you could have been killed!"

That stopped me. I didn't want to play anymore. I ran up our driveway and across our lawn and into our house. The side door was always open. I ran through the living room and up the stairs and flung myself onto my bed.

I could have died.

My mother had not heard the screeching tires or known that I'd almost died. But what if she had heard? What if she still didn't come?

I felt alone in the universe. No one had been there to help me. Not even my guardian angel, whom I prayed to every night.

And I had forgotten what Daddy had told me.

Stepping off curbs could be the end of me.

Left, right, front.

Watch.

CHAPTER 1

JULY 1993

"What, Mom?" I asked, leaning over her. I looked down at her thin face, her straw-like hair, her arm with the sagging skin, the plastic tube straddling her nostrils.

She was so weak, but her hand held mine as tightly as it could.

"I want the priest."

"I know. I called the rectory and told them. He's busy."

Mom wanted a priest to bring her communion. I felt annoyed at her for insisting on a priest because the Catholics didn't allow women to *be* priests. But my mother had her faith, she was dying of lung cancer, so I kept calling and asking for the parish priest to come. Sister Yvonne showed up instead.

"I want the priest," Mom kept saying.

I don't know why. I'd gone to church with my parents on my trips from New York over the years, and their priest barely spoke to the people, not even greeting them at the door when they were leaving. Mom always criticized his sermons. When she'd been in the hospital last year, she'd sent the nurse out to bring him in. He came in all right, poked his head through the door and said, "I'm sorry. I only go to my parishioners."

For all of that, Mom still wanted him. I supposed that for her it wasn't real communion unless a priest gave it to her. That the fingers that consecrated the host should give her the host.

I sat up, still holding her hand.

3

"I'll call again."

She eased her head back on the sofa pillows.

Her day now consisted of roaming the apartment from bed to sofa, winding the long nasogastric tube around the dining area to get to the living room couch. The tube led to a four-foot-tall oxygen tank that breathed throughout our apartment.

She'd been a lifelong Catholic, come hell, corruption, or Vatican 2. In our old parish, the one where I'd grown up, she'd been active in the Altar Rosary Society and the choir, and the priest had been a friend. Once we were all out of school and they moved to Ohio, she took up golf, spending a lot of time with her friends on the course. But she and Dad attended church every Sunday. She never gave up smoking.

I called the rectory.

"I want to speak to Father Jennings."

"He's in a meeting."

"Please ask him to call."

"Have you made your pledge yet?"

I hung up.

He didn't call. After a few tries and listening to requests for a pledge, I located a church bulletin in a drawer and found the number for a woman in charge of the Altar Rosary Society. I called her.

"My mother is dying. She is a life-long dedicated Catholic, and she would like to have Father Jennings come one time – just one time – to give her communion. Okay, she hasn't given a lot of money, and my parents didn't pledge this year, have you heard of medical bills, but they used to, and Dad donated free Pepsi to *Mr.* Jennings. She has cancer, and cancer care is expensive. I hope you never have to find that out. But *Mr.* Jennings won't return our calls. Not even to say no."

"What do you want me to do about it?"

I couldn't believe this.

I said, "I'm a writer from New York. I'll be writing a letter to the town newspaper. He is supposed to visit the sick."

"He has plenty of meetings and other obligations."

"My mother is his chief obligation."

I wasn't lying. I was a writer. I lived in New York, and I wrote for a medical journal. And thank goodness, this Ohio town had a newspaper. I knew it liked religious news. They'd covered the story about "the vision" for two weeks a few months before. Ah, "the vision." People looking at paint peeling off a building in the moonlight thinking it was a vision of Saint Joseph holding the baby Jesus, and people came from miles around to see it! Even *Newsweek* picked that up.

The woman on the phone said, "Oh, well, you don't have to do that."

Indeed, after about two hours, the late Father Jennings called me, mumbling about his meetings. I had no sympathy.

"You are a priest," I hissed. "You are not taking the right meetings. You should be grateful my mother really does want you to come."

When he arrived at my mother's sofa, after a few polite words, and possibly confusing her with me, he asked her, "Why are you angry at God?"

And let me be clear, I was not angry at God. I was angry at Father Jennings. The two are not interchangeable.

But my mother, she pushed herself up on the mostly skin and bones for arms, and she had to take five breaths to reply to him, and her angry reply brought the man to tears. And me.

"God is...get...ting...me...through...this."

I will never have my mother's faith. Never.

He took my mother's hands and he said, "Peggy, you bring God to me."

I forgave him then. We helped her sit up to receive communion, and she believed, I knew, from the hope and the faith in her eyes, and I wondered if I would ever have that faith again, faith lost somewhere between...well, I forget. Just lost.

Father Jennings came every week from then on. He always stayed just below an hour, sometimes just holding her hand.

He told this story at her funeral. To me he said, "She changed my life. I'm not kidding. Oh, me of little faith."

Mom was a priest that day, don't you think? She didn't change the bread into Christ's body, or maybe she did, but she did change an idiot priest into realizing what his job was.

I was, to be honest, disappointed in her for preferring a man to give her communion, a man with a collar, but she was from another generation. She thought most of the Vatican 2 changes were idiotic. She clung to her faith in the pre-Vatican church – well, it *had* lasted for centuries – the Latin masses, the old hymns, the strict requirements for fasting, and she wore a hat to church until she had to stop going.

I confess, I missed those days, too. I'd loved the mystery of the Latin Mass, the ceremony, the sense that God was present. Then came Vatican 2, and we were singing, "He's Got the Whole World in His Hands" over and over for months of Sundays with guitarists from a local rock group until we got new hymnals and monthly "missalettes" with the Mass in English. We knew the priest was puzzled and confused because he faced us now. We could see his confusion. Instead of the mystery of what he did, we could see he was just like us.

Mass had been personal for us long before, kneeling to that Latin, listening to gorgeous music that went deep into our souls, knowing all Masses around the world used the same language, and what that meant to us. Our souls participated. Vatican 2 wanted participation, but we had been participating. Hadn't they known that?

Along with Catholics of my generation, however, I leaped into the new ideas when I thought they were good. In college, I sang in a folk group, and I took part in Masses where we sat on the floor and shared feelings during the sermon. Even so, my anger grew at my Catholic faith that felt it was fine for women to bake the bread and clean the table but not good enough to hold the bread and consecrate it. My anger grew more when I found myself arguing with a priest on campus duty.

"God made people in His," and I quickly shifted the pronoun, "Her image."

"His image. Man is made in God's image," said the priest. "That's in the Bible."

"In English," I said. "It also says that God says 'Let us go down' to see the humans made in their image. Male and female. Women are also in God's image."

"No, no, no. God created women as an afterthought. To help Adam."

He wasn't kidding.

That was when I left the male concept of the Blessed Virgin behind in favor of a powerful Cosmic Mother. It took some mental adjustment, but once I'd said "She" often enough, the earth looked different. It just did. It was brighter, the people more real, the sun and moon more brilliant. When I welcomed God the Mother into my public prayers during Mass I got funny looks when I changed "Lord" in the psalms to "Mother," and changed all of God's pronouns to "She." Well, I alternated, thinking "He" should get equal time. I got laughed at, nervous laughter, perhaps because I was invading the Holy of Holies or something. It was college; we were supposed to be doing things like this, but I was the only one doing *this*. Was I the only person who felt this way? Why didn't my friends feel more powerful by calling God by feminine pronouns? Why did they feel threatened? Or moved to laugh at me?

When I moved to New York City, I felt alone and isolated. I was angry that the American church hadn't split from Rome and its archaic and unforgiving "doctrines." I did a lot of things those days – performed in musical revues, did an off-off Broadway play, sang leads in operas since Broadway didn't like lyric sopranos for almost a decade, preferring belters, screamers, and little girl voices. I took a lot of jobs that liked fast typists. That eventually led to editing and writing jobs, then to a job writing medical history columns for a journal while I sang in small groups and played the cabaret circuit.

I would come into Manhattan on Saturdays to browse bookstores, and I found "feminist theologians," and I bought and reveled in these books unveiling the history of goddesses and also of important women in Christian history. The world around me was struggling with what the Equal Rights Amendment meant, and one day, coming out of the subway, I encountered signs that said, "Woman are human beings," and I was stunned. Because for some reason, that was a shocking thing to see. I was used to thinking that women were above all that. The shock of that sign told me that I was as caught up with male superiority and that my feminist theological quest at the time was akin to trying to catch up to the boys.

Oh, no.

Well, this was all in my head. I had no place to work out these ideas. Until.

When I moved from Queens to Manhattan, a freelancer on my journal turned out to be a neighbor, and she stopped me when I passed her house walking to the grocery store.

"How would you like to join a church choir?"

Ruth. Scrawny, fiftyish, energetic, shrewd Ruth. How did she know that my mother was dying, and I needed – something. So, I joined the church choir, which turned out to be of a Protestant church that had done away with ministers. Imagine! How many mortal sins did I catch when I joined this group? Lay people led the service and cared for each other, and they hired preachers from all different denominations to give the sermons.

I had stopped reading the Bible when I came to the part where Lot wanted to throw his daughters out to the crowd, but listening to these speakers, I realized that the Bible contained fascinating stories. And ethics. And social justice. All one needed was insight into the conditions under which they were written. And, as some of my feminist scholarly reading had revealed, the Bible make references to the female god and to goddesses. Even at the creation of humanity.

Perhaps I should try again. Perhaps I could go home and see old things as new.

Churches love newcomers, so they elected me president. I wished I could have called my mother, but she had been gone for three months, and my father wouldn't have cared.

"Hey, Mom, I'm head of a church!"

She would have laughed, but she would have been sad that I wasn't still a Catholic.

My little church rented space from Saint Philip's, an Episcopal church, and I decided to try its more liturgical service for Easter. It was as close to a Catholic Mass as I could get, and I wanted to honor Mom's faith.

The procession came up the aisle and I realized that, whereas the smiling Vicar, Rick Campbell, was a man, the celebrant that day was a woman, a Mother Frances. This tall woman came last in the processional.

There she stood, behind the altar like any priest doing what every priest does, including the holding the host and the chalice at the Consecration and giving a magnificent sermon – I couldn't tell you what it was, because I was falling over onto the seat of my pew and physically trembling, and when communion came and she offered the host to everyone, one by one, I couldn't go up. Not because I was a baptized Catholic. These Episcopalians welcomed everybody. Mother Frances said so. Nothing like the "unless you are…" note in Catholic missals, barring any nonbaptized Catholic.

I felt my mother, I wanted to call out to her, "Look! Look!" I wondered if she would understand. We'd never spoken about it, and she had wanted communion from a Catholic priest. Was it because the priest was a man? Or that he was highest on the parish totem pole? Or just because a priest coming would show her respect? We'd never spoken about it.

Someone tapped my shoulder.

I picked myself up and turned.

"Are you all right?" a man whispered. A big man.

I nodded, tried to smile.

"It's – she's doing that."

It's all I could say. For I could be her.

The guy nodded. "Yeah. Peace." He patted my hand. "I'm Peter."

She was doing every single thing that men had done for centuries, and the earth did not tremble. I thought of the wasted talent, the stupidity of frightened men.

The congregation stood, but I knelt as the priest blessed us. As *she* blessed us. And Rick Campbell, the Vicar, stood at her side, smiling, not the least bit threatened by her presence.

We were all just people.

They were singing the last hymn and coming down the aisle. I tried to sing. Couldn't.

But I rose.

CHAPTER 2

JULY 1993

T he last Sunday in July was the last service for the Community Church until September. I was thrilled. There would be only three weeks until my stint as president would be over. I loved them, but I needed to explore the world I had re-entered.

But as for the fancy that I could be "called" to be a priest, well, that was silly. Lost in a romantic sea of possibility, I had checked. Alas, to begin a "process," that is, the journey toward ordination, one had to be sponsored by a church that was part of a denomination. My church was independent. It was a church because it said so.

I didn't have anyone to talk to about this feeling, this strong push saying move move move. But move where and how?

It's just a silly fancy. I'd been reading a book called *Defecting in Place*, about women claiming responsibility for their own spiritual lives that church could not fulfill, and while that seemed a lonely quest, I really felt that was to be my own path. I would be a church unto me, in other words. But how lonely was that?

Then, on the last Sunday of July, Dr. Richard Forrest gave the sermon. He wasn't much of a speaker, he spoke softly and almost without inflection, but what he said…!

Now my understanding of Moses leading the former Israelite slaves from Egypt to the promised land pretty much centered on Charlton Heston and the *Ten Commandments* movie. Dr. Forrest, based on his scholarship that he briefly outlined, viewed this event from a sociological perspective. Canaan – the promised land – had been divided into oppressive city-states, and people of those city-states eventually joined with the incoming Israelites to create a revolution – and a new land. And as he told this story, he remarked, briefly, about the feminine aspect of Yahweh. Just a glimpse, then gone, but it hit my spine and I knew it was another nudge aimed at me.

I knew I wanted to study the Old Testament – or, as he called it, the Hebrew Bible – with him.

It wasn't just what he said. It was the collision in my head with the feminist theologians emerging from more inclusive theology departments. I'd weep while reading them at the liberation of my own soul as it began to peek out and say, "I am here, too, and I deserve to be here."

It was a new time, women getting ordained in several denominations, women speaking out, women being the voice of churches. With them came whole new ways to think about things Biblical and church.

I burrowed into Elisabeth Schussler Fiorenza's *In Memory of Her*. The German scholar shared the same sociologic vocabulary of Dr. Forrest– all those models, hermeneutics, and frameworks. But I read. And here was her point:

The historical role of women, and not that of men, is problematic because maleness is the norm, while femaleness constitutes a deviation from this norm. (p.42)

Now was the time to change that norm.

Dr. Forrest taught at the New York Theological Seminary. I hadn't heard of that place, but when I looked into it, I was delighted. All the classes were at night because most of the student body worked or were pastors and could only come in the evenings. Seventy-five percent of the student body were African American men and women. Ten percent were, like me, white women. Ten percent were Asian men and women. This was New York City. This was the United States.

I needed to hear other voices.

As for a call or whatever? I would wait to see what happened.

I called the school and asked if I could audit a class taught by Dr. Forrest.

"There's the Introduction to the Hebrew Bible," said the registrar. "That would be two hundred dollars to audit."

Two hundred? To study with Dr. Forrest? What a bargain!

"Monday nights," she said. "It's a large class, so we rent space from General Seminary."

Even better. The Episcopal seminary was a few blocks from my apartment.

"I'm signing up," I said.

And that was that.

But life was going on back in Ohio with Dad.

Some woman who had not had any contact with my father since the late 1960s – she'd been a friend in the town I grew up in but from which we'd moved – called him up and invited him to visit her!

He drove from Ohio to Virginia and back to Ohio.

And called me up.

"I'm going to marry Helen Trackowitz," he said.

"You're going to what? Who?" Had I gotten amnesia for a year?

"You remember her. She went to our parish. She was in your mother's bridge club."

Your mother. Not Peggy. Now I knew there was trouble.

"What? When?"

"Probably around October. I have a lot of things to do here."

"What things?"

"I'm moving to her place. I'll have to get rid of a lot of stuff here."

"Dad! It's so soon!"

What stuff?

"Don't worry. When you get to be my age, you don't want to dally. You remember her. It's not like she's a stranger."

I had no idea what to say. I'd never had my father want to get married before.

"I want what makes you happy," I said.

Did I?

Dirk called me up ten minutes later.

"Do you believe that crap? That whore?"

Whore? The woman was in her sixties.

"She went right for him."

"Well, he is a catch," I said. "All those widows were after him."

"He shouldn't be doing this. I'm going to stop it."

If anyone could talk to Dad, Dirk could. They'd been pals all Dirk's life. He was the son, the lawyer, he could do no wrong.

CHAPTER 3

SEPTEMBER 1993

I was only auditing this class. I didn't have to do anything except sit and listen. But I could not contain my excitement at being handed a twenty-five-page, single-spaced syllabus.

I wanted to explore every nook and cranny.

I could already feel my imagination lighting up.

Professor Forrest's soft voice drew me and the others in as did his conviction.

After the lecture, the leader of the small group to which I was assigned, Maria Vega, proved to be a down-to-earth human. A short young woman with short blonde hair, she was a graduate student at Columbia and was writing her thesis about ancient seals, carved hundreds of years before Christ, yet with pictures that resembled Gospel stories. One showed two women standing at what looked to be a tomb. These women, she explained, were two goddesses grieving a god who had died, and they were waiting for his coming to life again.

This hit a few students hard, and they just muttered, "Coincidence." I didn't say anything, but I felt a door open to a whole world that understood the story and the hope of spring returning with women spreading the story. Just like the Gospels.

I was going to be challenged. I was going to listen.

As I crowded with the other students on the way out, someone tapped me on the shoulder. Turning, I saw a woman with a pixie face and an owlish look – the glasses, I realized – with a long, thick braid down her back. Like me, she was one of the few white people in class.

13

"You go to the Community Church across the street, don't you?"

How did she know that?

"Yes…"

"I'm Meg Madigan. I worship at Saint Philip's."

Not "I go to Saint Philip's" but "I worship at Saint Philip's."

I tried to remember if I'd seen this Meg among the hundred or so people leaving the church while we were going in.

"Sure, I think I've seen you. I'm Janene Shannon."

"Which way are you going? I'm heading to Fifth Avenue for a downtown bus."

"I go as far as Seventh."

We crossed Ninth Avenue. I tried to think of something to say.

She said it as we dodged a turning car. "Does Community Church ordain people?"

"Oh, no," I said. "I'm just auditing."

"This? This is the toughest course in the school."

We'd reached the corner, and as I stepped up to the sidewalk, she beat me to it and practically glared at me. "Are you trying to avoid getting grades?"

Well, say what you think, dammit.

"I'm interested in the Old Testament. Not everybody has to be ordained. You do, I assume?"

"You want to be ordained," said Meg. It was like an order.

I just laughed, and I switched the topic. My choice, or hope, was a private thing now. "Doctor Forrest is the top Biblical scholar in the country."

"How do you know that?"

"He preached at Community."

"I hope he preached better than he lectures. What a monotone."

I looked across the street at the old tower of Saint Philip's. Back in its nineteenth century day, it must have been an impressive structure, a Gothic church with a bell and clock tower soaring above the neighborhood.

"He talked about the feminine aspect of Yahweh. Really interesting. Why do you want to enter Holy Orders? What's the path to being a priest?"

"Funny you should put it that way. I used to be a nun. Yes, I'm

14

on the ordination path, no, I should say process. I'd love a path. Tree shaded, pretty flowers, benches, a forest nearby."

"Do you think God is calling you?" I had to ask.

"I've got a gut feeling that says I must, I must, I must. I couldn't tell you if it's God."

We dashed across Eighth Avenue before the light changed.

"I used to be Catholic, too," I said. "Unless I still am as the catechism says and I'm deep in mortal sin for missing all those Sundays since college. What do you have to do to be a priest?"

"An Episcopal priest," Meg said. "Oh, dear God, it's so convoluted. And they're still figuring things out now that they're ordaining women. As soon as I took off my veil, I couldn't be Catholic anymore."

"And you let your hair grow."

She laughed, a throaty, almost a choking sound. "Yes, I grew back all the hair I'd missed for so long. And I got married – to an ex-priest, but he died. Cancer."

"I'm so sorry."

"That was in Ohio. I moved here. I teach English at a Catholic boys' high school uptown."

"Do they mind that you wandered off the prairie?"

"I haven't said. They just assume I stayed Catholic."

"I still don't understand why women just don't walk out."

"They're hopeful, poor things. You're an ex, too?"

"I used to be. When I was in college, I thought the American church would break off with Rome. No, they just wallow in whatever you say, holy daddy. That is, the few who chose to stay."

"We have lots of ex-Catholics at Saint Philip's. A lot are gay men who just threw up their hands at it all. Or the church kicked their support organization out."

"My mother stayed until her dying breath. So, you had to strip off the veil and the habit?",

Meg did a sexy twist, her braid dancing around her shoulders. It seemed to have a life of its own, like a serpent's.

We were lingering over the movie posters of the theater just before the corner.

I said, "I spent the summer reading feminist theology. I stumbled on this whole section at the Barnes and Noble on Sixth. Wow. Carol

Christ, Audre Lord, Elisabeth Fiorenza, Merlin Stone, and even some Native American and Greek mythologies. I read all of Robert Graves' Greek mythology volumes. His footnotes are fascinating."

"I don't like myths, but I do like Merlin Stone and Audre Lord. Yes, the clouds have opened up and there's a whole bunch of women's voices being heard now. What a time to live in." Then she turned toward me. "Auditing? I Don't think you're doing this just for fun."

We started walking again, toward Seventh Avenue.

"You're doing this because you think you might want to get ordained. Right?"

"I'm doing this to be free," I said. "Free of grades."

"I'm doing this to be free, too," said Meg. "Free of this annoying voice in me that says I should do this."

We had reached the corner of Seventh Avenue, a few steps from my building. I could have said goodbye then, but I didn't want to. I wanted to keep talking.

"But you must have a call. What's that's like?"

Meg laughed. "That's so esoteric, Jan. Can I call you Jan? The Episcopal process is lined with dragons and fire pits all along the way. First you have to get in as a postulant. That's where I am. No, not even that, not even at step one. I'm an aspirant. Thanks to my nun education, though, I'm almost through with seminary except for a few courses. And thank God, I found a great parish to be in. You have to go through a period of discernment to formally decide. The Vestry votes on you."

"The Vestry is Saint Philip's governing body?"

"Yup."

"But how do you measure a person's call? It's so ephemeral. They make it so mystical, as if God speaks to you in a field or from a burning bush. There's a ray of light, and there you are, falling on your knees. How do you even describe such a thing? And if you did, wouldn't they decide you're a nutcase?"

"The Vestry would unanimously vote me a nut case." Meg laughed. "I lost one vote, but I was still in. After that, the Rector – that's Rick Campbell, you know – he submits your name to the Canon – the officer - who oversees the process and then the wheel starts to turn. Mine hasn't turned yet. Three members of the Commission on Ministry interview you, and if they like you, you get scheduled for a convocation of sorts, a weekend where the members of the Commission interview all the aspirants. Then they vote on you. If they like you, then you get an appointment with the bishop. And if *he* likes you, and only then, then you're in the process. You go to seminary, you write the bishop on Ember Days or something like that, and on you go. It's supposed to take three years, but there are shortcuts."

It sounded terribly complicated. "But you're going to seminary."

She shrugged. "Yeah. I just have to take four courses and then a class on Episcopal church history. I thought I'd get it all done. People do that in different orders, and the diocese likes it if you do it their way. But it's political. It's all political. They just yak about a call from God. Oh, there comes my bus. Where are you going?"

I pointed to my building. "There. Nice meeting you."

"Come to Saint Philip's," she said, as the bus pulled up. "We're fun. And you won't be in charge of anything!"

"Don't tempt me!" I called as she climbed on.

As I walked to my door, I reflected on how cold those process steps seemed. How can one measure how close to God you are? How does anyone measure it so that the Bishop of New York would understand? It seemed political. God was calling, not the bishop, right? Or so some said. Women only started to be ordained in the past twenty years, and now all of a sudden, we're getting calls from God?

What about all the women before who had those calls?

Back in my apartment, I sat on the sofa in my tiny living room and thought. I liked Meg. It was as if God had reached down and given me a big sister. I would go to Saint Philip's service. I was unsure about a lot of things, but I'd found a stimulating world and had made a stimulating friend. I could see her as a priest. But I couldn't see me as her, though I wanted to be. Sure, smart, determined, strong.

That wasn't me.

CHAPTER 4

The Episcopal service reminded me of the Catholic Mass of my childhood. Not the Latin mass but the post Vatican 2 Mass (once it settled down), with everything in English. Even so, the feeling of respect for mystery, for something beyond us, reminded me of the best of that old, now- forbidden- after-two-thousand-years, Latin Mass.

The symbolism and ritual at Saint Philip's jogged my memory and my heart, as did the seriousness, or I should say reverence. But there were also smiles from Father Rick Campbell and the altar party. As opposed to the priests' rattling off words as if they had no meaning, which I was familiar with from my Catholic days, Father Rick spoke the words with care as if they were being said for the first time.

Those words reminded me who I was and that I was part of not only to the ceremony I was observing but to its past, a past that hurtled back to a time when God walked the earth, an eternal now, one that encompasses past, present, and future. Yet I cautioned myself: these words I now heard and the gestures and movements that went with them were close enough to younger, safer times when I went to Mass with my family, once a whole family. The words were that close to old secure days. Contrarily, I also felt as if I stood on a cliff, alone, watching the beauty of the earth beneath. A bit like being at Yosemite, climbing alone up to the top of the waterfalls. Safe and dangerous at the same time, God always present.

Mother Frances had transferred to Chicago. I was sorry to hear that.

Father Rick gave the sermon. I felt the poetry and the urgent call to Now. Listening, I felt strong, confident.

...The women and men of God are more often those who have encountered the deepest darkness in themselves and in the world.

18

The gospel paradox is that in the same moment…that same light takes them into God's life and transforms them into uniquely powerful instruments of salvation."

"Times of transition are difficult…But the stormy, painful time can also be times of real growth, real spiritual growth. In our transition we can, if we will, if we have faithful eyes, see beyond that whirlwind, to the gift that God is. Now.

…I think out of the forge of life here, God has planned such things, rare beasts, unique experiences, as will part the waters before us. Please…feel the body we are, working together. Feel the love we bear one another – the often difficult love – and those around us reach out. That love is Christ. And nothing will ever separate us from that love. Indeed, we will be upbuilt by that love, into whatever God is now calling us to become. Wow."

And the sign of the peace! Back in Catholic days, the words, "Let us offer each other a sign of peace" simply meant smiling at people around you, maybe reluctantly shaking hands, and it lasted a minute if that. It always felt awkward and forced. Nobody wanted to do it.

But at Saint Philip's, everybody charged into the aisle like a grand homecoming with people hugging as if they hadn't seen each other in years. Father Rick dove into the aisle with everyone else, greeting and hugging and sometimes hugging people twice on his way back up the aisle.

Meg pushed her way down to one of the back pews, where I stood in some shock, and gave me a hug.

"This is fantastic," I said.

"Yup."

Father Rick came over and gave Meg a hug. His smile was warm, a burst of sunshine. He looked like Santa Claus except that his gray beard was shorter and trimmed.

Meg said, "This is Janene. She's in seminary too." I felt his arms wrapping around me and pulling me in toward him, a real bear hug. Like my father used to do. When I pulled away and looked up, his warm smile beamed down at me. Even the top of his bald head beamed.

"Peace, Janene. Welcome to Saint Philip's." Then he was gone, and so was Meg, who plunged back into the crowd.

A tall, thin woman, hair all gray, took hand and my hand and shook it. "How do you do, I'm Betty, Father Campbell's wife. Welcome to our service. You go to the Community Church, right?"

"Yes. Peace to you," I said, shaking her bony hand. She didn't hug me.

A short, stocky black lady with gray hair grabbed and hugged me. "I'm so glad you're here! It's a madhouse, but it's the best worship ever."

"I'm Janene," I said. "Meg invited me."

She backed away, her smile seeming to stretch across the aisle, her teeth like big white blocks. "Great. I'm Paula. Welcome. I'm so glad you're here! It's a madhouse, but it's the best worship ever."

She'd repeated herself, and I wondered if that was a slogan they could put over the door. Probably true.

There were only a few black people. Even that seemed good in the gentrifying neighborhood, and I noticed plenty of men kissing. I had never seen that, but they made me smile.

Everyone settled down as Father Rick made it back to the altar, just as another black woman grabbed me and said, "Welcome to Saint Philip's. I'm Norma."

"Thank you!"

"This is what I tell everyone. There is a gift for you here at Saint Philip's. All you have to do is find it."

"I think I just did," I said, hugging her back.

The woman in front of me, slim, elegantly dressed in a tan suit and wearing a little black hat with a feather, turned to offer me a hand. "Peace," she said. "Hi, I'm Ellen."

I shook her hand and said, "Janene. Peace."

Everyone was sitting down. I sat.

Father Rick began a series of announcements. This meeting, that service, the Vestry, and so forth. Then he said, "Walk in love, as Christ loved us and gave himself for us, an offering and sacrifice to God."

The Eucharist continued.

Eucharist. It meant the entire service, the Mass, not just the communion part. Eucharist means thanks, gratitude, in Greek.

This banquet was come as you are.

The choir, small but well balanced with women and men, sang an anthem while Rick and the servers prepared the Offertory. John Gregory, who directed the choir, played the organ at Community Church.

When the basket came around. I put a dollar in. A broad, tall man said, "Thank you" and moved on. A young woman, a little plump – reminding me of the fairy Merriweather in Walt Disney's *Sleeping Beauty* cartoon – prepared the altar while Rick sat listening to the choir. Glancing at my bulletin, I saw that this woman would be Lily Forest and that she was an ordained deacon on her way to priesthood.

It was so like and so unlike my old Catholic Church, and it was also unlike Community Church, which resembled a business meeting. I had been working to change that, and people were listening to me.

Still, I wanted to stay here. This liturgy was more home to me.

But I did love the "we're a church because we say so" mentality of the Community Church. It remained a group of caring people, and I felt bad that I couldn't devote more of my time with them for now.

The next Sunday, I went back to Saint Philip's and listened closely to Rick's sermon:

"God holds His arms out – it is what He gives – come, let me embrace you. Come and be with me, and I will comfort you."

Baptized Catholic or not, I joined them around the altar for communion.

After the last hymn, Paula landed at my side and said, "Come to coffee."

"I have Community Church," I said, lamely.

"Come on."

I followed everyone out the front door, shaking Lily's hand, getting another hug from Rick, and down the steps of the church and up the steps of the Rectory. The hallway and the rooms contained laughter and boisterous talk. Paula took my arm and pushed our way through to the table loaded with coffee, juice, cookies, bagels, and cream cheese. I took coffee and worried about spilling it in the mob that filled the three small parlors of the downstairs rectory. Everyone was jabbering and moving around to greet people.

"Hi, you're new." I recognized Ellen.

"I've lived in Chelsea for about three years."

"I'm on the Vestry. Welcome." She held out a hand for me to shake. "What brought you to our church?"

"She's the head of Community Church," said Paula, her glasses glinting from the chandelier overhead. "Isn't that great that she came to our service?"

"How good of you to visit!"

"No, she's going to join us. She's going to seminary. She's in Meg's class."

I felt that Paula was taking ownership of me.

"She's ex-Catholic. That man in the dress who hates women drove her out."

That was an odd way to describe the Pope. Dress? Rick was wearing the same type of vestments and garb. I wasn't sure how to take this Paula.

Fortunately, Meg joined us. As did a serious, bookkeeper type fellow in a gray three-piece suit who shook my hand and said he was Tom and the Senior Warden.

"That sounds like a prison," I said.

He laughed. "A prison for the Warden. It's the strange title for the senior officer on the Vestry. Warden Junior's over there. His name is Chris. The thing is he's so tall and I'm so short, so I should be junior, but he is. Hi. Who's this?"

Meg said, "She's Janene. She's head of Community Church. She's in my seminary class."

"I thought I recognized you. Are you going to be a priest?"

"I'm just auditing."

"You're doing it for fun?"

"I love it. I come home from class, and I just sit and think. Then I watch *LA Law*."

"Are we brunching?" asked Paula.

Rick walked up. "Good having you. Do you think you'll continue to be coming here?"

I made a quick decision. "I'll straddle both churches."

"Good." He smiled. "Look, if you want, since you're in seminary, I always ask the seminarians to give a sermon every so often. Would you like to do that?"

A sermon?

I laughed. He couldn't have been serious.

I batted my eyes. "Father, this is so sudden!"

Everyone caught my joke and laughed.

"Just call me Rick. You and I would meet and discuss it of course. If you're going to keep coming to our services, we can consider it part of your training. See if you can get some credit for it."

"And you can volunteer for stuff," said Tom.

I made a face at him. "But I'm just auditing this class."

"You never know," said Father Rick. "Let's give it a whirl."

This was whirling a little too fast.

Meg said, "Oh, for heaven's sake, Rick, let her sit down, sip her coffee, have a cookie, and then snag her." She whipped her long braid around so that it almost encircled her waist on her other side. Quite a trick.

"Thanks," I said.

I realized that everyone called the rector Rick. Not "Father."

"Speaking of food," said Paula, "are we brunching?"

"Our cookies aren't enough for you?" countered Tom.

"Give me your phone number," said Rick. "I'll call you and we'll make an appointment."

I gave both my home and office numbers, somewhat bewildered.

He went on, "I know you have responsibilities with Community Church, but I'm thinking of a slot in a month. Could you come this Wednesday afternoon? And the Wednesdays after that at about three?"

"I work. But my office is a block away. I could come in early, work through lunch, and leave at three and then go back." Charley, my boss, wouldn't mind. Things did tend to get hectic at around five.

I pulled out my calendar to make a note while Meg clapped her hands.

"I gave a sermon last month," she said. "Does anyone remember it?"

"Something about being kind to people," said Tom.

"It was not," said Paula. "She was talking about the non-inclusive language in the Bible."

23

"Wouldn't that have taken a few hours?" I grinned at Meg.

I saw Jill from Community Church coming into the hallway and checking the church's mailbox. She saw me with the Episcopalians, gave me a "huh" look, and walked back to the door. I felt guilty.

"Aren't you brunching?" asked Paula, hooking her arm into mine.

"I have to step into Community Church. Where are you going?"

"The Galaxy." A local diner on Ninth. I'll tell them you're coming."

I rushed off, going the back way and waving, and John, the choir director, stopped me.

"If you're going to come to the ten o'clock, you could sing in the choir. Thursdays at seven thirty."

I just laughed. "I'll get back to you!"

I went to Community Church. An ex-convict gave a beautiful sermon of penance and rebirth, and we were all in tears. I thought, what a gift this place was. I would remain torn about it.

It was easy to find the Saint Philip's crew at the Galaxy. At first, I didn't see them, but then I heard Meg laughing somewhere in the back. I moved through tables laden with bacon, eggs, and toast, turned a corner, and there they were in a little side room at a big table, and everyone was laughing.

"Here, I saved you a seat," said Paula, waving.

I squeezed in, waved to Meg and then to a waiter and ordered – what?

"Eggs Benedict," called out a plump bearded man at the end of the table. It was the man who had taken my hand at Easter. I smiled at him. Peter.

"Yeah, that – coffee – whole wheat toast."

"Did you do the readings for class?" called Meg.

"I was stunned that he considers the Bible a human creation."

I'd meant it as a joke, but then I wondered if I'd offended someone.

"Inspired by God," said Paula.

I said, "With love for God."

Paula smiled at me.

"How is Community Church?" that from a solemn looking fellow, quite good looking – somewhere between his forties and fifties with dark hair and a gentle pair of eyes.

"It's good."

"Janene's the head of the church," said the solemn man. "Hi, I'm Steven. This is Tom. He's only a warden."

"We've met," I said.

"I like the idea of your church," said Peter. "No ordination."

"No coronation, either," I added.

"Community Church isn't run by people who think they're closer to God," said Peter.

"Saint Philip's isn't run by someone who thinks they're closer to God," Meg protested.

"Yeah, but in general. And people go along with it. That's all I'm saying."

"When I get ordained, I won't think that," Meg said, bound for the offensive.

"Stop that," said Tom. "We're lucky to have Rick."

"Yes," said Meg.

"And you," he said to me, "the head of a church. How did you get to be that?"

"Nobody wanted the job." I grinned. "How'd you get to be senior Warden?"

"Yeah, right."

"If they'd offered a collar, everyone would want your job," said Peter.

"You work at the diocesan office," Paula shouted. "How do you do that every day?"

"I look for comedy in my life," said Peter.

The elegant Ellen said, "Meg said you were in one of her classes."

A woman whom I recognized as being Lily, the deacon at the Eucharist, and whose chest barely made it over the table, said, "Why are you auditing?"

I hedged. "I was interested is all. It's only two hundred dollars."

"And Forrest is the theologian of our day," said Meg.

"He doesn't act like it," I said. "He's modest and soft spoken. But his book is –"

"Impenetrable," said Meg.

I laughed.

"I'll need a translation," said Meg. "It's supposed to be an introductory text, but it's pretty dense."

I hurried to eat as most of them were on their second coffee. I listened as Tom and Meg went back and forth about some church financial issue. I admired her seriousness, her immediate grasp of the problems, and how she laughed self-deprecatingly. She'd lean over to the side and laugh – not giggle – and then straighten up and grin.

Tom said, "I admired Frances's preaching, but she could get a little too in love with Paul's ecstasy over the Crucifixion."

"Rick's sermons have me sailing over the hills," said Peter. "They're poetry."

"She's in Chicago now," said Chris. "Rick got her the job."

"Mother Frances was a little too evangelical for me," said Lily. "Remember her Good Friday last year?"

Meg put her hand to her chest. "Welcome Good Friday. Good Good Gooooood Goooooooooood Friday."

Peter, Tom, and Chris laughed.

Meg whipped her braid back. It hit Tom.

"Would you control your pet?"

"Why did you grow your hair so long?" asked Ellen. "How can you stand it?"

"Don't forget I was a nun for almost thirty years."

"It must take hours to braid," I said.

For answer, Meg fingered her braid, and, in a few moments, it was undone. She then separated her hair into three parts, and in not even a minute, she had braided the whole thing again.

"Wow," we breathed.

"We should have you as the feature of a street fair," said Tom.

The check came.

"Am I on it?" I asked, gulping the last of my eggs.

"Uh – yup," said Peter. "Twelve ninety-nine and coffee."

I took out fifteen dollars and handed it to Tom because everyone was handing him their money.

"Why is it always me?" he wailed.

"You're our financial wizard," said Peter.

"Because we trust you," said Paula.

"Yeah, yeah."

"He always complains," Paula said to me. "But he knows we love him."

We filed out of the restaurant, calling out goodbyes. Paula was the last to go, pausing to say to me, "I hope you become part of us."

Meg and I walked toward Seventh Avenue.

"Are you going to come over?"

I knew what she meant. Worship at Saint Philip's.

"Lots of work to do for class," I said, avoiding an answer. "Have you done it?"

"Nooo," she said. "I did the Ministry homework. What a horror that class is. All these men insisting that God made man first, so man is superior to woman."

"If that's true," I said, "then we should kowtow to the fish in the sea."

She laughed and I turned the corner to my building.

"See you tomorrow. I have to figure out what Forrest wants us to do."

"It's pretty easy."

"Oh, you braggart!"

She hurried across Seventh.

Even my squalid hallway seemed magically lit.

When I opened the door to my apartment, the answering machine blinked a green light.

First, I opened my mail. One envelope, the address scripted too legibly, came from Arlington, Virginia. An invitation from Helen? No. A blank card with the words, also too legibly written, "Our wedding is a private ceremony. Helen T."

I had to sit down for a few minutes and stare at my radiator.

Finally, I played the message. It was my brother Dirk.

"There's no sense to this marriage. I'm going to call the priest in Arlington and tell him what's going on."

For all my life, Dad and Dirk had been best pals. Dirk, three years older than me, the only son, had been the football, whiffle ball, basketball playing son of whom I'd always been jealous and ready to fight. Now that was all over. Now it was son against father. Our family was exploding, falling apart and down a hole, splintering – pick a metaphor.

Dirk said, "The priest should know this marriage he's going to do is wrong. Dad is out of it. In shock."

"I don't think you should get involved. He's dead set on this."

"Trust me. I'll call the priest tomorrow from my office. He'll think twice after we talk. This man just lost his wife!"

I hung up. Five minutes later, as if they were on the same wavelength, Dad called. He sounded like Nixon saying he wasn't a crook.

"Your brother thinks I'm grieving. I stopped grieving. I was grieving when your mother was sick."

No, he wasn't. When Mom was sick, he believed a miracle would happen. He didn't think she would die. Her death might have smashed his faith in God – and he'd always been a religious man – not outwardly but inside, where faith ran deepest and most private.

"Dad, we knew she was dying."

"You come to the wedding," he said.

"This is a private ceremony."

"She doesn't want me to come," I said. "She wrote me. Thanks a lot."

"I don't see why you shouldn't come."

Sure, I'd show up and she would be angry, and he would side with her.

We had been so tightly knit when Mom was sick, but when she died, we were blown to smithereens. The odd thing was that it brought Dirk and me closer when we'd never been close. I felt I had to hang onto him or else I'd lose my whole family, for my sister Jules – you never knew where she was. Usually, I didn't want to know.

As soon as I put the phone down, it rang again.

"Movie later?"

It was Meg.

"I have a ton of work."

"I was wanting to see *Flatliners*."

"What's that?"

"Something about seeing what's beyond death. Julia Roberts is in it."

"I don't like her."

"And Kiefer Sutherland and Kevin Bacon and Oliver Platt."

"I like Oliver Platt."

"So, you want to go? There's a five show at your theater on Twenty-third."

"Aren't you a teacher? Don't you have class preparations?"

28

"I've been doing the same stuff for years."

"Have you done your questions for small group?"

"I can do that in five minutes."

I pulled out the syllabus and chanted, "Characterize four major approaches to the Hebrew Bible. What are the advantages and disadvantages of each? Which of these approaches have you used or studied closely? If you are preaching or teaching on a biblical text, how would the four approaches assist you in understanding and explaining the text?"

"Right. It's all in the book. Come on. We can eat at the diner later."

"Okay."

I was easy. Besides, I wanted to get to know Meg better. I needed this friend.

Chapter 5

I would be preaching at Saint Philip's on the twenty-third Sunday after Pentecost. The Gospel for that day was the story about Jesus healing the woman hemorrhaging for twelve years and the young daughter, about twelve years old, who had died. Jesus healed them both. I wondered at the parallelism. A desperate woman and a little girl. A woman's bleeding ends. A little girl awakens; her bleeding will begin soon.

The feast for that day – I flipped pages – the maternity of the Blessed Virgin Mary.

Aspects of the goddess. Nymph, mother, crone.

Could I connect those to the Gospel?

I would let that simmer a bit.

I wasn't happy about *Flatliners*. It claimed to be exploring life after death, with medical students voluntarily dying for a few moments to see what lay beyond, but it turned dark and pretentious. Nevertheless, I retained my admiration for Oliver Platt.

"Wasn't that fascinating?" Meg asked as we settled into our booth at the Chelsea Square restaurant – well, diner.

"It just fell through for me, but it was an interesting story."

We didn't talk for a while but sipped our drinks in silence.

Then I said, "Church language is so … he he he."

"You don't mean funny, do you?"

"It sets up a world view, doesn't it? We get used to it so that it seems right, but it shuts us out. And it happens to God, grouped under that lovely exclusively used He pronoun."

"To call God a woman is shocking to most people," said Meg.

"But she WAS also perceived as a woman. Lots of times."

"You read that book, too?"

"Another thing that bothers me is how women were so marginalized in Jesus's time."

"But were they? We're reading books and analyses written by men looking at books written by men etcetera for a long time. Are we right to think so?"

"No women rabbis," I said.

"That we know of," said Meg. "When there were women goddesses, human women still tended the hearth."

We were getting far afield.

I shrugged. "I guess I get a little tired of the he he he of history."

"It will change once women are in powerful places – lots of them, I mean, not like being a queen." She laughed. "When Mother Frances was here, people would ask for the Father Mother."

I decided to ask her "the question." "Why do you want to be a priest?"

"Because I have to," she said quickly. "That's not the answer I'm giving them. Ask me another tough question."

"You left the sisterhood. How would being a priest be different?"

"Nuns can't have sex. Priests can. Well, except for the Catholics. But they will anyway. Were you ever married?"

"Not yet."

"I married a man who left the priesthood. We were marching away from the Catholic Church and how it could never change. He died. He thought it was inevitable that the Catholics would start ordaining women, at least in this country."

"It's become their trademark. We won't ordain women as priests. Ever. And who goes to Masses anymore? Women."

"Not you. You left."

"Sure did. I like being considered a human being. Still, at a Catholic church near Penn Station? They have a Mary mass – they held it before a choral rehearsal I was in. And after the mass, a long, long line of women wait before a statue of Mary as each woman kneels with her private petition – which they give to her. Maybe that's why women stay."

I bit into my sandwich. The familiar tuna fish – in the old days, Friday's lunch box sandwich. Fish on Fridays. The comfort of parents who loved each other. Tuna fish with mayonnaise brought it all back.

31

Even tuna fish can hurt.

"Yes, I left," I said. "Despite Mary worship, the church proclaims women aren't worthy, yet we are holy vessels of babies. I don't understand why women don't all walk out when they're not perceived as whole human beings."

"Well, we are at Saint Philip's. You should join the liturgy committee." Meg talked about how wonderful it was, as Rick gave them a pretty free hand. I listened and ate my tuna fish, thinking of Mom, the homemaker, cleaning the house and making great meals and laughing.

If I flatlined for a few minutes, would I see my mother?

Meg was saying, "Rick's church isn't like Grace or any of the big churches, the ones so visible they either tow the mark or incur wrath. It was different with Bishop Bulla. He was a saint – social justice, his ear to the ground. He came late to women's ordination, though. It was hard for him, but he came through."

"Why is it so hard for men to see women as human beings?"

Meg pulled her braid from behind her back and stretched out to the end of her bench. "Some do. Like Rick. He's special. We're lucky."

"He's so welcoming. I mean, the hugs!"

Meg laughed.

"And I'm giving a sermon. But it's his pulpit."

"It always will be. But he knows that's how we learn. I just wish Bishop Hiney was a little more special."

"Hiney?"

Meg laughed.

"Our bishop. It's H-e-i-n-e. Everyone says Hine, which is right, but it's too tempting. The Hiney pronunciation does get around."

"I would guess so."

Meg laughed. "Peter works at the diocesan office on Fifth Avenue, and he can't stand Hiney. Bishop Bulla hired Peter, and it was nice until he left. The good old days. Peter does accounting work, but he makes it his business to be in on the gossip. He can sense the wind changing for Rick since Heine came to sit in the cathedral."

"Heine doesn't like Rick? Does that really affect his decisions?"

"It's so painful, Janene. And so stupid. When they were both priests, Heine started a program to defeat national hunger. The program was really a fundraiser, but it did not raise much. Rick was a priest in Michigan then, and he got together with a few priests and with the cathedral in DC. He started a national educational program about world hunger. It's still flourishing. It's why we and so many other churches have a food pantry. Heine's program faded away after a little over a year. So, Rick irritates him. Stuff like that. Then there's who's in our church."

"Ex-Catholics and rebellious nuns?"

Meg tapped my water glass.

"Not directly. Lots of gay people. Peter says that he gets the sense that they think Saint Philip's is all gay men having sex during the Eucharist."

I had to laugh. "Hasn't he visited?"

"Sure, but he must think it's all a show for him. We do have a lot of gays who are ex-Catholics. They came mostly from Saint George's downtown. The new priest there is anti-gay, whatever you say Pope is okay, so all those gay Catholics, mostly men, came here because Rick is well known for giving an AIDS Memorial to anyone who asks, whose church will not do it. What would Jesus do? So, we have Tom and Steven, Chris, Robert, Peter, Joseph – a bunch of good guys all different. A few earn really good salaries and contribute financially and with their time. Some of them came with a precious understanding of how liturgy works. They're really smart, and we're lucky they came."

"The Catholics are so good at hospitality and loving their neighbor."

She laughed. "Another reason to love them. But the Episcopal Church welcomes everyone." She grinned. "We have to. Our numbers are falling. But we're keeping up. I'm glad you're with us."

"Why do people think that churches who think for you are better?"

"Not everyone," said Meg.

We parted with a hug on Seventh Avenue.

Back to Forrest and his approaches: the confessional religious approach, the historical-critical approach, literary, and social science approaches. None of them fit my bill. I would probably think along the lines of how Scripture used stories that were already old in myth. Stories told around hearths and fires by women and men, stories told to tribes, stories moving from tribe to tribe. Finally written down.

I picked up my study Bible and turned to Joshua. Not finding it interesting, I turned to Judges. We were only concerned with Judges 1 through 2:5, but the language – even in translation – was so archaic and so filled with weirdness and what seemed to be awkward transitions that I was fascinated. I paged through. An eye-popping story about a woman named Ja-el (El! A name for Jahweh!) and a judge named Deborah who sat and sang under a tree and the naming of goddesses startled me. I had no idea what was going on, but I was delighted to find what resembled remnants of stories about goddesses. Indeed, I found a reference to women making cakes for the Queen of Heaven and an Israeli campaign to destroy the Asherah poles. To get rid of the goddess, for only "He" was god.

Wow.

Judges was so ancient. It seemed messy because it followed the neat history of Joshua. Beneath that tidy tale – a glorious mess. I wanted to explore it.

Except that Forrest had only assigned the first pages of Judges. Dull stuff. Military stuff.

Just like a man.

I was auditing, so what did I care? I would write two papers!

I wanted to astonish – me and them – and prove myself the best – the auditor who topped them all.

I always remembered how this preoccupation of mine had begun.

Some years before, on a bus ride to New Jersey, I'd taken a little book called *The Lost Goddesses of Early Greece* that I'd just bought. In it, the goddesses spoke in first person. *I am Demeter. I am Artemis.* Reading this book caused a strange feeling in me. I looked out at the depressing scenes around me, but they had transformed. Even Route 9 on the New Jersey Turnpike, looked beautiful – radiant, glowing, filled with possible magic. I felt different! Was this power how men felt when they read the Bible or prayed to Our Father? I had an opportunity to recreate that feeling if I had the nerve.

Here, in the gospel I was to preach, were an old and young woman. The girl may have been twelve; the old woman had bled for twelve years. In the middle was a mature woman who could bear children.

Maiden, mother, crone.

But how could I make such a connection? How could I bring a bit of beautiful New Jersey Turnpike to Saint Philip's?

All this thinking fed me with an energy I haven't felt in such a long time that it felt new all over again. It was probably the feeling I had when I was so little that the entire world seemed a magical place.

I felt that God was encouraging me to keep going down the path.

I ventured into the library, hoping to find material about the women of Judges. Forrest's bibliography was helpfully filled with pages of possible articles and books to read, and thanks to the explosion of feminist theology, his list included new books and articles with feminist interpretations. My memory recalls that I flew from shelf to shelf, so that must have been how I felt.

I was pretty much alone in that library. I sat at desk carrels that students used on weekdays but not weeknights or on panicky Sunday nights. Every carrel I sat at contained catalogs, obviously paged through, for clergy clothes. Vestments, yes, and also an assortment of clergy shirts and types of collars. These students weren't ordained yet, and they were obviously fantasizing about dressing up.

Wandering through the shelves, the books at my fingertips, some a few years old, some going back a century or so, I realized I'd been a coward. I was denying myself a voice, hiding in the Audit Cave. I wanted more. I wanted to study as much as possible, and I might as well get credit for it.

I thought of my meager bank account. Writers didn't earn a lot, but I'd just been promoted to Assistant Managing Editor, so I could do this, thanks to the seminary's payment plans. I could go for a Master of Divinity degree. I would grab ahold of every scrap of knowledge that had once been denied to women, and I would enjoy myself.

Why hadn't I decided this at the beginning? Because I'd been scared? Because I didn't want to commit? Because I thought church was too patriarchal to be saved? Maybe it was, but there was only one way to find out. Do it.

I called Rick to tell him the ideas I had for my sermon.

"Show me something by Wednesday."

I hadn't convinced him, I guess.

The phone rang.

"Can you talk?" It was Meg.

"Of course."

"The bishop called Rick. He read Terry's letter, and he is going to ponder it. I have to go in and discuss the Creed with him."

"Who's Terry?"

"Oh, gosh, you don't know." She paused, as if to take a breath. "Terry used to be on the vestry. she's not coming to St. Philip's anymore. One day, after a meeting, I rode to Second Avenue with her on the bus, and I stupidly said that I thought the Creed was just a historic document, not really a list of things we had to believe."

"On the bus?"

"Yeah, I guess I was showing off. Anyway, Terry's so old school. She told the Vestry that, and it went into a couple of days of argument just before they were going to vote to let me enter the process."

"Oh, jeez."

"Rick broke the logjam by calling a vote and Tom spoke up for me and Paula, and everybody calmed down, so I got voted in. Terry voted no, but everyone else voted yes."

"But what's this about a letter?"

"She wrote the bishop about me."

"Why did she do that?"

"She's a bitch. No, sorry. Her mother is in charge of one of those breakaway parishes in Texas. They don't like women priests, and they are conservative about their theology. Anyway, now the bishop wants to talk to me."

"When?"

"Friday. I have to arrange for a substitute teacher. Oh, crap. I feel as if I'm going up before the Inquisition."

"Do the Episcopalians burn people at the stake?"

Well, that wasn't funny, but she laughed anyway.

Meg sighed, a long and dramatic sigh. "I don't know how Heine will take it. He doesn't like Rick. They're at opposite political spectrums. Rick is opening up the church. Heine is 'close the window and you'd better be pure.' If he doesn't like me at any point in the process, he can strike me out. Rick has friends on the Commission, thank God."

"Do we believe in the Creed even when we say it? I think it's some historic document we recite, but…"

"It's like a dance."

"It's like an elevator," I said.

"Huh?"

"Jesus. He's up in heaven then he comes down to earth then he goes down to free up the souls locked out of Heaven since Eve, then he goes to earth to rise from the dead, and then he ascends into Heaven. It's an elevator."

Meg laughed. "That's great. I wonder if I'm brave enough to try it out on Hiney."

"Just don't give me credit if it doesn't work!"

CHAPTER 6

In Rick's office on Wednesday, he didn't seem to be talking to me but to himself. "A stupid conversation blown up. So unfair."

He was taking this Creed thing seriously.

"Bishop Heine hates me, that's the trouble. It's all about his power. He's pulled in a conservative group around him, nothing wrong with that, but they are leery of ex-Catholics, especially women and gays. He doesn't like me because I've been out there, marching with Dr. King, working with Bishop Bulla, his predecessor, advocating for Democratic candidates – outside of church and the pulpit of course. Heine has a powerful group around him, and he is influencing them to suspect me because I got on a *Time* magazine cover twenty years ago."

I'd have to look that up.

He sat and looked at me with eyes that gradually lost their fury. "I'm sorry. I know I'm using up your time."

"It's all right."

He pushed a fist into his hand. "Meg must be ordained. She *must.*"

I wondered why he felt so fiercely about it. Her skills, of course. Her quick intelligence, her passion, her ease of speaking to difficult topics. She *should* be ordained and not tripped up by some stupid man over stupid stuff. How right Rick was to be so passionate about making sure that happened.

We turned to my sermon.

"Read what you have," he said. He stood up and looked out the window to Twenty-third Street.

I realized then that what I'd written was silly.

"It's Catholic," I said.

He didn't turn. "Haven't you heard? We're Anglo Catholic."

Whatever that meant!

I started with the Hail Mary prayer, which made him look over at me with a whimsical look as if to say, "I caught you."

I read.

"All that prayer and devotion to Mary – rosaries and May crownings and Blessed Virgin Saturdays and stories of Mary's childhood and adulthood. These filled my Catholic childhood, but I wonder. What happened to all those prayers? Who were we praying to? These prayers and devotions have been prayed for hundreds of years certainly demonstrate that there has been, and I suspect remains, an enormous need and hunger for Mary, the mother of Jesus. When I moved over into the Protestant world, unable to even consider walking into a Catholic church ever again, her absence remained painful and puzzling. Ironically, I had sacrificed this unique prayer life and worship of a woman to worship in places where women were considered equal to men before and behind the altar."

I peeked at him. He had turned and was looking at me, his gray eyes sharp, and yet he nodded.

"Go on."

I went on.

"For Mary and Jesus, each possesses a human side and a divine side. I probably don't have to explain that idea for Jesus, but with Mary, we certainly can point to her human side. Yet there is also this Idea about the woman who gave birth to God, an idea that has throughout church history, teetered on heresy. Yet the idea held on, powerfully. It is ironic that the churches ordaining women do not reflect that much about Mary. She seems to be a footnote. I wonder, where is she now? Where did she go?"

I looked up at him again.

He nodded at me.

"This is not," he said, "an Episcopal sermon."

"Anglo-Catholic?"

He laughed.

"We have enough ex-Catholics so they'll know what you mean. Go on."

I went on. He stopped me a few times to ask me to clarify something, to be more specific – I was so carried away by my own feelings that I flew over ideas I thought anyone would easily understand.

On Saturday, I headed back to the seminary library. The leaves were starting to change, and I thought, why not go to Central Park? Instead, I spent the afternoon looking up information about Mary – just to put my head where she could be. I found an article about Saint Jerome that made me laugh out loud.

It seemed that, when translating Genesis into Latin from Greek, Saint Jerome erred. The text of Genesis where God cursed Satan in the Garden had, in my family Bible, read, "She shall crush your head." Meaning a woman would crush the head of Satan with her foot.

Except that the Greek had said, "He will crush…"

Our family Bible had been a direct descendant of Jerome's translation, and it said in Genesis, God to Serpent Interpreted as Satan: "She shall crush your head." I'd read the passages so often during my juvenile attempts to read the Bible.

That text in Genesis was a mistake.

Ipse it said, not ipsa. Feminine instead of masculine.

Jerome's mistranslated ipse to ipsa. "She shall crush your head." This in the Vulgate that remained the Catholic Church's official Bible for centuries. So instead of a prediction of Christ, God's words became a prediction for Mary, his mother.

And that is why in nearly every Catholic church, a statue of Mary depicts her foot atop a serpent's head.

I also remembered, from hearing it from priests many times, that that text had been the proof that Mary must have been conceived without sin – the Immaculate Conception – declared dogma by the Pope in the mid nineteenth century because Popes could not err in matters of faith and doctrine, and so – it must be true. The entire reasoning was based on this text from Genesis.

And men accused women of being illogical!

I found a reference to Judith, the star of a book in the Apocrypha, in a note in my study Bible. I found that she had her song – as did Miriam and Deborah – and that she had done particular damage to a general's head. And Ja-el, also in Judges, the one with the name of God, who had driven a tent peg through an enemy's head.

"She shall crush your head."

Indeed!

Of course I went back the next Sunday, and this time during the Peace, I cautiously went into the aisle and was bombarded with hugs. Soon I was moving in the crowd, hugging, wishing peace, and re-introducing myself. During coffee hour, I wandered from group to group, always welcomed, and enjoying myself before returning to the Community Church. And once again, I joined "the gang" for brunch.

When I got to their table at the Galaxy, Tom was talking about needing money to fix the church's roof.

Meg said, "A street fair with special activities for kids? That would remind the neighborhood that we're here."

"That's a start. What else?"

"We could give tours," said Paula. "Talk about the history, the stained glass. People could give whatever they pleased."

"That's on the list. And Steven and I could get Christmas trees and sell them at a profit. Anything else?"

I said, "The church has great acoustics. It's a wonderful place to sing. Probably all that wood. Pianos sound better, too, and I'd bet any music would."

"But it's not a studio."

"Street sounds," said Steven.

"I could ask around," I said. "I could put an ad one of the trades."

"Okay," said Tom. "It sounds like a long shot, but it's a good idea. You guys are better than the Vestry. They don't have any ideas except a street fair, and Meg made that better."

As Meg and I walked toward Seventh Avenue, she said, "You're practically one of us now. What about Community Church?"

I shrugged because I didn't know the answer. I hated to be another minus on their attendance sheet, but I could only be in one place at a time. But I loved them for how they'd helped me get this far.

I climbed the five flights rather than take the elevator. When I got to my apartment, which I'd been dreading, and opened the door, I looked over at the answering machine.

No message.

Tomorrow was Dad's wedding. I'd put it out of my mind with all the work I was doing, but I'd made a plane reservation to arrive at noon in DC. I hadn't heard from him though, just that last call when he'd said he'd get Helen to say I could come and would let me know.

Why hadn't he called?

I knew why.

I should call him, but for the first time ever, I had no idea where he was.

Arlington – somewhere. He'd cleared out of the apartment in Ohio. He'd tossed most things at the auctioneer. Mom's things. Some of my things. He didn't care.

I thought. He liked Best Westerns and Comfort Inns. I called several in the Arlington area.

I found him at a Best Western.

His voice was groggy when he answered the phone.

You jerk. You went to sleep.

At least I knew he wasn't with her.

"What – what do you want?"

"You didn't get back to me. You said you'd call."

It was like talking to a stranger. Even his voice was different. Higher pitched.

"Well, are you coming?"

"Did you talk to her like you said you would?"

"I don't see why you couldn't come."

"Does she want me to come?"

Again, he hedged. "I'll make a reservation for you here."

"I'm not going to make a scene."

"You won't."

Didn't he know this woman?

"If she doesn't want me to come – you didn't even talk to her, did you? And you promised."

"I don't know what you want. I'm getting married."

"She's made it clear she doesn't want us around, and you've made it clear that you don't care."

"The way you all behaved ..."

"She didn't want us around. How were we supposed to behave?"

"Not you so much. I don't see why you can't come."

"If she doesn't want me, I won't come."

"I don't see why. I'll talk to her."

"You said that last week. You're afraid to talk to her."

"I have a right to a new life!"

"Yes, you do. Without your kids. You've made that painfully clear. Once upon a time, you treasured your family. Now all you want is a new life."

"I deserve it. I do."

"Yes, Dad. You deserve the life you want. Before Mom. Just erase her now that she's gone."

"No!"

"Your life before us. When you get tired of it, don't bother calling."

I hung up. A man I'd loved all my life had died. Enjoy the Witch. You'll be sorry.

I canceled the flight, but it was nonrefundable. I was also dipping into the ready credit to pay for seminary, and I lost the Diner's Club card because I'd paid it late too many times. The hell with that. I'd lost my dad.

Don't let it bother you.

I had things to do. I had a new life myself! I had a sermon to preach.

The money I'd get back if I was careful.

My father – gone – just like that.

Well, I had friends. They were my family now.

CHAPTER 7

On the Sunday I was to preach, Meg met me at church and held out the white gown that covered one from neck to feet.

"Do I have to wear an alb?"

"You're in the altar party. A guest preacher. Is that your sermon? Put it on the pulpit."

I joined the choir and warmed up with them.

"Good luck!" John called as I headed back to the sacristy. I realized as I hurried that my sneakers were visible under the alb.

"Damn. My shoes."

Meg laughed. "If they're looking at your shoes, you're in trouble. Or the pulpit fell. Here, do you know how to tie this?"

Meg handed me a long cord and showed me how to knot it around my waist.

"I'm going to take courage from you," she said. "Rick keeps asking me to preach but I put him off. This is one sophisticated crowd."

With those comforting words in my ears, I took my place in line behind the acolytes and in front of Meg, who was subdeacon, and Rick, who gave me a big smile and, of course, a hug.

We did a brisk walk to the back of the nearly filled church. I walked up the aisle, singing along holding my hymnal, looking up to smile, pretending to be relaxed.

Once on the altar, I sat in the chair next to Rick, and I felt a little silly because all I was going to do was preach.

Never had a service moved so fast. Suddenly, we were at the Gospel. Meg and Rick went to the center aisle as we sang the first half of a hymn. Meg held open the book and Rick read the story of the woman bleeding, of the child raised to life. All I could think was that my sermon seemed trite and useless. The miracle was Jesus bringing them to new life. It wasn't about the female image of God.

We finished the hymn. Rick and Meg were back in their places.

And everyone stood, expectantly. I have never forgotten that special silent moment at Saint Philip's, as the preacher of the day would step up to the pulpit, and look about at them all, ready to listen. Rick, a splendid and poetic preacher, had educated them to recognize God in the poetry that blessed us with signs everywhere.

Well, I wasn't Rick.

Still smiling, I looked over at them and switched on the light. Making the sign of the cross, I said, "In the name of our Mother and Father God, their Son, and the Holy Spirit. Amen."

That came off my lips without my thinking. It was their cue to sit, and they did.

I saw Paula clap her hands silently and there was Tom, grinning and shaking his head at me.

I began.

Jesus gave them both life. The woman. The daughter. He saw them, he felt for them, and he gave them life. It is easy to connect the woman and the girl, both unseen by their culture. Jesus does see them and recognizes them. By his touch – or his cloak's – he healed them. And he caused others to see them.

I improvised that on the spot, just to connect the gospel with, well, Jesus. Now what?

A woman, let us say a mother. Or an old woman, a crone. And a young girl, a maiden. Maiden, mother, crone – all aspects of a religion that lasted for thousands of years, including the time Jesus lived – we could say that Jesus recognized these two and offered them life.

No one was going to understand that.
I rattled off the Hail Mary. And, to the startled congregation, I asked,

So many people have prayed to a woman, the mother of God.

All that prayer and devotion to Mary I knew as a child – rosaries and May crownings and Blessed Virgin Saturdays and stories of Mary's childhood and adulthood. What happened to all those prayers? Who was I praying to?

Those prayers and devotions have been prayed for hundreds, thousands of years: apparently, there has been an enormous need and hunger for the woman we call Mary, Jesus' mother.

For Mary and for Jesus, there exists in our minds a human side and a divine side. We know Mary's human side, but there is also this Idea about the woman who gave birth to God, an idea that has through Christian history, teetered on heresy, but people could not let go of her. Where is she now? Where did she go? We barely mention her outside of the Catholic church. Is she dead to us? Unclean? Not worthy of our attention?

Lily leaned forward against the pew ahead of her and put her head in her arms.
Pay attention to the sermon. Not to their reaction.

In the Bible, we find that feminine imagery accompanies what those writers call the Wilderness and, in the Bible, and in traditions surrounding those of the Bible, more women wander in wilderness. They come from Greece and Turkey, from Syria and Sumeria, from Babylon, from Egypt, from Ugarit in the land of Canaan, along with the women in the biblical tradition who have been, gradually, silenced as the Bible took form. In fact, there are so many women wandering in the wilderness, forgotten or silenced, it's a wonder John the Baptist never bumped into them."

Mild laughter.

And all these women are somehow connected to the Idea of Mary we inherited. There are those from the Time Before, when gods, like people, were male and female. When goddesses were

46

mothers and more than mothers who danced in the cosmos and fashioned the earth, who were mighty warriors, who battled cosmic monsters, who had power over the serpents" – I said that slowly – "who moved forcefully through the stars and the earth's seasons, who were sexual, who were cosmic, who gave life – and who took it back. Madonna and child. Pieta. Ishtar of Babylon. Anat of Ugarit in Canaan. Demeter of Greece. Inanna known as Ma-ri-enna of Sumeria. Isis of Egypt. For thousands of years in the Time Before. They were lovers, they bore sons, they mourned the death of their sons and rejoiced when their beloved god returned to life, personifying the spring. And when they grieved, they went and wandered and searched in the wilderness until it once again bloomed with life. They were fervently believed in and prayed to. Where did they go?

For some reason, I looked up to the ceiling, and I was startled to see a gentle, glowing light circle the ceiling's midpoint. I felt as if I were somehow ascending toward it, and that it came down over us, wrapping us in its arms, and in those arms the church glowed.

I am not making this up. That ceiling was glowing.

I hesitated, and when I spoke again, my voice trembled.

All this is deeply embedded in our most ancient spiritual heritage. Biblical women join them: Hagar, Jeremiah's Rachel, the widow symbolizing Jerusalem's destruction, Miriam. And more. They are all there. Many of them, in one form or another, do appear in the Bible. Isaiah and the Psalms, calling upon old traditions, are particularly rich.

They were still listening. I felt it. And as I looked up again, I could almost hear faint music, like fingers sliding delicately across strings, like a harp. So strange, really. I wanted to stop and listen, but I felt that I had to keep on.

Here is an example of how these things work – In Ugarit, the land of Canaan, the goddess Anat crushed the serpent monster, just as Yahweh does in Isaiah 27. The Divine Warrior for the prophet Isaiah is Yahweh, who in the same tradition of the goddess Anat, battles chaos, meets his bride, and is enthroned. Who is the bride? 'Rejoice, daughter of Zion, shout aloud... for see, your king is coming to you, his cause won, his victory gained.'...the wilderness and the dry land shall be glad, the desert shall rejoice and blossom...

Faces before me – Paula, Lily, Peter, Tom, Steven – all looking up at me – Joseph, Norma, Ellen, Robert – their faces seemed to glow – that couldn't be true – and the light strings like a harp – I looked up and thought of doves. I don't think I saw them, but they were there in my mind.

The god who is female often represented the faces of death and destruction as well as of life and fecundity. And these things too lie in the wilderness, a liminal place between life and death, where there is barrenness and blossoming, grief, amazement, and newness of life...In the Bible, the barren and restored wilderness is portrayed with female imagery, in images of nature withering and blooming, of women who are harlots or crones or brides or mothers giving birth, or widows in mourning. Mary, who gave birth to God, inherits all this, with some siphoning off in false accusations to Mary Magdalene, but one Mary at a time.

No one laughed or chuckled. I looked up and saw Lily kneeling, her head in her hands. I glanced at John and the choir in the pews to my right and saw John looking at me intently. Beth, the loud alto, was also right there with me, I felt. All right then.

I continued, knowing I was far afield from the actual Gospel.

The whole idea of Mary, of a female force at work in the godhead, would not go away. Will not go away. That is frightening to some people. People resist the idea. It is unfamiliar. It is not part of the sign of the cross millions make several times a day. It causes an enormous struggle. But how can the mother of God not be divine, too? Does it affect our view of Christ if we elevate his mother to the godhead? Some early Christians worshiped a Mother, Father, and Son trinity. She resides in every other mythology and religion. Why not ours?

In some ways, because of this, the Mary worship stuff makes her different. She is neither human nor divine. She was put in some enormously lonely and barren wilderness apart – so apart – removed from essential humanity and yet not quite divine. Why has theology been so reluctant to put her there?" And I adlibbed a line that had bothered me but had not gone over with Rick. Too bad. I had to mention the Mary statue that was here. "Even here, she lives in the shadow, in the corner, passed by with little notice." I gestured to my left, where a foot-high statue of Mary did indeed live in shadow. "And we don't mind. We don't even miss her. Why? Maybe it is best to forget her, but how can we? Protestants have tried, but we still have that little statue at least. And she is there in one of our Tiffany-stained glass windows, between daughter and crone, accepting the angel and her fate of being mother of Jesus. Christianity struggled with the humanity of the idea of Mary.

When people accepted Christ, they gave to Mary beloved and passionately held ideas. Mary helped people embrace Christianity. She took over the temple of Artemis at Ephesus. Temples were rededicated to her. Many of the Gothic cathedrals were built over shrines of the ancient goddess: her churches have been built over shrines of Hera, Isis, Minerva, Diana, Artemis, Hecate, and by the 800s, she was the Queen of Heaven and busily interceding for sinners before an angry warrior God the Father.

I paused, looked up. The light was now descending to the full church. I thought I was crazy, that this could not be happening. Partly to keep my balance, I tightened my hold on the pulpit and looked down at the choir members, who with John, sat in the pews directly in front of me. John, in the second pew, saw my glance, and he put his hand over his heart.

Here's the question: If people were worshiping her in some form, because of a great hunger and need of her, where is she for us now? Where did she go? Does it matter?

When I was at a spiritual workshop not too long ago, our director asked us to seek inside ourselves a nurturing God, a wisdom figure, to in fact visualize a God and then draw that vision. All of us women drew feminine imagery – fountains, trees, an old woman weaving baskets. After the workshop, we went to the chapel to pray the daily office with the sisters. There are no feminine images in our corporate Christian prayer – it seemed like a different language that had no use for our needs. After our long meditation, the change produced a painful spiritual wrench.

And now I paused as I came to my punchline.

How in God's name have we women been nurtured by Christian corporate prayer? We have all been wandering in a wilderness, only this one does not have her.

So, what was I saying?

Between the nymph and the crone is the Mother, and did he think of her as he healed? Oh…It is not that we elevate Mary to divinity or maybe we do – to a divinity close to the full creation in God's image – not separate from human groundedness or cosmic dream, not confined away or separate, but a manifestation of the physical miraculous creation of earth and stars, the miracle of our bodies knit with our souls. She is human. She is divine. Her power, with the power of God, heals. With her, the trinity explodes with power, unable to contain the vastness of the incomprehensible, the eternal mystery that is God: the regeneration and miraculous recurrence of the seasons, the stars that move around us, and their stories that light our way to find her.

Because we shall always seek God, even in our loneliest moments. And when we seek God, she is there.

Now let us come out of Wilderness.

As I said that, I felt the darkness returning to the building. I couldn't even see faces in the back.

Let her come out with us. In this extraordinary, sometimes frightening time we live in, it might be good to contemplate one more thing, a mystery we have not pondered in a long time but one we cannot leave behind, one that ties us to the dim recesses of our deepest spirit, and to the earth and stars that we are. Let us heal. Mary, and those of her sisters, maiden, mother, wise women – will, like creation, groan in travail and then deliver to us newness and amazement and mystery.

Do not forget her, the woman who gave birth to God. Then we shall all be healed.

Amen.

I turned off the pulpit's light switch, stepped backward down off the pulpit and went to sit next to the acolytes.

My first sermon was over.

We stood for the Creed.

"We believe in one God, the Father, the Almighty-"

It seemed so wrong. Next to me, though, one of the acolytes, tall, willowy Nancy – matter of factly said, "Mother, the almighty," and it gave me such a jolt that I felt the world had changed. It hadn't. Everyone else went on with the Creed as usual. I half wished they had stopped.

After the prayers of the people and the confession and forgiveness, Rick called out, "The peace of God be always with you."

He had changed it from "the peace of the Lord." He'd made it inclusive, well, as much as he could. God calls to our minds a guy who looks like Santa, but it is really an inclusive word.

The great gabfest of Saint Philip's peace began, people hugging and calling out, "Peace be to you! The peace of God!" That peace for which there is no understanding. I hugged Nancy and Norma, the acolytes, and Meg came bounding over.

"I didn't want to leave the wilderness! Oh, what you did!"

John jumped up the steps and hugged me hard. "That was beautiful. I was in another place. Now you get in your soprano place."

As I did, several came to offer me the peace, all of them looking for words. What had I touched? What had touched me? I was thinking that it hadn't hung together, but they all seemed to have caught something I said – I wonder what it was.

Rick flung out his arms, giving me a strong bear hug.

"How you spoke it was as good as what you spoke."

What had the sensation been like? A real manifestation of something here, something greater, something lifting me up into the light. It had certainly felt real. Had I invoked something? The feminine God?

No, that was silly.

Well, I would not forget the experience, and I would try not to define it.

"You have a thing," Peter said to me at coffee hour. "You took what must have been a lot of research and made it poetry."

"But it meant something," said Paula, hugging me hard. "It was about goddesses – still in Scripture if you look for them."

"And Mary. The Catholics don't say she's a goddess, but to all intents and purposes, she is."

"Isis was worshiped for longer than Christ," said Peter. "We've worshiped God for how long? Does that make Him real?"

"Her," said Paula.

Tom laughed.

"As long as that makes people laugh," I said, "we had better keep saying She so we get used to it as much as we are with God being He."

Steven gave me a hug. "When are you getting ordained, Janene?"

"I'm not in the process."

"You should be," said Paula.

"Why not?" asked Tom.

"Oh, she'd never make it through Heine," said Peter.

"Rick would fight that," said Tom.

"We'll soon know about me," said Meg. "My BACOM is coming up."

"Bacon?" Paula looked confused. "Are you going to throw up?"

Meg giggled. "No, it's BACOM, Paula. The Bishop's Advisory Commission on Ministry. It's when the Commission attacks."

"The process!" I said, grandly.

"Some of Bishop Bulla's people are still on it," said Tom. "They're Rick's friends, and that's good."

"I hope so," said Meg.

After a long brunch, during which we had a glorious discussion about how the Catholic church, which most of us had been raised in, both elevated Mary and brushed her aside and how we could bring her back to the Episcopal church in some way. It was lively, it was more delicious than the eggs benedict.

Afterwards, Meg and I walked to Seventh Avenue.

"I'm going to have a rehearsal for the BACOM. I really dread it. Rick is getting all his priest pals together. Wednesday night."

"Are you worried?"

Why would Meg, so definite and confident, be nervous?

"How do you explain a gut feeling? I can't rationalize it."

"They'll help you."

Easy for me to say. If this process made someone as steady as Meg nervous, it might send me under my bed.

"You should think about signing on. You have a powerful presence."

"I doubt that sermon would get me through the Commission on Ministry."

"Yeah. Hey, we could get a church together. You could give the sermons and I'd run the Vestry."

"That's not how the Episcopal Church works."

"Well, when we've both been priests for a while."

"You're afraid," I said.

"Yeah." She whipped her braid around.

"Fear is no reason to not do something."

She shrugged.

"How's your Dad?"

"Lost. I'm going to see them in January, but they don't know it yet."

"Can we review for Forrest's test? It's a quarter of the grade."

"Okay. Call me later."

"I was thinking of going to Rome for Easter break. Why Don't you come with me?"

Well, I certainly wasn't going home for Easter.

"Okay."

"I love you, Janene."

Meg hopped on the bus, leaving me with my mouth wide open. How long had it been since someone had said that to me?

My mother.

Trying not to cry, I bumped into people trying to cross Twenty-third Street.

How I wanted to call Dad and tell him about the day. Instead, I prayed to Mom. Then I pulled out Forrest's study sheet.

I'd earned a 98 on his first test – the highest in the class. I knew that because he'd announced that the highest grade had been a 98, and one person had gotten it.

I was thrilled. I'd found where I should be. All of me.

CHAPTER 8

I studied harder, competing with myself, writing notes. I covered such terrain as history-like themes in Genesis through Joshua/Judges, the Covenant Code, Pharoah Akhenaton and Atonism, conquest sagas, different editors' contribution to the text, parataxis in Hebrew poetry, Conquest vs immigration or social revolution.

The phone rang. I picked it up before checking.

"You aren't here," said Ruth.

"Hi, Ruth."

"We need you. Why are you with Saint Philip's?"

I dodged. "It's the seminary. I need to do field service with a minister supervising me." I wasn't yet in Supervised Ministry, but I had spoken to the Registrar, and they said if Rick signed off for me, they would count the time.

"Are you going to be ordained? I heard you preached a lovely sermon. Why didn't you tell us? We'd have come."

"I wasn't sure how it would go."

"Don't forget us. You're going to be our first ordained minister."

"I'm not in any process. I'm just ..." I didn't know what I was. "Ruth, in all honesty, I hate to do this, but I'd better resign. I'll still come to church every so often, but I'm technically in field service at Saint Peter's. The seminary wouldn't recognize the Community Church."

Ruth said, "Some things aren't up to us. Just don't forget us."

"How could I? You brought me back to church."

She sighed. "Yes, that's what we do. People who are unsure about church come in, stay a bit, find out they like church after all, and go and join another church. And you know what happens?"

"What?"

"They quit and never do church again. Maybe you'll come back here?"

I couldn't answer. How could I?

"You'll still be our first."

I didn't feel guilty. CC's vice president was a stable and thoroughly nice guy and was a better replacement for me than me.

I became a part of Saint Philip's. There every Sunday, in the choir, getting to know everyone, everyone greeting me at coffee hour. I joined the liturgy committee.

One Sunday, I'd been assigned one of the readings. I hadn't even skimmed it, just went up to the altar with the citation in my hand. The book on the reading desk was already opened to the correct place. I found the beginning verse and read.

"Let us all praise famous men."

I stopped. We were celebrating All Saints' Day, and the reading celebrated famous men?

Shannon, you know what they mean.

No, I didn't. I could have just added, "and women," but instead I looked out at the congregation. Then I closed the Bible and went back to my seat.

No one moved. No one said anything.

"Men," my fifth-grade nun teacher had told us, "includes everyone. When you don't know what pronoun to use because a group is made up of men and women, and you want to say he or she, no, you use 'he'. "Men" is used as a collective word for everyone. For instance, 'all men are created equal.'"

How handy. You keep saying "Mankind" and "men are made in God's image" and so on, and pretty soon all the men have the good jobs and the only pictures you see in the newspaper are of men, or if women, they have men's names like Mrs. Edward Shannon. And pretty soon, women are invisible, even if they are there.

Let us praise famous men indeed.

No one protested. The Gospel reading went on as usual. At coffee, Meg squeezed my hand and Rick gave me an extra big hug and said that he would order an inclusive language lectionary.

"We'll be praising everyone," he said, smiling at me.

But one of our older parishioners, Donald, protested. "These inclusive language things are written up so fast that they leave out the poetry. God is in the poetry."

"But Donald," I said, "we can't keep calling God 'he'. It doesn't even match the original Hebrew."

"The word 'he' includes women."

"Oh, Donald, the word 'she' includes men."

I just thought that up, and Rick laughed. Donald shook his head and walked away. I felt sorry I'd said that.

I went up to him and apologized, but he just smiled and said, "If we're not arguing about something with friends, then what kind of a place are we?" He then added. "So many things change. It used to be that you stand for worship, kneel for prayer, and sit for instruction, but now it's whatever you feel like doing."

"Of the three," I added.

"It used to be so simple to explain to children," he said, "now you have to explain in paragraphs."

I applied for a passport. I didn't need it until Easter, but in my busy life, I knew I'd forget.

Jules called and shocked me.

"You went to the wedding?" I practically screeched. "You weren't invited!"

She was unimpressed. "It's a public ceremony. He's our father."

"Okay, well, what happened?"

"Nothing. He ignored me. I know he saw me. There were only ten other people in church – Uncle Dick and that bitch's family. Dad saw me when he came in and walked right past me. He didn't come around for the Sign of Peace."

"He doesn't want anything to do with us. We don't exist." I couldn't believe I was saying those words so matter of factly.

"He was always Mr. Get Here for Christmas Because We Should All Be Together."

"He died, I guess,'" I said.

"I went out on the sidewalk. He didn't say a word. She didn't of course. I went up to him, he turned away. They got in the car for the reception, and I followed. They made a lot of turns. He was trying to lose me. Finally, I just gave up."

"Jules, I'm sorry."

"I couldn't not go."

"I know."

"Will we ever see him again?"

"It's not going to last. It can't. And then what?"

"He'll never admit it. Maybe give it time. You've got me. Call when you need to or leave a message. It's pretty hectic here."

Phone down.

Dammit Dad. To not recognize Jules! And walk right past her! You and Mom made her!

The hell with him.

CHAPTER 9

"Bravo," said Doctor Forrest as he handed back my paper and my "extra" paper. I paged through my extra and found it loaded with his pen written comments – finishing up with a list of books I should look at. Almost on every page, he had written, "Never thought of that." The grade? A-plus. A combined grade for both.

Students complained about him, but I floated. I loved. Love for the wonderful Old Testament, filled with old stories and legends, some discreetly buried and not meant to be taken literally but wonderful, old stories, nevertheless.

Now, a month dealing with The Flood.

It was all so interesting, looking at the Bible with critical eyes. I kept reading it, referring to the books I kept finding in the library, and going back and forth as the words peeled off from the old reading of a story too old to mean much to a new story that had everything to do with me, with women, and opening up windows into my soul, into my mother's soul, and her mother's…I was so excited.

Even so, the mundane must interrupt.

The liturgy meetings made me impatient. There was something in the atmosphere that intimidated. I hadn't taken Pastoral Liturgy yet, so I was slowly coming to understand Episcopal liturgics.

Meg and Lily kept tossing around the word "rubrics," making it seem like some gigantic rule book. But a remark from a classmate, going through the Episcopal process, made me drop my jaw. "Rubrics" were simply the words in red typeface in the Prayerbook – essentially the stage directions.

The hot topic at another meeting: Planning for Lent had to start now because time flew after Christmas, well, that's what everyone said.

"Are we going to mea culpa?" Lily asked.

I patted my chest with my fist and murmured, "Through my fault, through my fault…"

"Through my most grievous fault," said Peter.

"I don't mea culpa," said Rick, pretending to be haughty.

I laughed, as if that had to be a joke.

"Cover up everything in purple?" asked Lily.

"Let's not," said Meg. "Sin, sin, sin. That's not what Lent is about."

"It's not?" asked Peter. "Purple means penance."

"No, it doesn't," said Meg. "Lent just means longer. As in the days are getting longer. It has nothing to do with penance."

"What did you do last year?" I asked, trying to help.

"Doesn't matter," said Meg.

"It is the season of penance," said Donald. "No matter what it's called."

"What do the rubrics say?" asked Lily.

I flipped through the Prayerbook, knowing to look at the red directions.

"Nothing."

"What would we cover up?" asked John.

"The statue of Mary. The statue of the child Jesus. The cross on the altar."

John gave a short laugh. "What would be the point of making Mary, little Jesus, and the cross invisible during Lent?"

"I don't know," said Rick.

"Let's not," said Meg. "Some people come into the church for Lent and need the statues."

Like me. They were one link to the Catholic in me. If you went into a "too Protestant" church, there were no statues. Even so, the statue of Mary was so small.

The next agenda item involved Community Church. The ten o'clock Episcopal service had grown so long that their noon start kept getting pushed back.

"Yes, that doesn't make them happy," I said. "If I were still there, I'd complain."

"We need to cut something," said Meg. "How about my sermon?"

I tossed a pen at her.

We went back and forth. Everything took a full discussion with possibilities and problems. Put everything in the bulletin and tell people to read it? But Meg said there was a lovely give and take with the community during announcements. Give and take? Why should that be in the middle of the service? The Eucharist wasn't a meeting, said Donald.

I finally spoke.

"Put the announcements in the bulletin and tell people to read the bulletin after the service. If there are questions, they can ask them during coffee hour."

"No, no," said Meg. "I don't want to give up that conversation."

"It's always joyful," said Rick.

"How about just trying it for Lent?" John asked.

Oh, he was a gift. Didn't speak much, but when he did...

"Good idea," said Rick.

"And our service, unlike the days, will get shorter," said Rick.

"Next item," said Meg. "Who is singing the Exultet at the Easter vigil? Count me out."

"What is the Exultet?" I asked.

"The opening chant at the Easter vigil. It's generally sung by an ordained person, but Rick opens it up," said Meg. "How about you?"

John smiled at me. "How about you?"

"I don't know it," I said.

"Good idea," said Rick. "You have a lovely voice."

As Meg and I walked toward Seventh Avenue, she stopped and said, "The announcements are great. We become a community."

"They're all in the bulletin."

"People don't read the bulletin."

Why was she so crabby about a thing like this?

"Tell them to. I get a sense of community from the service itself."

Meg shook her head. "No, a sense of community for what we do together, not just our feelings in the service. So, what if we go over a set time?"

"The Community Church pays rent. We have a responsibility to them."

"You're just biased."

I stopped. "I happen to understand what it's like to wait for you guys to finish up while you are still doing stuff during our time. A few minutes is one thing, but sometimes it's ten or fifteen. It's rude."

"It's just that you said the obvious only if you don't understand our community."

"Everyone agreed to it. Just for Lent anyway."

"It's going to stick, I know. Well, see ya."

That braid whipped around so fast that I had to step back.

No hug.

Her blazing eyes, her accusatory tone. I didn't want to lose her friendship, but on the other hand, I didn't want to lose myself either. Why was she so upset?

I zipped up my jacket and walked home slowly. Even as I unlocked the door to my building, I felt a sense of loss, of even terror, of not wanting to be alone. And when I opened the door to my apartment, I heard the familiar sound of the radiator hissing and the drip from the radiator from the floor above. I grabbed a towel and put it on the radiator so I wouldn't hear the steady dripping. Of course, it was too late to call the super.

I understood better about Meg when I met with Rick.

"I invited several people to come and work with Meg to prepare for the BACOM."

I vaguely understood.

He sat, looked me in the eye with such concern, even fear.

"She could not articulate anything at this meeting. You know Meg. She's more than outspoken."

"Right."

"But she couldn't even say why she felt called to the priesthood. I was horrified. These were friendly people. It's important that she make it through the BACOM. She must be a priest." He punched his fist into his hand. "She's – God calls her to it. If only she could articulate it, but why can't she? She's never at a loss for words."

I stopped my chuckle when I looked at his face.

"She's kinda stubborn," I said. "And she was mad at me after the liturgy meeting."

He smiled. "Yes, she is stubborn. About the right things. And she *must* be ordained. *Must.*"

I left his office, thinking suddenly that that had been my time, and all we had talked about was that Meg should be ordained.

I worked late at the office to make up for the hour's time with Rick and grew absorbed in Greek theories about the heart. Charley, who had waited for me to hand in my column said, "This is interesting. Get some pictures from the Bettman Archives."

When I got home, I found a message from Meg.

"I am so sorrrry! Call me."

I decided to let her wait. I had homework.

I made a point to wave to her when I got to class, and at the break, I hurried over to her, but she was heading across the hall. I couldn't tell if she'd seen me, but I needed sustenance. I followed the crowd to Frank's Deli across the street. Frank didn't close his deli until the seminarians flooded in during night class breaks.

It was just a tiny bodega, but Frank, a smiling Italian, was ready for the onslaught of some sixty theology students, most of whom had skipped supper to get to class. Pots of coffee were ready, sandwiches were prepared. Naturally, we all called it the Loaves and Fishes miracle. Frank greeted us as "the ministers of tomorrow" and we grabbed our coffee and sandwiches, paid him, and left dollars in the tip basket. He called us "wonderful students," and made us feel as if we were doing something important.

I carried my coffee and sandwich back to the room where my small group met. Maria came in a few minutes late, carrying a pile of papers and a coffee cup. I felt some sympathy for her. She carried a full load at Columbia University and also had to grapple with us.

Now she said, "I have caught up on your response papers. I'm so proud." She started handing them out and when she came to me, she said, "Another great paper, Janene. You've been doing a lot of work."

I finished my sandwich, and as students came into the classroom, I went across the hall to where Meg's small group met. There were still a few minutes before the bell rang. Meg was looking for her notes, her face a study of grimness.

I sat next to her. "So why in God's name do you want to be a priest?"

"What do you know about it?"

"Rick is upset. He spent my whole hour talking about you."

I could see her reaching for a sharp retort, but she just said, "I don't want to talk about it."

"Why not?" Weren't we friends? She had helped me, but I couldn't do the same for her? "It's just me. Wouldn't it help you to try to articulate some things?"

"No."

"Maybe you don't want it hard enough after all."

I went back to my class and had a fun time. Some men were confused that Rahab was a harlot, and the Bible always did seem to favor harlots.

I asked, "What do we call men who sleep around with lots of women?"

That sent someone to the Bible dictionary to prove that harlot meant sacred prostitute and not a woman who engaged in casual sex, but some guy said that was wrong, too.

Maria smiled ever so sweetly. "Prostitutes in ancient times were likely to be working in the religious establishment."

"What?"

"Look it up. Sacred prostitutes."

"Who said that sex wasn't sacred?" I asked.

The class ended in laughter.

Outside, I found Meg, waiting for me.

She was nice again. But I'd better keep the subject off of church.

"I got my passport," I said.

"I'll check flights. Rick said you should sing the Exultet. He has the music for it. Did he tell you?"

"No. You took up too much of my time."

"As I should."

Her bus came, and she jumped on, her braid making a huge wave behind her.

Rick asked me to continue to help rehearse Meg for the BACOM and gave me suggestions for questions. I grilled her at McInerney's Bar after class on Wednesday. She answered slowly, pulling the words from some difficult place. I told myself that this didn't matter. What mattered was how she felt inside. I peppered her with questions and wondered how I would answer them.

"Why do you feel called to be a priest?"

"What do you feel capable of as a priest? Rector? Priest in charge? Interim? Hospital chaplain? What?"

"Tell me what you do at Saint Philip's."

"Why did you leave the convent?"

"What priests have inspired you?"

"What is your favorite psalm?"

"How would you exegete the story of Adam and Eve?"

"Who is Christ?"

"God, you're rough," said Meg. "I'm glad you're not on the committee. Can we have some more beer?"

"It's past eleven."

She was certainly meek. Her answers had been halting, although from what I knew, her answers were an improvement.

Someone at the next table called, "What were you two talking about?"

"The last judgment," said Meg.

I took a gulp from my Manhattan.

Meg said, "Bishop Hiney hates Rick."

"Hates?"

"Rick's popular. He has a natural power base."

"He does?"

Meg shrugged. "A few of his friends are on the commission, but their time is almost up. I'm sneaking in under the wire. But he has friends all over – in the Midwest, in California and Washington, and certainly in New York. He's got some power, but I don't know how much Hiney fears it."

"Rick said you must be ordained. He was quite firm about it. He must think you have the chops, so you shouldn't worry."

Meg laughed. "Yeah, that would make things easier for him."

"Why? Will you be his assistant?"

"Maybe temporary associate until I get a job. Lily's going to work in the office, by the way."

"Huh?"

"Sandy left. In the office? She's getting married and won't need the job. Lily's stepping in as office assistant and she and her kid are moving into the top apartment in the rectory."

"Is that a good idea? What if you need to fire her?"

"It's just for her year of grad study. She'll start in January. Why would we fire her?"

"Okay." It wasn't my business anyway.

When I came into church on Sunday, ready to join the choir, Rick waved me over to him.

"We had another session. Thank you so much. It went far better."

"She'd done a lot of thinking."

"You pushed her. Thank you." He paused. "I owe you a dinner. You and Meg and Betty and I – we should make it a movie night."

"I need that soprano," John called.

Rick hugged me. "Thank you,"

Rick sure had a spring in his step.

After the sermon, Tom got up and said, "I just thought we should all know that recording projects in the church are going gangbusters. Checkers Recording was here for a week, and they scheduled six more weeks. The word got out. You know how musicians talk." He grinned at John and us in the choir.

"And we sound so nice when we do!" John called out.

Tom pointed at me and said, "I want to thank Janene Shannon for suggesting this. It looks as if we're going to fix our roof and not feel helpless about it." He sat down. Then he sprang back up. "There are plenty of announcements, so do read the bulletin."

"Little victories," John muttered to me as we got up to do the anthem.

Dad called.

"Your sister came to the wedding."

"Yes, I hear you successfully lost her in the traffic."

"She wasn't invited."

"Neither was I, although you tried to pretend I was. Would you have tried to lose me, too?"

"I don't know why you don't want me to be happy."

"You're never happy! Ever since this whole thing began, you have yet to be happy!"

"Because I have miserable children."

"You wanted me to come to your wedding. Very brave, doing something she didn't want. You didn't even have the nerve to talk to her. All she wants is a man, an escort – and there you were."

"We knew each other when you were kids."

"Biblically?"

I couldn't resist, but my father wouldn't have done that. Yet I wasn't sure who my father was right then.

"Your mother said she was a lady."

"What?" I laughed. "Were they ever friends like Florence and Lee and Jerri?"

That brought a deadly silence.

He shouted back. "Your mother wanted me to be happy!"

Oh, after her death, he referred to her as "your mother."

"Yes, she did," I said quietly. "So do I."

"No, you don't. You wish I had died instead of her."

"To me you have."

"Don't be so dramatic."

"Have a good life," I said. "You are no longer a part of mine."

He hung up first.

The shock wore off the next afternoon at work, at which point, I fled a meeting and rushed into a stall in the ladies' room and bawled as quietly as I could.

He had turned on us so easily. He just didn't want to see us anymore. I thought we'd be drawing closer after Mom died.

Instead, I didn't have a family anymore.

CHAPTER 10

Some general moaning in Forrest's class on Monday – test results. Meg got an 89. I'd gotten a 98 again.

Why do I keep getting one wrong?

Frank, blessed be that little bodega owner, handed out free cinnamon rolls! Warm cinnamon rolls!

"It's almost over," said Meg as we walked back to class. "Except that Isaiah paper. What are you doing for Christmas?"

"I don't know."

I felt bitter.

Meg took my arm.

"Have Christmas here. We'll do a bang-up Christmas Eve at the church, and I'll get a turkey and stuff it and have a banquet with as many of the gang as can come."

"Have you ever made a turkey?"

"No, but I'll get a cookbook. And Peter is a great cook."

"Uh huh. At your apartment?"

"Sure."

"Wouldn't you be going home?" I asked.

"That is home. My parents are gone. My brother died two years ago."

"I'm sorry."

"And he was a priest."

Now I understood her better.

Meg's apartment was larger than mine, which wasn't saying much, but her rooms were wider, and she had a tiny bedroom, where the cot she slept on took up most of the room. The bathtub stood in the kitchen, covered by a wooden plank that served as her counter. But she had a nice sized living room – no table, though. I pointed this out.

"We'll eat on the floor on the countertop. It'll be fun."

"I'll get a little tree for the middle."

"There you go!"

The semester ended. I got an A. Meg got a B-plus in Forrest's class and an A-minus in Foundations of Ministry. The next semester, I would be taking New Testament and Theology with the much-celebrated Tina Collins and the unknown Irving Dale. It struck me that most of the professors were white, and I was struck by how that bothered me. I had realized how important it was to hear from people who were not the same color as I was. I always thought of myself as unbiased, but I'd grown up in redlined towns that had kept blacks out of the town's borders. Crazy. Now they took up ninety percent of classes.

Rick preached.

Out of the forge of life, God has planned such things, rare beasts, unique experiences, as will part the waters before us. The whole church here in Ephesus represents change. Thinking changed – in an old world. Ethics changed – in an old world. Lives changed in the midst of an old world. Feel the true dimensions of that life we share together. Feel the body we are, working together. Feel the love we bear one another, the often-difficult love, and those around us reach out. That love is Christ. And nothing will ever separate us from that love. Indeed, we will be upbuilt by that love, into whatever God is now calling us to become. Wow.

After church that Sunday, Robert reviewed the subdeacon's role for me. He impressed upon me that the subdeacon is responsible for the entire service going smoothly, that we had to make sure everyone would show up on time, prepare the Altar Book with the proper pages for the day with the ribbons in their proper places, and set out the vestments for the correct liturgical color. The sacristan would set up the offertory table, which the sacristan could arrange as she saw fit. The altar had to be set up with the proper liturgical color and the proper vessels and cloths.

We walked through a Eucharist together. I loved how the soft spoken and sincere Robert was careful that I did things right – the walk to the altar during the procession, how to "mark" the Altar Book with my finger subtly placed at the end of each line so that the celebrant wouldn't lose his or her place, when to go down the steps with the Bible and where to turn and how to hold the book when the priest and I were in the center aisle and the priest read the Gospel, how to handle the offertory vessels, how to offer wine at communion – and how to clear the altar after communion. Robert emphasized, "This is your time. Don't rush. Let people quiet down. The work is over."

We debated about bowing before the altar.

"If the Holy Sacrament isn't there, why bow?" I was reverting to Catholic speak.

"The altar represents Christ's tomb."

"But He's risen. He's everywhere."

He laughed and let it go. "There's no hard and fast rule. You should do what feels right."

I loved our Eucharist and wanted to learn from it. A time of Thanksgiving, a time of gathering together in a circle around the altar, seeing us close up, accepting the gift of Christ living inside us, the gift that was also a responsibility. There was so much joy in how Rick celebrated, and it spread to all of us, so that we were dancing and hugging and happy, too, that inner light of celebrating.

I took notes, but while listening and walking through everything with Robert, it didn't feel overwhelming. My Catholic background helped a lot, and when I was home, I made detailed notes to help me remember.

I was nervous that Sunday, but as we went up the aisle during the opening hymn, I made sure to smile and to walk with a bit of a bounce.

During the service, I absorbed each word, each gesture. They were symbols, leading to the past that led directly to where I was standing. They led to something else, too – God's presence among us.

It felt good to share the service with my friends, to feel the bond of that community, and to participate in a ceremony ages old with a sense of Now. Yes, capital N. After communion, I took my time as Robert instructed. I brought the chalice back to the offertory table. Next, I took the paten and hosts back, covering the consecrated hosts with the white cloth, the purificator. Then on my way back to my chair, I touched the linen cloth covering the altar, lightly, with a smile. I felt the ceiling grow lighter; I felt the community with me in the light.

I had never thought such things before. The vessels and even the cloths symbolized our community struggling to do right. And the people were the most important part of the service – not the props, not the vestments or the Mass itself – the people were the most important because they – we – were the ones God loved most of all. That love was enacted in how we treated each other – with joyfulness or compassion or grief.

I also loved giving the chalice to the people at communion, one by one, letting them dip the bread in the cup if they wished, wiping the cup gently with the white cloth purificator if they sipped from it. All these people I loved, taking in Christ. As a Catholic, we had been taught that the bread had become the real body and blood of Jesus. The Episcopal Church speaks of accepting Christ symbolically, but it is a real, genuine acceptance. I think, how can Christ live in me and of the others taking in Christ, symbolically, imaginatively – these are real ideas. An idea built on imagination – which is real, you know – and reaching back to Christ who invited us all to participate and work for the kingdom.

And there is God.

At the quiet time after communion, one of our older ladies, Cleo, stood up, walked into the aisle, and sang "Alleluia, Hear God's Story" with considerable spirit and foot stomping. Those of us on the altar followed Rick and stood and smiled. Then Cleo, obviously heavily medicated, sat down again. Someone said, "Alleluia!" No one laughed. After all, what she did came from her heart.

That is what I loved about this church. The acceptance no matter what.

I cleared the altar of the vessels, taking my time as Robert had advised. I took the Altar Book and closed it with a loud clap. I picked up its golden pedestal and carried it to a stand on the side.

This was a lovely period of quiet, of just being present. I tenderly smoothed out the white altar linen, imagining it as Jesus' shroud and knowing he was rising from the tomb, and went to sit with the choir to perform an anthem. To me, those few minutes were the sweetest.

We processed out, singing. Rick stayed at the door to greet people, and as I started to rush up the aisle to start the clearing up, Rick grabbed my hand and pulled me in for a hug.

"Really nice job," he said. "You seem more alive and more at peace than any time I've ever seen you." And he smiled that big smile of sun rays. I loved the man and "if only he weren't married" raced through my mind. Oh, silly. Rick was a gift in my life, the father replacing the one I'd lost. I recognized that, and I was grateful for it.

I skipped up the side aisle and saw Robert holding up his hands and clapping.

John met me at the steps. "You have a presence," he said.

Whatever, but being subdeacon felt like home at the altar, perhaps because it was so like the Catholic liturgy of my childhood that now presented itself as deeply resonant with profound implications.

After brunch, Paula, Meg, Lily, Ellen, and I went out to see the movie *Aladdin*. Then we told sad stories about ourselves – we had a good time together and a relaxing supper. We all felt light and filled with magic.

And we had a big, tight group hug on Twenty-third and Seventh before going our different ways.

CHAPTER 11

Papers. Homework. Writing medical copy on a tight timeline for my job. Studying. Church. Singing. Studying. And then… Christmas.

Like many old New York apartments, Meg's door opened to the "kitchen area," with a small refrigerator and stove, opposite of which was the bathtub, covered by a wood plank serving as the counter. The kitchen area opened to a small square living room space with some comfortable chairs and a woven carpet over which Meg had laid a bright red tablecloth. The tiny bathroom and bedroom were down a narrow hall.

Robert and his partner Richard, Peter, Paula, and Lily wandered about, looking at Meg's copies of Renaissance art on her walls.

I had expected to sniff turkey when I came in, but Meg's turkey sat stark naked in a pan on her counter. When Robert let me in, she was peering into a cookbook lying flat on the counter.

"You haven't put the turkey in yet?" I asked, amazed.

"I didn't dare," said Meg. "I might kill it. It says breast side down in the recipe. What is that?"

"You have to be kidding," I said. "You have it upside down."

"Oh."

"I take that as a cry for help, and I'll answer," said Peter.

I had brought mashed potatoes along with butter, tomatoes, prosciutto cheese, an apple pie, and, at Meg's specific request, canned cranberry sauce. While Peter showed Meg what breast side up meant, Paula, Robert, his boyfriend Ralph, and I played charades.

Once the beast was done to Peter's satisfaction, there wasn't any room in that little stove for it. We were busy fixing the gravy, potatoes, and stuffing so that bird rested on the living room floor.

We sat on the floor, hilariously toasting and joking and drinking the wine Peter had brought. I forgot being sad and felt grateful.

At home, I opened presents Dirk and Jules sent me. Nothing from my father, not even a phone call, though I'd sent him some books about World War II. I called Jules, and we talked about her kids. Same with Dirk, who called me. We did not mention Dad.

I would call Dad. He had to be himself sometime. He couldn't keep being this other person. What could that be doing to his insides?

"I can't talk to you now," he said.

Boom.

The phone rang as soon as I hung up.

"Coming? I'm down at the diner."

"Oh, yeah, I'll be right down.

Meg and I had started going to the movies every weekend. We'd have dinner at the Malibu diner first and then cross the street to the multiplex movie theater and make our choice.

We talked about classes, about the church, about people we knew, about politics, and then...our conversations began to be repetitive. Meg would describe an interview she'd had – part of the process – and I would hear her whine, "It was so paaaaaainful!" An interview with a priest who was a woman brought her comment, "It was so patriarchal. I can't get brainwashed."

"No one could brainwash you."

Or she would say things like, "I couldn't possibly work in a parish that insists on Rite One. It's so patriarchal. It's so groveling on the ground toward God. Insisting that we're all such sinners."

"Well, we are."

"Not groveling on the ground sinful. Women took that so seriously because through the ages, we've been treated like the great tempter. Get on the ground and grovel. No."

"It doesn't hurt our souls to ask forgiveness."

"The imagery is all about groveling on the ground. Women shouldn't ever have to say anything like that."

"We all want forgiveness for something, and every something is huge in our hearts."

"Society pins the blame on women. We're made to feel guilty for everything. It's Tertullian, or whoever first pointed a finger at Eve and called her the devil's helpmate."

"But to know you're forgiven? Remember going to Confession and coming out and feeling like a new person? The sense of freedom? All our sins wiped off the board? I'm talking men and women."

"You don't have to grovel as if before a king to do it."

"It's beautiful language, though. Old."

"And it should die. No Rite One for me."

"If we talked about it as a church, though…"

"No Rite One. It's a crime with the church playing the power of God it doesn't have."

Okay, I agreed with her, but I felt that Donald and others loved Rite One, and they must have seen something noble in it.

Rick assigned another sermon. Jonah. Jesus telling about the laborers in the vineyard. Sea and land. Came from my gut. I wrote most of it in a furious mood while at the counter of the Chelsea Diner, sipping four cups of coffee.

Anger can feed. When it moves, anger feeds and it can feed good things, it can give energy for good purposes. But it can go on and it can build walls and hide you, and how do you forget anger when you're surrounded by not only your wall, but everyone else's?

In the question is the answer, in the anger is the love, in the loss is the rebirth, in the numbing work of the vineyard is the struggle in the belly, and in the struggle is the anguish, the anger, the working out, and there is the recovery. Aren't Jonah and the vineyard really true? – in a way we can't grasp but we will grasp, truer than all the ways of living and visions of God anyone has ever had, true, for God keeps turning season, and faces, on us.

"Please don't tell me that your father is God," said Meg.

"That wasn't where I was going."

"It's funny. You pour on metaphors, but that's only on the surface."

I had to take that seriously. "Rick, too many metaphors?"

"Almost," he said. "Next one, though, keep it to earth. Just so we know you can preach simple."

"Uh huh."

He laughed. "I know. Look who's talking."

CHAPTER 12

M eg's BACOM loomed over the next weekend. Rick had announced it at the service, and he was organizing a prayer group for that weekend. The community, already well versed in Bishop Heine being not a friend to the church or to Rick, wanted to help as much as possible.

I fervently wanted Meg admitted to the ordination process. That would solidify my love for the Episcopal Church. Love me, love my friend.

That Saturday, I met Paula, Lily, and others for a quick lunch at the Chelsea Diner, and then we joined the prayer service for Meg. I even said a few Hail Marys.

The phone rang. Rick hurried to get it and returned in a few minutes.

"She said it was tough and, in some cases, ludicrous and painful, but she had some friends there, or she felt that." He sighed. "One more day. We'll meet at four."

I went straight to the library at General Seminary, where I spent most of my Saturday afternoons soaring through the shelves, making notes, fascinated by the storytelling of the simple and glorious Judith, the woman who saved her village.

The book's humor was magnificently subtle. The enemy cut off her village's water supply by damming the waters at the *bottom* of the mountain! Thinking that their sins caused the drought, the entire village put on sackcloth and ashes, even the animals.

Judith thought that was nuts. She scolded the elders for their weakness and claimed that she would get rid of the bad guys, thereby freeing the waters (to run uphill, remember).

Judith returned home and took a bath – remember, there's no water!

– put on her finest outfit and took her maid and a bag down to the enemy camp, where she enchanted the enemy general and stayed with him for three days. Each night, Judith and her maid passed the guards on their way out of the camp "to pray," carrying a bag with her. The general, smitten, grew to trust her, and so on the third night, Judith gets him drunk, chops off his head, puts it in her food bag, and she and her maid leave the camp "to pray." Used to seeing her going and coming, the soldiers didn't think twice.

Judith and her maid hurried back to their village, where Judith showed them the general's head, rousing the village to hurry down below and defeat the army– disheartened and frightened by their general's death – and free their village and the waters!

Even the author of the book had fun – the animals in sackcloth, Judith on her roof, Judith with water when no one else had it. The author started the fun by setting the story in several different historic timelines.

And Judith personified several goddesses with her upraised sword, her bathing, her beauty, and her power.

She's been pretty much forgotten now, but for a long time she was quite popular, and Gothic cathedrals contain many images of her.

Judith and Mary. Judith destroying the enemy by sawing off a general's head. Mary, crushing the enemy, her foot over the serpent's head.

In my old Catholic missal, on feasts of Mary, a few lines from the book of Judith are used.

This path was just so much fun. Smiting serpents, monsters, giants.

The next day's BACOM news was simply that we didn't know.

"They were nice," she told me on the phone. "But it was that cold kind of niceness. So I don't know what's going to happen."

We would talk on the phone several nights a week, quizzing each other for tests and planning our imminent trip to Rome. I hunted down places where we could stay, and she made the airplane reservations. We also planned to go to Florence, Assisi, and Pompeii.

For Fat Tuesday, the parish held a party in the rectory, complete with pancakes, dancing, and board games. Even cleaning up was fun. Ash Wednesday was somber. I thought of my mother, whose ashes lay in Arlington Cemetery, and I wondered – but she is more than dust, right? She is in heaven, right? After all her faith, all her prayers, all her pondering her Catholicism, all her common sense, all her doing her duty and her love for her family, right? Right? Right? Dust? What are you saying?

Now, even while heading into final weeks and papers and flying through the library and the joy of final exams, here came Holy Week.

Palm Sunday began at General Seminary with a short service and then, waving palms, we processed across Ninth Avenue to the church where John was ready with the hymn as we entered. We processed up the main aisle, around the church and back up the main aisle.

"But we don't go anywhere," Meg muttered to me. "Just around in circles."

I practiced the Exultet, the chant that opens the Vigil service. Rick gave me an older version, which included a tribute to "the mother, the bee" that helped make the wax for the Paschal candle. Very charming. Robert offered to sing it for me, to show how it went, and I suspected he'd wanted to sing it. He sang it solemnly, but listening, I thought that one shouldn't be so solemn when entreating people to rejoice. Hey, this was the night! The night Christ conquered death. Did I believe that? I thought so. Yet I struggled with death. If he'd conquered death, where was my mother?

With all that going on, I took off the end of Holy Week.

Before going to the Maundy Thursday service, Paula, Ellen, Lily, Meg, and I met for a quick dinner at the Galaxy, and we were quite giddy. Even Ellen, who was finalizing her divorce, joined in with puns. Meg was recovering from the BACOM and making fun of the questions she got, like, "Don't your glasses keep you from being close to people?" It just felt so good to be with what was now my real family.

CHAPTER 13

The thing about the Triduum, the three days, is that the services don't end. They move from one to the other, never finishing… beginning with Maundy Thursday. The last last supper. And something more.

I wasn't interested in foot washing. Too literal.

The thing is that Jesus emphasized this act as a teaching moment – his ministers must serve, not be served.

Rick welcomed everyone to get their feet washed. Whispered instructions ran through the pews – remove socks but leave pantyhose on being the most urgent. I didn't much want to get in line, but everyone in the choir did, so not wanting to be sitting alone in the chairs up front, I got in line. Stupid reason. My turn approaching, I sat in one of the chairs and slipped off my shoes. Rick and Lily, who was subdeacon, knelt at Tom's feet. Rick dipped his hands into the water and washed Tom's foot and vigorously rubbed it, then dried it and kissed it. Watching, I felt Tom's vulnerability and openness, as well as Rick's humility. Lily, I noticed, was more tender than Rick with her washing, and her kiss longer.

Rick touched my stockinged feet. He didn't look at me but went to work, and he gave my foot a wet massage that sent shivers up my spine. His rubbing felt downright sensual. He kissed my nylon encased foot. I wanted to reach forward and kiss his hands or his head.

He moved on, standing, kneeling, washing, kissing, a lot to do for a man of sixty. I slipped on my shoe and scurried to sing with the choir. Even though Rick had only washed one foot, I felt as if I had been totally cleansed.

We received communion, mindful that this commemorated when

Jesus called his disciples his friends and asked them, when they gathered, to do so in memory of him.

Jesus is betrayed, deserted, arrested.

We are silent.

Rick approached the altar grimly. He stood, eyes closed, hands on the altar that had been cleared of all vessels. He looked down as if summoning his energy, and then he wrested the altar cloth away in what almost seemed a violent, sexual act. I thought, it is the violence of grief. Now the servers moved quickly to strip the chancel, picking up chairs, vessels, books, cloths. All the furniture, every vessel, every book, everything had to go so that nothing was to be left.

This symbolized, and in fact made us feel, total, cruel grief at Jesus's betrayal and subsequent suffering. All left Christ alone, all his friends, even anything that would remind us of them. If it wasn't stripped away, it was cloaked in penitential purple.

Yet a part of me wondered – had they abandoned him or had they been killed? Was the abandonment of the apostles another way to blame the Jews for Jesus' cruel treatment by the Romans? No wonder why many people are so surprised that Jesus was a Jew.

The consecrated bread was moved to the side altar, Mary's side, and it was as if it was hidden there, inside her. Several of us stayed, some moved to the side pews to be closer. The rest of us left quietly, but we would return. We would watch with Jesus.

After the service, a few of us paused at the corner, but we were quiet, perhaps even afraid of the night. I walked home, wishing I could reconcile with Dad.

I sat and cried over old pictures. I guess I was still hurting.

At quarter to eleven, I walked back to church, giving the signal rap at the door. I heard footsteps. Donald opened the door. We smiled, didn't speak. He left. I shut and locked the door.

I was glad it was a warm evening. I wouldn't have to worry about there being no heat, or, if there was, have to put up with the boiler clanking.

"Would you not watch one hour with me?" Jesus asked his friends who could not. We, however, watched with him all night. Eleven to midnight was my hour. I went over to the side aisle and sat in the front pew. I'd brought my rosary.

The church creaked, but mostly, all was quiet except for a few honking horns outside. The noise seemed so distant. I wondered what my "watch" meant. Was it symbolic? Did it mean something deeper? What did waiting with Jesus mean for me? Was this too silly?

I moved in front of the pew and knelt before Mary's altar, where the consecrated presence rested. Flowers crowded the altar, and the scent was sweet. Why did I kneel there? To be close? To ask for favors? I questioned my sincerity, my understanding. Where was my life taking me? I brought up my Catholic prayers – the rosary, the Memorare prayer, the act of contrition.

I walked around the church, stopping at each station of the cross. So many years before, my mother had gone to the Stations, taking me, and I can still hear her voice, still our priest's voice, wonder why Jesus "had to" die on a cross. It still made no sense.

I went up to kneel at the steps of the main altar. I recalled my sense of when I was a child, believing, wondering, accepting, not fighting the whole business. For wasn't this asking me, where are you beyond the big talking? Beyond all your As in class? Where are you? Who are you to God if you're even there? And if not, even if there never was a God or a Jesus, except in the same dying/rising God of all mythologies, here we have created him and struggle with his teachings and isn't that good? Or does it lead to abuse?

Oh, if you are there, help me, help my mother, my father, help us all.

I stood up, turned to look at the whole church.

That great organ in the back choir loft presented a magnificent sight with its long, gorgeous pipes. Built in 1848, it was the church's first organ. But despite its grand appearance, it was silent now, having been vandalized. But it's something to look at and see, to remember how grand our visions of church once were. How people would do the best work for churches. Indeed, the balcony that wrapped around either side of the church from the loft, and the wood carvings on the balcony, were done by a parishioner of the time.

That great organ, wasted. And the great organ on one side of the chancel, also broken. Useless giants. Too expensive to fix.

I returned to my seat and tried simply to float away.

As soon as I closed my eyes and took some slow breaths, I could see in my mind's eye a waterfall. Cold white water pouring into a wild river, rushing under a wooden bridge, and all-around cliffs -- great mammoth cliffs reaching almost up to the sky.

I was at Yosemite.

Some years ago, I'd discovered that park for myself, stunned by its beauty and considering it my spiritual refuge. I'd since gone back every year, taking a cabin alone, breathing the pines, discovering the quiet in my soul. Looking up at El Capitan and Half Dome, I could feel God's power and love and the cleansing power of the Merced River through the pines.

I wouldn't be going this spring. I'd be going to Rome with Meg.

A sound. A rap.

I remembered where I was and grabbed my purse and hurried to the door to unlock it.

There was Ellen.

I nodded, let her in, and waited until I heard her turn the lock with me outside. I walked home, breathing calmly.

I had never felt this way before. I felt part of a greater something from the thousands of years before we were born, thousands of years before Christ, thousands of years before that and, oddly, after. The man/God, the dying God, the goddesses who give birth to, mourn, and raise the God – the God of our time, put to death we are told by a mob who would tear apart the sacred tenets of their own religion to kill him. But no, that made no sense. The God of our time was put to death by the earthly powers. Put to death once and then forever after, every year, nailed to that cross, year after year after year we do it.

And yet, resurrection.

And yet, life.

And yet, hope.

Just believe it.

Had this been my mother's secret?

"Come to me…all you who are weary and burdened…and you will find rest for your souls."

If only I knew how.

Close to noon on Friday, I returned to the church. A few people were sitting on the side, at their vigils. I took one of the center pews. The choir would be sitting somewhat together in the pews for this service.

The altar was stark, empty, as was the chancel, and save for but a few chairs, everything was gone. The church seemed abandoned and lonely.

The liturgical procession processed in silently, the altar party wearing the gray sacks of Lenten array.

Meg read a psalm.

Tom read from the Paul's Letter to the Hebrews.

John and I went up to the altar to sing the Passion. John sang Jesus. I sang the Narrator. I realized how the Narrator underlined the story and drove it relentlessly. We could not stop this from happening. The mob still cried, "Crucify him!" Pilate still cried, "Shall I crucify your king?" And the crowd cried, "We have no king but Caesar."

Joseph, yes, that foul mouthed, funny, courageous guy who'd lost half a leg to AIDS, represented Jesus. As he took the form of a cross, I bent down over his feet and washed them with my hair. This was part of a play Lily had found in one of her classes, and it added poetry and a grim solemnity over the story.

Only a week before, a crowd had hailed Jesus as their king.

Jesus had been considered a king and a son of God as kings were.

"Then," I sang, and I really did not want to sing.

"He bowed his head and gave up his spirit."

I knelt, facing the congregation. Everyone in the pews, kneeling, bowed their heads. The others in the chancel knelt. The others knelt in their pews. We stayed still, silent, drawn into the horror and the grief.

The gospel is political, I thought. The gospel of love is always political. Because love for all is such a frightening notion. So we search for people not to love, to condemn, whether by skin color or political belief or nation or size of their bankroll. For every person we choose to hate, a piece of our soul crumbles. But mustn't we hate evil people – Hitler? Saddam Hussein? My stepmother?

John tapped my elbow.

I stood up, taking his hand and a deep breath.

I sang. "And they laid Jesus in the tomb."

John began to sing, "Were you there when they crucified my Lord," and we joined in. I noticed that my voice sounded fierce. Well, we were all there. He died because of our sins not for them. But most people don't want to see that. It's easier to excuse our murder away by saying it had to happen. It was God's will. No, it was our will.

We sang a hymn that, just by its tune, broke my heart, "Ah, holy Jesus, how hast thou offended."

Rick and the acolytes processed down the aisle, where Rick picked up the large wooden cross covered in purple.

Lily cried out, "My people, what wrong have I done to you?"

Rick sang in a monotone, "Behold the wood of the cross."

The procession moved up a few steps.

We genuflected. We crossed ourselves.

Rick pulled down a bit of the purple cloth, revealing one arm of the cross.

The procession moved a few steps further.

"Behold the wood of the cross." Rick sang, a note higher.

Again and again, they moved forward until they had reached the altar steps and the Cross was fully exposed. Lily laid it across the steps and placed a pillow at its foot. The procession, beginning with Rick, lined up before the Cross as Meg and Lily held it. Rick knelt and kissed the Cross, remaining there for several moments. Then he stood to hold the cross. Lily and Meg each took a turn. Then they turned to us.

Now I had always wondered what the heck this was all about – people all ages – and the elderly the most devout – kneeling slowly, bending over awkwardly, and kissing the nailed feet of Jesus. Meg, Lily, and Rick held it up so you wouldn't be lying on the floor, but still – wasn't this somehow idolatry? What was the point? We couldn't rescue him.

As I stood in line, I thought, or are we the friends – we who did not abandon him.

Didn't I have a confirmation name, one I had chosen?

Mary.

Both Marys, Jesus' mother and Magdalene, had stood at the cross. For sure.

Would I have stayed?

I knelt and kissed Jesus' feet. I did not know whether to grieve or to call myself an idiot. I thought, I am here. As my grandmother did, as my mother did. With the women, who stayed by him. But would I have stayed? Would I have been afraid of the Romans coming for me?

After a quiet Communion served one by one in line, Rick dismissed us. The procession simply walked to the sacristy, while we sat quietly, unable to leave.

Rick returned to ring a bell at the side of the altar. The bell sounded thirty-three times, the age of Jesus at his death. At each strike, the bell resounded in our souls. Rick would pause, then strike again.

The ringing made me flinch for a corrupt world.

Then silence.

We filed out quietly.

CHAPTER 14

Three days in the tomb? More like a day and a few hours.

After a quiet Saturday, we were back at eleven that night.

Back in church – well, not in church – we robed in the sacristy and then gathered around the brazier in the cool crispness on the church's porch.

Rick held up a finger.

"Too breezy to light the fire."

Robert held the Easter candle, marked with resurrection symbols, which he tenderly touched every so often.

"Let's go in," said Rick. "We'll light it inside."

Rick pushed the brazier into the dark church where people waited with their unlit candles. Rick kindled the flame.

John scooted up the aisle to get the fire extinguisher.

"Oh, you of little faith," I whispered when he landed back next to me.

"No damn kidding!" He handed the extinguisher to Tom and hurried back to the organ. In the dark.

Silence returned. Rick offered a prayer, the fire grew, and with a taper, Rick lit the Paschal candle.

Robert led us down the aisle – I was behind him also wearing an alb and hoping not to trip – into the darkness of the church, Robert's one light for us to follow. The tall candle's aura reached only so far, so save for that flickering light, we were in pitch darkness. The flame formed a half oval above the candle, some of it touching the top of Robert's head.

He stopped, turned, sang, "The light of Christ."

I took a step forward and lit my candle from his, turning, focusing on Meg behind me, I found the wick of her candle, lit it, and down the procession the flame went as Meg turned to light the candle behind her and so on.

We walked further up the aisle, the narrow, faint light casting a tender aura over us. The church itself was invisible. Only our light marked reality and the shadowy figures in the pew.

Again, Robert stopped.

"The light of Christ," he sang.

"Thanks be to God," we sang.

Now we shared our candle fire with people on the ends of the pews, and they shared their candle lights. I could make out Paula, Joe, Norma, Nora, Joseph, Tom, Steven, Chris, Peter, Ellen, others.

The church grew in some pale light, gentle, comforting, like the safety of night when you were five years old and had just been tucked into bed.

Again, we moved forward.

Robert stopped at the foot of the steps.

"The light of Christ!"

"Thanks be to God!"

He mounted the steps and placed the candle in its holder. I climbed up and went to the eagle desk where my Exultet music lay. Only candlelight would guide me, but I could already tell that the light was growing. Anyway, I knew the piece by heart and would only glance at it.

The congregation glowed in halos spinning around them, a larger halo enveloping them all. The rest of the church seemed shadowed, not quite there.

We were floating in a space that had no time.

Rick sat in his chair in the center, signaling others to do so.

I plucked a note out of the air. I smiled and lifted my arms. I was one Exultet singer who would not be solemn.

The light, people, the light is coming! See, some of it is here! And it's growing!

"Rejoice now, heavenly hosts and choir of angels,

And let your trumpets shout Salvation

For the victory of our mighty king."

I was Miriam at the Red Sea. Mary at the Annunciation. Deborah under her tree, watching the battle. Judith in victory, holding up Holofernes' head before her village. All those jubilant, singing women. Mary Magdalene should have been given a song. Perhaps she had one, but the guys writing the Bible didn't put it in.

This was all sung as an a cappella chant, but I had rehearsed a pulse to it, mostly emphasizing consonants. So, it was a little jazzy. I felt lifted up. I leaned forward. And in my arms, in that light in the high ceiling I had seen before in the faces of my friends, in the old song I was singing, in the shout of rejoicing that had been shouted for centuries, I felt the power of consolation. Do not despair. This will never die. It lives again and again. No matter what.

I was offering hope that you could see.

And that is how I realized I was a priest.

I ended, raising my arms, "May Christ, the Morning Star who knows no setting, find this candle ever burning – he who gives his light to all creation, and who lives and reigns forever and ever. Amen."

I was almost in exultant tears.

Slowly, I returned to earth and my chair.

For a moment, silence.

I felt completely calm, completely right. My feet settled, one beside the other.

Rick said, "Let us hear the record of God's saving deeds in history, how he saved his people in ages past, and let us pray that our God will bring each of us to the fullness of redemption."

I thought of my mother, but I was brought out of that by Peter reading the story of creation, and every time he stated God's order, "Let there be," he snapped his fingers. We laughed. He was bringing out the humor in the story that, once upon a time had been just people telling stories by the fire, and these stories contained humor. In fact, the Bible stories were downright funny in many places. They've just been so deadened by study that we've forgotten to hear them.

When Nan got up to read about the Valley of Dry Bones – and she read it dryly! - we all found it audaciously funny and laughed our heads off. But there were unfunny reads, too: Abraham willing to sacrifice Isaac, for example. But the flood story was funny, too, and there was triumph at the end in Miriam's song after the Israelites crossed the Red Sea into freedom.

After we had renounced Satan (again!) while renewing our Baptismal vows, Rick stepped forward and called out, "Alleluia! Christ is risen!", and we rang bells and sang "Gloria in excelsis!" We danced in the aisles and hugged, like a great Peace.

Christ was alive in us, so of course we danced.

It may seem ludicrous to celebrate an event more than two thousand years old – and one many believe did not happen and many believe could not happen. I always thought so – until our Vigil. Because I felt it. I did feel it.

Yes. Even if not literally. Even if you do not believe one bit of the story. Even if you do not believe that Jesus was Christ or God or even ever alive. Because what we say when we say Christ is risen is not to celebrate an old story but one that is forever and ever new. The hope cruelly dashed and nearly destroyed by the mobs and the weak leaders of our world do not and cannot destroy us, even if the hopes lay in the tomb for a time. They will rise again – the friends, the followers - they will rise again and proclaim the good news and bring back the hope and the understanding that it *is* real – and that's not the Creed, no no – it is what Christ proclaimed – compassion, justice – feeding all, security for all, justice, compassion, and forgiveness – not in a Miss Nancy way, but with a firm understanding of realities. That is why men and women poured out of this new movement to tell all the nations.

Unfortunately, when the church became an institution of power, it forgot where it came from and why it was there.

But by telling the stories around our warm fire, we could remember and bring back the hope.

Rick preached.

This good news – does not fill us with peace. We cannot be sure what happened. We are released into the abyss of bewilderment...There is that in us that is always striving for life. And there is that in us that is afraid of real life... We each of us carry within ourselves, to some degree, a place that is walled in, sealed up, utterly cut off from human communication. Neither we ourselves nor any other person can enter this place...The glorious, good news of Easter is that in the night...while all of us were sleeping, the stone

– that huge and immovable obstacle that assuredly no one could ever move – has been rolled back! Yet…The walled-off place, the place of death, still stands. The habits of pain and paralysis that a lifetime has inscribed in the flesh are not dissolved instantaneously.

As we danced and celebrated, sang, and shared a meal, I realized what a bountiful feast Easter symbolized. It meant there would be unimaginable grief but healing and recovery from that grief.

And perhaps that is what it meant to me because I needed to feel that way.

It was the gift of the day.

I didn't get home until after midnight, and when I got up, I still had the glorious hope and the feeling that the hope would become reality. The old hymn found me:

O day of peace that dimly shines

Through all our hopes and prayers and dreams

Guide us to justice, truth, and love

Delivered from our selfish schemes.

May swords of hate fall from our hands

Our hearts from envy find release

Till by God's grace our warring world

Shall see Christ's promised reign of peace.

(Words by Carl P. Daw, Jr., sung to *Jerusalem* by C.H. Parry)

CHAPTER 15

Meg pulled up before my apartment building at three o'clock that Easter Sunday in a blue coupe. I put my bag in her trunk.

"Passport?" she asked as I dropped into the seat next to her.

"Check."

"Tickets? Oh, I have them. Check! Cash? Credit cards?"

"Check, check!"

I'd never been in a car with Meg driving, and I have to say it was illuminating. She furrowed her brow, glared at other drivers, and even yelled at them through the glass.

"Repent, you denizens of the devil!"

I have to say I laughed.

When traffic stalled, I started a Taizé chant.

She said, "Move it, sinners! God's coming to get you!" She laughed at herself. "I get behind a wheel, and I am the queen of the world. Oh, my foolish people!" she cried. "Why do you get in this lane and slow down?"

Then she sang along with me.

We arrived at Newark Airport and parked in the "God knows when we're gonna come back" lot. We checked in, checked our bags, and presented our passports. Mine was blank. Meg's wasn't. They pulled her aside and took her to a glassed-in room where they interrogated her – over what, I couldn't say.

After a quarter of an hour, when I was giving up hope of seeing Rome, she emerged from the room, passport in hand, looking just as amused.

"They always do this."

"Why?"

"Because my passport says I've been to Israel and Saudi Arabia."

"When? What?"

"They were tours. Catholic mission tours – nonpartisan nuns in Saudi Arabia. I went to Jerusalem because I wanted to go."

"You aren't just a mystery wrapped in an enigma. You're an enigma wrapped in an enigma."

"And cute, too. Hey, you should bring food on the plane."

"Don't they serve us?"

"Polly want a cracker?"

I got a turkey sandwich and a bag of chips. We found our gate. We picked our seats from a diagram.

I talked about the vigil service. She said, "I'd never heard the Exultet sung like that. You were so happy!"

"The words say 'rejoice' – you can't tell people to rejoice looking grim."

"It's an ancient hymn, so everyone's so solemn, but you're right. And hey, you have some presence."

I was about to tell her that I'd pretty much made my decision when the attendant announced our flight, and we jumped into the line. We got on board. It was a big mother of a ship. Past first class, the cabin had two long aisles and three rows of seats. I found our seats by a window.

"You want the window?" I asked.

"I want to sleep. I didn't get any."

"Now you tell me."

The seats were wide enough so that we could put our food bags between us and put the seat arms up. I looked around – the plane wasn't entirely filled. A few empty seats were scattered throughout. An attendant came through and told us that our food bags had to go overhead.

Meg grabbed a roll out of her bag, and we fastened our seat belts.

In those days, I loved to fly. I had full confidence in pilots and engineers, and I loved take-off – especially in a big plane. It felt so secure and exhilarating – the race down the runway, the engines growing louder, the feeling of immense power all around me, and the breaking free from the earth. I felt triumphant and proud.

Once airborne, I peered at little New York and took a folded up *New Yorker* out of my purse. Meg emitted a soft snore.

I went through the cartoons, then returned to the main story, determined to be informed. The first essay concerned the Security Council's resolution to end the Gulf War, the Kurds fleeing the Iraqi army, and who wanted them?

Soviet Jews were fleeing to Israel.

Doctors were on the verge of curing cancer again.

And people in East Saint Louis suffered in dire poverty.

I looked up –

The Atlantic lay beneath me, a blue-black mass, and around us, a blackness, - except for small patches of light, as if the sun's rays were trying to escape the water. Then I saw it on the horizon – the rising moon! It was looking right at me. Tenderly held by the night sky, it now rested, all of its white light upon the waters.

"Meg!" I called.

No sound.

I watched as the silver moon rose and brought more light to the blackness of the water, which little by little transformed into a soothing dark blue.

What human could have seen this sight more than seventy years before? I sank back in my seat, watching as the moon rose higher into the blue/black sky. She was fat, filled with light, bursting with it, her lights playing on the black surface of the Atlantic, leaping up and down, lighting up patches of the great ocean. I watched until she was no more, the Atlantic disappeared, and we were sailing in blackness.

As if we were God before She created it all.

I thought of how I'd felt the first time I went to Yosemite, that joyous sense of the discovery of God's awesome work, and I was glad I'd come this way instead of going there this year, that I could feel that divine force in other places.

The jabber of liturgy, of classes, of my job faded away.

I slept. I woke up. I read and made notes.

During the period in which John of Patmos wrote, the heavens hung low. The cosmos, represented by the bodies of light in the sky, contained portents and needed to be understood and consulted. We have lost that... Kapelrud claims that Anat was Jeremiah's Queen of Heaven...his reference to the Queen of Heaven and baking cakes for her can be compared with the act of baking kamanu cakes for the Babylonian Ishtar or the selanai cakes offered to Athenian Artemis. In all cases, the round cakes represented the moon.

I slept.

I woke up. My eyes felt dry – I'd slept with my contact lenses in. I dug my eye drops out of my purse. Meg was still sleeping.

"Ladies and gentlemen, we are descending into Rome."

I jabbed Meg's arm.

"What?" she yelped.

"We're landing."

"Why did you jab me?"

"Because you were sleeping."

"My first sleep for two days."

"Why?"

"Oh, stuff."

Rome before us, lighting up. The same Rome where Saint Peter had gone, where he had fled and then returned to face death. Rome, that sent Pilate to Jerusalem where he condemned Jesus. The same Rome that united a world under a mighty power. The home of popes, Michelangelo's art, and churches almost as old as Christianity.

Rome.

CHAPTER 16

Thank God Meg knew her way around and what to do. After we got our bags, we exchanged our money, found a train to the city, and from where that left us, we got a cab. I couldn't believe I wasn't looking at pictures. Rome was real.

And that of all my ancestors.

Streets seemed narrow – or perhaps that is my memory. Our pension – which I'd picked out of a guidebook - started up a flight of stairs in a dark alley. We plowed up with our bags and ended up in a lovely gold and blue sitting room. We found our little room with a bathroom two doors down. We slammed our bags down and, with our guidebooks in hand, hurried down the steps and out to Rome.

We passed the Trevi Fountain.

Alas, the Pantheon was closed.

"Let's get a coffee there," said Meg, pointing at a plaza with a streaming fountain in the center. The sun was warm, a guitarist leaned against the fountain, and all around us, people held quiet conversations in different languages.

"I could stay here all day."

"Welcome to Rome." Meg flung her braid behind her and smiled at a waiter coming over.

I was ready to order in Italian, but we had not fooled the waiter, who spoke in English right away. We ordered our coffees and settled back.

At the next table, a man and woman were quarreling. In English.

"Why did you have to take her?"

He was tall – even in his seat, thin, salt and pepper hair, early fifties, kind of stuffy. She was brunette, great cheekbones, early twenties.

"She's my wife, Gina."

"What kind of reason is that?"

Meg glanced at the couple with a perplexed expression. I just grinned.

"It's the Oscars. I can't show up with you."

The Oscars! Billy Crystal riding in. *Dances With Wolves* – which I hated.

Gina said, "You jerk. Who cares? You're a sound engineer?"

"I was nominated! If I didn't take her, I'd never hear the end of it from her. And others."

"You're not going to hear the end of it from me. I'm the one you're going to marry after you dump her."

"Treating me like dirt when your wife is so – a bitch. She makes your life miserable. I'm the one you love. Don't you have any guts?"

He stood up, tossed some money down and covered it with a saucer.

"I'm damn proud of what I did. Warren was happy with my work. It was one proud moment, and I would have hurt my wife too much if I hadn't brought her."

Warren Beatty? I so wanted to ask.

The woman got up and hurried away.

"Gina!"

The man ran after her.

"What a jerk," I said.

"Let's go," said Meg.

We wandered to the Trevi Fountain, tossed in pennies. We wandered back to our pension, smiled at people in the parlor who smiled back.

I'd thought we'd talk before we went to sleep, but Meg just buried herself under her covers and didn't say a word.

The next morning, we grabbed a pastry and coffee and headed for Saint Peter's, having taken care that our arms were covered as required! We crossed the plaza and covered our heads. Meg lent me a silk scarf in a delicate blue shade as I had completely forgotten about that rule for women, since Vatican 2 had helped destroy the hat business.

"It's a magic scarf," she said. "It'll take you to your heart's desire if you take it to a sacred place."

"It's lovely! How do you know it's magic?"

"I know." She grinned.

The scarf was lovely, with shots of blue and silver and transparent areas where you could look through it and see the world transformed into blue and silver. It was magical. I tied it around my head and knotted it.

Once inside that great basilica, we walked up to the tomb of Pope John XXIII, which Meg wanted to see first.

"He brought us out of the Middle Ages."

"Only to see *us* go out," I added.

"It could have been different, but the church wouldn't go along with it."

"He couldn't see us, Meg. Anyway, that 'you are Peter and upon this rock I will build my church' business wasn't anything Christ said. The writers put that in later. We learned that in class. Who made all those old men the boss of our souls?"

But she would defend him. "I think he would have come around to ordaining women. I think he was murdered."

I'd heard that, but I didn't believe it. Anyway, I was more concerned with the people, not the so-called leaders.

"I once met a woman who, on hearing about taking communion from a woman, said, 'I could never do that!' How do people learn to feel that way?"

"How can they unlearn it is what we should be thinking. Hey, let's climb the steps to the roof."

"Why?"

First, we walked through the massive cathedral. The trouble is, it was so massive that now I don't remember much about it. We got in line for the roof and took the elevator that only goes part way. On the first level, we went over to the fence, looking out beside Jesus and the apostles and the view of Rome – some of the statues of the apostles carried small crosses, which made me weep. What would they make of all this?

Meg looked out at the city solemnly, tossing her braid. She took my hand but didn't say anything. I had nothing to say either.

Until –

"Up? It's all stairs."

I gritted my teeth.

"Up."

First, we went to look down at Michelangelo's dome and his mosaics –the most extraordinary beauty. And the chair of Saint Peter, Bernini's baldachin.

Then - five hundred and fifty-one steps to the dome.

I was apprehensive. I'd been sitting all day for almost a year. I grimly read a warning about how dangerous the climb could be. Narrow steps curving round and round and no banister.

But I followed Meg and took that first step up.

I held onto the walls. We slowed; we caught our breaths.

Did Michelangelo do this at age seventy-one?

Then narrower steps – a window with a view – I could barely look down at the shrinking city – more steps, walls narrowing in further – would this never end? Would the walls only get narrower and pin me in? You'd think we'd have heard about that. Someone up there stopped, so we stopped. It was growing very warm. I wiped my forehead. What if someone had a heart attack? How would they get help? I thought about an earthquake. The world beneath was far away now. Heaven awaited. It was certainly getting closer.

A level floor. We stopped, panted, and thought we were done, oh no. More steps! People above and below gasping. Stopping. Up again. Walls closing in and in.

I reminded myself of the Mist Trail at Yosemite, which was over six hundred steps. I had climbed that.

I kept going.

The steps widened.

I could hear people breathing heavily.

Heaven seemed closer. Do people breathe in Heaven?

A banister appeared! I grabbed at it, pulled myself up with it.

More curvy, narrow steps. I wondered if whoever designed the Statue of Liberty had been inspired here.

Who sweeps these steps?

I felt dizzy, and then – air.

Rome was far, far below. A little city, not so mighty after all.

We grabbed something, I forget what, and stood gasping and feeling our sore limbs.

"We could hail a plane if we don't want to go down," I said. Meg grinned and made a gesture to punch me.

We faced south and looked down at Rome and the square and at Bernini's colonnade – embracing all, as it was supposed to do.

Except it does not.

The Castle Saint Angelo.

The Coliseum – largest amphitheater ever built.

The Pantheon.

We stayed there for almost an hour, resting on a circular bench, as people came and went.

"I want to hug this city," cried Meg at one point.

"I want to hug the city and soar into the sky over it. Meg, why do we feel this way since we both left the Catholics?"

"But this is where it all started. When Peter came here."

"Do you think he did?"

"Now I do."

"Yeah, all this does make you believe or want to."

That was all we said. We watched the sun and the light change on the statues as if they were giving witness to the day.

Finally, Meg said, "We have to go back down. I'm hungry, and I don't want to kill any pigeons."

Just the thought of going down made me feel dizzy again, but she was right. We had to go down sometime. It was still tiring as our legs were sore. At first, I thought, I never saw people going down, but there was a different staircase for that – the same curves, though, and tricky to negotiate with shaking legs.

Finally, we made it.

We sat.

The Mass was nearing its end. It couldn't have taken long.

Meg said, "Should we run back up? Hey, where's my scarf?"

I put my hand on top of my head, on my shoulders. When had I last felt it? I thought I remembered holding onto it on the roof.

"I don't know. Oh, geez."

We got up and retraced our steps to THE steps.

"It's up there somewhere," I said. "I 'm so sorry. I'll get you another one. Maybe someone will find it and turn it in."

She was upset. "A dear friend gave that to me, and now it's gone. How could you lose it?"

"I didn't do it on purpose. I'm really sorry. I'll get you another."

She strode ahead and nearly ran out of the Cathedral. How could she run? I followed her, but my legs hated to move. When I got outside, I couldn't see her in the crowd.

Well, damn you. It's not like I did it on purpose.

After a few steps, I had to lean against a wall.

I could not see her. I dug into my purse and didn't know if I could afford a cab. What about a bank machine? I had to laugh. The Vatican was a bank machine.

I pushed through to where I saw cabs and a line of people. Where was the pension? I had to dig further in my purse to find the paper I kept with its address.

It took almost half an hour to get a cab.

I had enough money, thank God. At the pension, I sank into a parlor chair and after a few minutes rest, made my way up to our room.

No Meg.

I took advantage of the empty pension and took a bath.

Still no Meg.

I worried.

She came back at eleven, very late.

"Did you eat?" I asked. I had run across the street for a sandwich.

"Yeah."

"I'm sorry. You know that."

"I shouldn't have given it to you."

"Did your friend die? Was it the only thing left for you? Tell me about her."

She glared at me for a moment, went to the bathroom, came back in her robe, and climbed into her bed.

"What are we doing tomorrow?" she asked casually.

I wished she'd have talked to me about her friend. Or was it her husband who gave it to her? But I didn't know how to ask. So, I was glib. "Stuff. The Coliseum and there's an old church on the other side of the river. Oh, our host used to work for the railroad, and he can help us with good connections when we want to go to Florence and Pompeii."

"Okay."

Well, at least she said "okay" to our going together. I had the feeling that she really hated me. I felt scared. I couldn't lose her friendship.

CHAPTER 17

O
h, that time in Rome. In the morning, Meg would be ebullient and funny, then as the day wore on, she'd be somber and clam up, and I would feel in the way so I would go off by myself. In exploring churches, I realized that Judith's story had been a popular one; the old churches had her story carved somewhere in their structure.

Meg and I did go together to a church on "the other side," the Santa Maria in Trastavere, well, that brought us a little bit more together. An old church, one of the first built, with gleaming, golden mosaics – art that could take forever to absorb.

Meg stopped, pointing at the apse.

"Look. They are equal."

She meant that Jesus and Mary, both seated on thrones in a painting upon the gleaming apse – some figures were in shadow, but these two were lit – Mary and Jesus sat enthroned, and they were, as Meg said, equal. On each side stood men, or so it seemed, several in typical church garb.

"Mary," I said.

Meg gripped my hand. "Isn't that fantastic."

It was profound. Christ's humanity was our humanity, and if God had taken part in that, humanity and divinity had come together and could not be separated – even by death.

I wanted to kneel down right there.

"Equal," said Meg.

"Divine and human," I said.

We split up to absorb the art, allowing for privacy. It felt right.

Her life in pictures. Madonna. Child. The Virgin's life – born, the

Annunciation of the angel, Jesus born, the Magi visit, bringing Jesus to the temple, and abruptly, her death.

So much should be in between. So much more. But it's hard to argue with an artist or artists who have been dead for several hundred years, and this work was exquisite and still alive.

I wandered to a dark part of the church; it seemed like a storage space of works of art in cartons.

Here I found a stunning picture of Mary and her baby. The face was both stern and tender. How could that be? Then, in her right hand, a sword

A sword shall pierce your heart. I remembered.

Was she holding the one that would kill her or was it her weapon to defend her child?

I remembered all those women I had uncovered with right arms upraised, gripping weapons. Fight! Liberty! Equality! Of one cartoon depicting Susan B. Anthony lifting her right arm to vote – and a man stopping her because in 1874, only white men could vote without interference.

But…they are equal. Jesus. Mary.

I joined Meg, who was praying. I chose to do that, too. We were alone in this beautiful church where faith had been so strong so early – and so different from the one that evolved. I prayed for peace and for my father. I prayed to my mother.

Meg nudged me.

"Let's go eat."

It wasn't far to a dinerish-looking restaurant. I ordered fish. She ordered spaghetti and insalata mista. She was bubbling all about equality in the early church.

I listened.

At the pension, we laid out our plan to see Assisi and Pompeii.

Meg started talking about the woman who hadn't been able to go to the Oscars.

"I feel sorry for her."

"You're crazy. The man's married. He's using her. She should realize that."

"I'm taking a bath."

When I got back, she was already asleep. Or pretending to be, face down, her braid slicing her in two.

Assisi involved a train ride, a bus ride, and a lot of Italian. Once there, I loved it. It felt like a wonderland of Italy, surrounded by lush fields. I stayed by the wall just to look at those fields before heading to the basilica and the frescoes possibly created by Giotto depicting Francis' life. Meg split off to explore the town.

I took my time in the basilica, savoring the art and its faith. I left as a crowd of tourists entered, and I climbed up the street, finding souvenirs for both Francis and his love, Clare, who had outlived him. I wondered about them, about her, about how strong and single-minded she must have been. And how much of them continued to live, even if it was simply in Blessing of the Animals services, although I doubted Francis would have liked the idea of bringing the elephants into the cathedrals. One should go to them to bless them. Church had a way of awkwardly recognizing the beautiful.

The town felt sacred. Assisi is like a trip to heaven if you love rolling green hills.

Eventually, I made it back to the basilica.

Declare poverty, and all the jewels in the kingdom are yours. I hadn't realized that Francis' own body rested there, where the greatest artists all went to honor him. Their art exploded with genius and love. All for a young man, something like a hippie, filled with love for people, for creatures.

He died young, forty-four – perhaps not young then. Of poverty.

He was never ordained.

The lower church was simple, earthy. I found a sweet portrait of Francis, and his eyes gentle, kind – his whole demeanor kind and yet – weary. I wanted to hug him. Other portraits of him set him off, away, in elegant vestments. They weren't him, despite the artists' good intentions.

I paused by the tomb. Francis, I thought, show me your way and your courage.

Outside, I found Meg sitting on a stone.

"I can't go in."

"Why not?"

"I just want to sit here and look. Almost time for the bus."

I sat next to her.

She flung her braid back, and I had to dodge it.

"Do you have to hang around me so much?" she asked.

I was stunned.

"We split up this whole time."

"You're always trotting along."

I stood up and walked away.

I didn't sit with her on the bus to Pompeii. There, I searched for the pictures on the walls. It was warm, and there was little shade, but I forced myself to concentrate on what the pictures were saying about these people who'd had lived and had passions and fears and loves and who died so awfully.

I don't know where Meg went. I didn't care. The bus would honk when it was time to go back to the train. I walked, smiled at the pictures, tried to make them out. I wandered to the amphitheater and did a little soft shoe, entertaining a few tourists.

The bus honked.

I picked an empty seat. She didn't get on and the driver honked again. She ran across the yard, peered into the bus, and found a seat up front with a woman.

When she got out, I hurried over to her. She had the tickets.

I followed her to a little room that was empty.

I sat across from her.

I must admit, I prattled on about Assisi.

"Will you stop chattering?"

"What's with you?"

"I loved my scarf."

The scarf!

"If you want, I'll climb back up to the roof to get it."

"Don't be silly. It probably flew into the wind. Or someone took it."

"Don't be vindictive over an accident. Maybe I'll write the bishop."

"Yeah, I'm such a pill."

"You are right now.

She looked at me and smiled. "But you wouldn't do that."

"Just try me. You've been one royal pain. You can't forgive anyone anything, can you?"

"But you lost my scarf."

I turned to the window to watch the lovely hills, the vineyards. I didn't want to miss this part of Italy.

I didn't talk to her for the rest of the trip. I was sorry, yes, very, but it was a *scarf.* If it was so important, she shouldn't have brought it on the trip or given it to me.

Back in Rome, we grabbed spaghetti at some little place. We ate fast and quietly. A couple shared our table and Meg talked to them in sketchy Italian, laughing. I didn't laugh. We walked back to the pension. I stayed downstairs to thank our host for his help and look through some of the newspapers.

Meg was gone when I woke up. I was glad and sauntered around the city – I went to the Pantheon, walking on that precious floor, looking up at the dome. We are, I thought, whom we love. With this thought, my eyes filled with tears. The immensity of everything I had been seeing caught up with me.

I went to the little museum with Artemisia Gentileschi's self-portrait and cried over it and other paintings. I went to the Sistine Chapel. There was, of course, a line, and when I went in, there was Meg, lying down on one of the benches and looking up at the ceiling, collecting amused laughter from the other visitors.

I had to laugh, too.

She sat up, waved, and laid down again.

A guard came over. The guards there are, well, colorful, with big helmets.

"Get up." He spoke English. He must have assumed.

Meg sat up, quicker than I thought she would.

"It's how he saw them." She grabbed my waist and sauntered off with me to the other end of the ceiling.

"You should have brought a ladder and a scaffold."

"Isn't this amazing? Where's God?"

"Right there." I waved at the Santa Claus-like figure pointing at Adam. Yes, he's the guilty one, I thought. Eve was still in heaven, watching warily from behind God's arm.

"She has a beard, Meg."

"Well, when you get to be a certain age…"

"How long have you been here?"

"All day."

"Well, I'm going to start looking. I wrote a story based on this ceiling."

"Tell me."

"Later."

She was just pretending to be interested. I wasn't going to chance it.

I walked away and looked up at Michelangelo's ceiling. He'd had trouble with ordained people. I empathized.

Over dinner on some piazza, after she asked me again, I told her the story I'd written. "We – my family – my town – were in church. There was a great explosion – huge. When someone opened the door, all was blackness – nothing above, below, or to the sides. No earth. Nothing. We still survived, our own little planet. Radios were silent. Our parish alone had been elected to survive – or had we been rejected? Arguments began right away. Who were we? Why were we? It seemed to be God's or someone's will that we survive – we're not even ON anything, nothing lay beneath us. And we had plumbing! And a stockpile of food in the basement! Why? People preached the end of the world. People preached the beginning of a new world."

Meg listened, played with her food. "So church is leaving the world?"

I wouldn't answer. "My character didn't fit in either group. She felt it was a church that could not see outside itself. She told everyone that there really was a world out there. No one believed her and pointed to the black windows where once saints had held up their hands in holy praise. One day, she just ran for the doors. The others, left inside, thought she died."

"Did she?"

"What do you think? I had Hayden's Creation singing as she leaped out – the creation of the earth."

"What were you saying?"

"The real sacrament is the world, our earth. That's where Jesus came. That's what God created. But I was also making the point that individual churches get so wrapped up in themselves."

"Is this part of your discernment?"

"I wrote this a long time ago."

"It's part of you."

"What are you so mad at me about?"

She looked away.

"It was just a scarf. Who did it belong to?"

"Someone I loved, okay? Shut up about it."

"Is he or she dead?"

"The more you love a person, the more you're hurt when they are thoughtless about you."

"I wasn't thoughtless."

"I don't mean you."

"I mean you."

She shrugged.

On our last day, we went to Florence, wandering through museums and plazas. Holy pictures, sainted halos, solemn faces, gentle Jesus.

All so much though. Too much to really settle it in my brain.

We were on the plane when I turned to her and said, "I'm going to tell Rick I'd like to start discernment officially."

"That is why you've been so weird. Now we can really be pals."

We couldn't be pals before? And *I* was weird?

I shrugged her off. I was going to have to learn to do that and not depend on her for so much, even for close friendship.

I remembered stepping off the curb. One foot could do so much.

We breezed through customs. We only brought back our darkness. When we were collecting our baggage, she said, "We should go somewhere else together again."

Oh, right.

We picked up her car. She rattled on about the General Ordination Exams (the GOEs), and I couldn't wait to get away from her. I didn't need to feel judged.

CHAPTER 18

We were both at church on Sunday, and Rick announced our safe return to great applause. Then he said, "Our prayers were answered. The bishop has agreed that our Meg can be admitted to the postulancy."

The place erupted with cheers and hugs.

As I congratulated her, I couldn't help feeling jealous. Of what? Her acceptance? The applause? Or just that she'd made it that far? She'd made it through the barriers of Heine's dislike of Rick and of our parish. It could be done. I could do it, too, and I didn't have any of Meg's problems. So why was I feeling competitive?

After the Eucharist, I tracked Rick down at his office. He was talking on the phone. "It took all I had. Bulla's people were still on, thank God, but they're ready to move on. And I could call in favors for two. The others would not budge. But she got a majority to approve her, and the bishop went ahead. It would have looked suspicious if he hadn't. Anyway, what a relief. It's all settled for now."

He looked up, saw me, waved me in.

The office was dark, for the shade was drawn over the one window. Everything appeared as if it had a pall of darkness over it, the desk, the filing cabinet, especially the several bookcases that crowded the place. Usually, it felt cozy. Today it felt tense.

He hung up, came over to hug me – of course – and said, "Great, isn't it? Meg said you two had a wonderful time in Rome. I envy you both."

"It was quite an experience. Rick," and I went right for it, "I would like to officially enter a period of discernment."

He stood looking at me for what seemed like a long time. My heel planted itself firmly. I pushed down on it and stepped fully down onto this road.

Finally, he spoke. "For the priesthood?"

What did he think it was for?

"Yes." My foot stepped off the curb. The heel planted itself down firmly. I pushed down on it and stepped fully down onto the road.

He smiled. He opened his arms wide for a hug. "That is wonderful." Another hug. "I'll form a committee."

Ah, the Episcopal Church. How many committees does it take to change a light bulb.

Two days later, Rick called to say that Steven and Michael Gregory would be my discernment committee. Steven had wanted to be a Catholic priest, but he'd given it up for teaching theology at Fordham. "After all, I'm a gay man," he told me on the phone, "although I've found that the Catholic priesthood is a perfect hideout for gay men. I don't want to hide out, and I'm not good at being a yes man."

I said, "Despite my just seeing the crushing power of Rome in its buildings, Catholicism is dying. It's lost almost all moral authority, it degrades women, it's nothing. I've found pictures and documents of very early churches, and they combine cultures in the art – Greek gods, Christ, you name it. Catholic means universal. It means it embraces all and welcomes all. But now it's become authoritarian, and you say what I say because I have God's truth in my hands."

"Wow."

"Sorry."

"Leaving it was painful. It was my mother's church, and her faith was strong."

"You'd go back?"

"It's not there to go back to."

I wondered if Steven might have issues with me, but he was smart, funny, and focused. Michael was another thing entirely. He spoke in a cloud I couldn't see through. Would these men understand me? Would I understand me? Would they pick me apart like so much lint on a sweater? I thought, well, Shannon, if you can't take the heat…

When Rick announced my discernment during announcements, Paula jumped up and hugged me.

I had to write something for the discernment meeting.

I decided I should become a priest when I stepped off the curb on West Twentieth and Ninth Avenue in New York.

After the intense scholarship of Forrest's Hebrew Bible class, New Testament felt like the eighth grade.

For one class, Tina Collins stood there in her gold lame outfit, all aglitter. She was showing us what sort of place Corinth was, but that was as deep as the class went. She went off on wild tangents about husbands and kids, and I felt robbed. I'd been told she was just the greatest. At least, we had a quiz every class, identifying quotes, and Meg and I would quiz each other on the phone the night before class.

After Tina's class, which always ended half an hour early, I would sneak into Angela Stetson's seminar on Paul. She waved me in, and I sat in the back. She created a person who was human and, surprisingly, admirable. I had never liked Paul and his attitude toward women, but she made me rethink him as a human being. Angela spoke through some of the feminist angst. She warned, "In thoughtful scholarship, in all scholarship, men write as Peter Brown has said, using women to think with."

I kept up my library Saturdays.

Wandering through the stacks, I found a book about Lakota spirituality, and on the shelf above it, a history of religion in the New World. I pulled it down and flipped through the pages. It was an old text. Fifteen hundreds. I leafed through it, putting my other book down on a nearby desk. After reading a few lines, I had to sit down.

The author, a Catholic priest, was against trying to convert the "savages." No, it's a waste of time. they were a step below creation, a taunt to God. They should all be eliminated because, clearly (!), the new continents were for the Christians. Everyone else should be eliminated, for the savages were insults to God and had probably evolved from the beasts.

I tried to find who this man was, and according to the forward, written during the nineteenth century, the priest was a man of God who had visions and who declared that the new world was Europe's by right. No, Christian by right. I couldn't understand the logic. I couldn't understand it at all. I copied a few passages to include in my paper, although I wasn't sure how I'd handle them. This attitude of his lasted for centuries. Christianity above all and kill the rest. It didn't belong in my paper, but it had to be written about, carefully, accurately. One more topic for the list, an important one.

At home, I went to my bookcase and took down one of the books I'd bought at Yosemite, *The Sacred Hoop* by Paula Gunn Allen, a Laguna/Pueblo Sioux, and she was citing the Keres Indians of Laguna Pueblo.

In the beginning, Tse che nako, Thought Woman, finished everything, thoughts, and the names of all things. She finished also all the languages. And then our mothers, Uretsete and Naotsete said they would make names and they would make thoughts. Thus they said. Thus they did.

This she had taken from Anthony Purley's literal translation from the Keres Indian language of a portion of the Thought Woman story. Purely was a native-speaker Laguna Pueblo Keres.

I remembered reading this at Yosemite, sitting on the banks of the Merced, wild and rolling in the spring, and how much the passage had spoken to me. How much of Thought Woman, when summoned -- and when I thought of the other women of the goddess wilderness, when they were summoned -- filled me with a light that dared me to believe.

And that stupid Jesuit wanted to kill these people.

CHAPTER 19

The phone was ringing when I got home.

"Hello, Janene."

Why, it was my father.

"How are you?"

"Good." He sounded fake hearty.

"Good."

"Helen treats me very well."

"Good."

Was that what this call was about? Just making sure I knew that?

"I was hoping you could come to see us."

"Really?"

"Yes. We don't talk anymore. Now that the wedding is behind us, there's no reason we can't all get together."

Why, he was a family man again.

"I went to Rome."

"You did? We're going to get a cruise to Alaska."

"Lots of things going on you didn't care to know about."

Silence.

"Look, I'm calling to make things right."

"Can you? The things you said to us? You weren't you. You never talked like that before. Now you want to be pals again? You don't even know you hurt us or how. Did you know that in hurting us you hurt Mom? It was never the wedding. It was your need to push us away. And now you want us back?"

A voice screamed.

Apparently, Helen had been on the line. I wonder if Dad knew that.

"How dare you talk to your father like that? How dare you hurt him?"

"Helen, how nice to hear your voice."

"He's crying. What you said to him was insulting. My children never talk to me like that or to him. They respect your father."

"Anything to get out of your house fast. Where are your children, Helen?"

"Stop it!"

I didn't want him to cry. He was two men now. Before and after. I was two women. A child wanting her father and a woman wanting to kill him.

"I want to talk to my father. Although you're such a joy to talk to."

"You be nice to him, or I will not welcome you in my home."

"I'll be nice to him. But I don't care about going to your home."

Dad came back on. "You made her cry."

"That makes three of us. I don't want to fight. She insists on being cruel, and you just stand there."

"I don't want to fight either."

"I'll see if I can get to DC soon. I'll let you know."

"Okay." He sounded as if he didn't believe me.

I opened my mouth to insist, but he had hung up.

Oh, Dad, I so understood your need to get away, but you ran away from us – I guess we reminded you of your pain. But you left us without the man Mom loved.

I'd thought we would spend some time honoring and remembering Mom, helping him get back on his feet – getting him a different apartment – going through things carefully – that sort of thing. Nope. Not one month later, he was in love with someone else. Someone who didn't want us. It was more important that he have a new life. We just reminded him of Mom. Too painful.

The job was hard that week. The publisher of our journal told us we had to kill our cover story, which meant another story would have to be pulled in, a new cover concepted, and the thing would have to be edited, copyedited, set, and laid out in three days. We worked late nights. I had to skip class. Meg was taking her GOEs, and I had to miss the parish gathering to pray for her.

Our publisher, Mike, and Charley, our managing editor also stayed late, and while logging some pages, I yelled within earshot of both, "I'd better get a lobster out of this!"

Mike yelled back, "Guaranteed!"

He went right to his phone and reserved lunch at the Palm for the next Monday.

Charley yelled, "You should have asked for a trip to Palm Beach!"

"Too late!" called Mike. "You only get one wish out of this genie!"

At least, I was lucky in my job.

And I had to give another sermon. I worked it in my head.

Meg said, "The thing was hard. I'm glad it's over." But she said it on my machine. I didn't have any time to stop anything I was doing. Finally, Sunday came and my sermon.

I preached about the Samaritan woman at the well. As expected, when Jesus told her that she had had seven husbands, the congregation tittered. I went to the pulpit and immediately told them under what conditions a woman could have seven husbands during Jesus' time. Handed from man to man, brother to brother. Then I decoded the gospel, thanks to some reading I'd done, to give the woman such joy and freedom that she ran through town praising him. It was a story about self-forgiveness, about our forgiveness of others, of opening our eyes to see the truth of love.

Rick seemed pleased.

Meg announced that she passed the GOEs, although scoring Inadequate in Ethics. We cheered.

Mike, Charley, and I took a substantial three-hour lunch at the Palm. We had three drinks, which made me able to open up a bit about the problems I had with my father. Just the facts. Mike was an old-fashioned Italian guy, and family was first with him.

"Your dad must have a broken heart," he said.

I said, "I want to go to Washington and Arlington and see them. Maybe cool things down."

Mike said, "The cardiology convention is coming up. Why don't you cover it? It's in DC. Take them out to dinner on us. That's not primary care, so I don't expect a story out of it, but you never know."

I dropped my little fork into the melted butter.

"Oh, thank you. I promise I'll go to the meetings."

"I know you will. But your Dad needs a nudge."

Nudge? More like a push over the cliff.

It was something to have people care about you.

I put in the paperwork.

I called Dad.

"Figure out where you'd like to go to dinner. It's on the journal."

He couldn't answer.

I heard him call out. "Janene wants to take us to dinner."

He was asking her permission to have dinner with his daughter.

I waited nearly five minutes while they spoke quietly.

"We'd love to," he finally said.

"Pick the restaurant." I gave him the date and information of my arrival and departure.

He said, "Thank you, honey."

I nearly burst into tears at that. He hadn't sounded so nice or kind or thanked me since the funeral.

The phone rang right after. It was Meg.

"I'm getting ordained deacon next month! Rick got approval that I get on the fast track! Because of my age," she laughed.

Wow. She was speeding right up that ladder.

"Will you be one of my sponsors? I've asked Lily, too. Rick will present me."

"Sure."

"They're having a meeting at the Cathedral – I'm going to try to get you to sing a psalm or something. Would you?"

"Depends on the something," I joked. Then I remembered. "When is it? I'm out of town the weekend of the fourteenth."

"Oh, this is the week before. Thanks! I've got to run."

"Congratulations. I thought it took longer."

"Heine didn't want to, but Rick still has friends on the Commission. Just in time. Most of them have terms up soon. I want to be a priest by my fiftieth birthday."

"Otherwise, you'll turn into a pumpkin again?"

"A rat. See you Sunday! Can you believe it?"

Meg's deacon ordination proved impressive and long. I sang the psalm way up high in the cathedral where the organ hid out. Afterwards, I thought we'd all go to dinner, but Meg had other plans and Rick had a meeting. Lily and I had dinner near the cathedral, and she kept playing with her collar.

And talking about it.

"You can't wear it all the time. You shouldn't wear it on the street unless you're on business. I shouldn't be wearing it here." And she giggled.

She didn't take it off, though.

Big party at church on Sunday. At coffee, Meg swung her arm around me and said, "Why don't we go out west this summer? We can fly to LA and meet some of my friends there and head into the desert like Moses."

Now that all the tension was over about her ordination, maybe things would be better.

"Sure. We could spend a day or two at Yosemite. Want me to try to get reservations?"

"Okay!" She turned when Rick called her name, her braid flying against my face.

CHAPTER 20

I flew into DC, but I stayed in Arlington so that I'd be close to where Dad and Helen lived. First, I had to cab it to the DC Convention Center to register and pick up my schedule. I sat in on a few meetings and found it difficult to concentrate. That night was The Dinner.

I cabbed it back to the Arlington Sheraton, showered, changed. Waited for the phone. Half hoping it wouldn't ring.

It rang.

Dad's different voice.

"Jan! Hi! We're in the lobby."

"I'll be right down."

Since his wedding, Dad's voice hadn't sounded right. It still didn't. A bass baritone, his voice had always been deep. It had gone up a few notes – it was fainter. As if he'd lost part of himself.

I stepped off the elevator and there they were. Dad looked good – thinner – still tall, still handsome. Helen's head came up to his shoulders. Her hair startled me – it was bright yellow and styled like a little girl's baloney curls. She wore a tiny hat on top, like a matron from the 1950s television shows, and a light brown coat over a light brown dress.

I hugged Dad. He kissed my cheek. I shook Helen's hand, and I placed my other hand on top of hers and said, "It's good to meet you at last."

That last was a deliberate dig, but I said it with a sweet smile. Neither of them seemed to get it.

"Let's stop in the bar for a drink," said Dad.

That was strange. When we'd gone out to eat in the Before Time, Dad had always ordered his drinks when we sat down to dinner. But this was his new life, so into the bar we went. We took a table. Behind us, at the bar, a few men were watching, and cheering on, a football game.

We ordered drinks.

I asked how they both were doing.

Dad said, "Wonderful."

"Your father is getting to know the city," said Helen, quite formally. "It's so lovely in the early fall. And I have made him walk because all these years, he did not take care of himself."

She smiled at me, and I knew she was digging at me.

"Yes, she takes good care of me," said Dad. "And driving is a challenge here, but I'm getting used to it."

"Good, I'm getting in a car with you!"

I meant it as a joke, ribbing like the old days, but Helen snapped, "He is a very good driver."

"Of course he is."

She wasn't going to get my goat.

"Have you decided what you're going to do?" I asked Dad. He'd jabbered about volunteering to work with the State Department or checking if the soft drink industry might want his expertise. Well, neither was going to happen, but I hadn't said so, and let him go on about his dreams of his marriage and His New Life.

He said, "I'm singing in a men's choir. A bunch of us old fogies."

Dad was sixty-nine. Not too much of an old fogie. He still had his hair, well, it was thinner and salt and peppery, but it was there. His own father had been bald in his fifties.

"He needs to rest," said Helen. "He has had a hard time of it."

I shined her a serene smile.

"Where did you decide for your dinner?"

"Filomena's – it's a lovely dining room with a view of the Kennedy Center."

Dad asked, "Did you work today?"

"I covered two meetings." I lied.

Helen said, "Your father needs to watch what he eats. He was so overweight when we married."

She said it like a dig.

"She takes care of me," said Dad again.

I felt as if he were in a fog. Walking in his sleep. Biding time.

"I'm glad," I said, still smiling serenely.

Helen smiled.

"It's her job," I said, as a joke.

Helen said, "Yes, it is the wife's job. He hasn't had anyone looking after him for quite a while."

I was not going there.

I said, lightly, "Mom was sick for three years."

"Oh, but not so sick until the last year," said Helen, her baloney curls bobbing. "She used to cook him a steak every night. She might as well have made it poison."

I looked at Dad. He looked tired. He also looked down at his drink.

"And why didn't you go home to take care of her at the end? Take the burden off of your father."

I took a long breath. "Mom wanted me to stay in New York, but I visited every two weeks. She said she liked thinking of me in New York."

"Yes, some women spend too much time fretting over their children, and they forget their husbands."

Ever hear about seeing red? It happens. Really. Red flames shot out of my eyes. I stood up, and I screamed at the baloney-curled harridan, "Don't you ever talk about my mother! Ever! How dare you criticize her? You're nothing compared to her! Absolutely nothing!"

The people in the lobby turned to watch, as did the guys at the bar.

I felt time stand still. Yes, that really happens too.

"For God's sake, Janene," Dad grumbled.

"You're just going to let her criticize my mother? Your wife? Remember her?"

"Sit down. And she's not my wife now."

Helen stood up and with all the dignity those baloney curls could muster, she walked away.

"I expected civility from you at least," Dad grumbled as I sat.

"What about you? You're just going to let her walk over Mom? That's what you just did."

He flinched.

"I have a new life. Your mother would understand."

"Your new life is without her children. *Your* children."

"I don't interfere in your lives."

"We weren't interfering. We were panic stricken because you were – are – acting like a different person."

"I grieved when she was sick. And I'll have you know that your mother said Helen was a lady."

I looked at him blankly, and then I laughed. I shook my head. "Is it going to be 'your mother' now? What happened to Peggy? Or can't you say her name anymore?"

"This is my new life. Your mother smoked. She wouldn't stop. She died. I loved her, and she thought Helen was a lady."

I sighed. "Don't you know? Mom was making fun of Helen's pretend prissy ways. Helen was not the kind of lady Mom admired. Did she visit with her? Gossip? No. It was a joke, Dad. You married a woman Mom made fun of, only because you wanted to get away from anything that reminded you of her. Including me and Dirk and Jules. I understand that part. But Helen's no lady. She turned you against us because she wants you to only depend on her."

He stared at me, his face bloating red. He was angry.

I touched his hand. Even though I'd already lost him, I had gone too far.

"I want you to be happy, and if Helen makes you happy, that's good."

My cop-out seemed to settle him.

"She does."

Well, he was away from the sickness, the fear crawling over us, the despair at God pulling Peggy away inch by lung inch. Give the guy a break.

"We should go."

Helen spoke like an automaton, not a living being.

I thought she meant the dinner was off.

"The reservation is for seven."

I pulled up my purse, but Dad said, "No. The drinks are on us."

Oh, make me feel bad.

Outside, Dad led us to the car. I got into the back seat and Dad drove, cursing at the traffic. I'd never heard him curse. Even "damn." But "fuck them?" Unreal being in the back seat and the woman next to him wasn't my mother.

We got a table with, yay, a view of the Kennedy Center, all lit up.

"We've gone there several times," said Helen. "We've sat in the President's Box three times."

As a volunteer at the White House Greetings Office, Helen could grab opportunities like that. They were probably available to a lot of people, but I pretended to be impressed.

The whole thing felt surfacy. We were going through the motions. Saying the polite and proper things to say.

I helped that along. I talked about ballet and singing, and I mentioned that I was being considered for ordination.

That surprised them. It even seemed to frighten Helen. She dove down into her meal, barely looking up. I just smiled at her, complimented her choice of restaurant, praised the food, the view, the beauty of Washington, blah blah. I asked about her job. I asked about her daughter.

I paid for the dinner, which impressed them both. As I put down my Visa card, I remembered another dinner.

Not two years before. I'd called Dirk and said, "Let's take them out to dinner for Dad's birthday. Let's surprise them. We'll show Dad that we won't forget him even after – after Mom should die."

We did surprise them, and we all went to Mom's favorite restaurant in Toledo and enjoyed a fine dinner, aware that it was the last time all of us would be "going out to eat," something we'd done so often as a young family.

Mom had her oxygen tank sitting by her chair, and a man at the next table came over and said, "Excuse me, but what is that?"

"It's my own private still," Mom said.

We were quite merry. Dad gave a toast, saying, "Of all the times we've been together, this is the best. This is the best time of this family."

I swear that he meant it.

The waiter brought the check. I looked at my brother and sister and lifted the little tray with a grin.

"We'll split it."

"Oh, no," said Dad.

"Oh, yes," I said, pulling out my wallet.

Jules said, "I – I left my cash home."

Right, Jules. I grinned at Dirk.

He grinned, pulled out his wallet. Pulled out – nothing.

"Oh, no," he said. "This is the wrong wallet. My cards are in the new wallet, and I forgot – oh, jeez."

"Well," said Dad, "I think I have the right wallet."

"Oh, no," I said, and I pulled out my Visa card.

"Is that yours?" Mom asked.

She took the card to look at it, handed it back.

"You have your own credit card?"

"Sure."

"I never had my own. You hold onto that."

I put the card on the tray, feeling that I had impressed her more than ever. She was so thrilled and proud at such a simple thing that she, and most wives, couldn't have gotten in her own name.

We had our picture taken, five smiling people, all desperately hoping for a miracle that never came.

She grew weaker. In a few months, she couldn't leave the house for long.

I think of that dinner almost all the time I pull out a credit card.

This time, it felt bitter.

We got back in the car, and the next stop was their apartment.

I felt that I was in a fog when we took the elevator to the sixth floor.

Once inside the apartment, where Dad was married to another woman, Dad took off his coat and tie and mixed a Manhattan. I asked for a Coke and worried. This was his third Manhattan. Were we driving him to drink more? Mom had always – now that I thought about it – monitored his drinking. Two Manhattans at the most. One if we were in a restaurant and he had to drive home. She would say, "Not now," and he would obey.

I said, "What a nice apartment."

Helen said, "Come into the den."

I thought, oh boy, a shootout.

Instead, she showed me pictures of the wedding. At the church. Taking vows. After the ceremony.

"Very nice," I said.

"It was lovely. Why didn't you come?"

At that point, I knew she truly was insane.

She took my hand. "You were right to defend your mother. My daughter would do the same."

I couldn't answer.

"He hadn't had sex in four years while she was sick."

I knew that wasn't true, and it seemed as if it wasn't something he would have told her. She must have just guessed that.

"A man has needs," she said.

This prim, baloney-haired, prissy, so correct woman spouting this all of a sudden! I almost laughed and slugged her. How sweet of her to rescue Dad from his "needs." I'm sure she had needs too, and Dad was a catch.

Back in the living room, Dad sat silently while Helen talked about her daughter and her daughter's husband and something or other.

I had to get away from them.

We'd agreed that he would pick me up the next day – Sunday – for brunch, their treat, and then we would go to Arlington Cemetery to visit Mom.

I insisted on getting a cab as I didn't want Dad to drive.

I fell onto my Sheraton bed. I wanted to cry but I couldn't. I wanted to sleep but I couldn't. My old life, childhood, had simply gone away, replaced by this new reality.

I wanted to sleep but I couldn't.

Brunch proved quiet, all smiles and politeness.

Dad had a pass into Arlington Cemetery that allowed him to drive right to the columbarium, right near where Mom's ashes were. I'd never been there. He'd moved Mom's ashes there when he married Helen.

He planned to have his ashes join hers.

It first struck me as impersonal, but then I heard the splash of the fountain and realized the columbarium was in an enclosed courtyard. You could feel the love inside it. Arlington, my God. You can't help loving when you walk through the fields with those white markers in the ground.

When Dad pointed to a top shelf with his name on it and his rank of lieutenant, and his birth year, and then Mom's with her birth and death years complete, Arlington became personal and awful.

Right away, I noticed that her birth year was a year off.

I didn't say anything. I would change it, but it was a bit of a joke I had with Mom right then, for he'd given her an extra year.

Dad said, "She was the most courageous woman I have ever known. And she had such faith."

Well, finally he had said something about Mom. And he'd waited until Helen was safely locked away in the car.

He reached up to the marker, tracing her name, then his own.

"This is where I will be," he said. "Just as we wanted."

His voice had grown deeper, just the way it had always been, and his voice caught just a bit, enough for me to hear the depth of his grief. I realized he had not found a "new life," only a way to pass the time until he did join Mom.

I reached up to put my hand next to his, touching the cold wall with her name, her remains behind that slab, so close.

I couldn't cry.

He grabbed me in a huge hug, pulling me in close, so tight, and he bent his head over mine, and he sobbed so loudly, and that was me sobbing too, and as we stood there, gripping each other, weeping, I realized – how stupid I'd been. He and Mom had sold the beautiful house Mom loved because of the medical bills, for Mom hadn't turned sixty-five and qualified for Medicare until four months before her death. He'd gotten some money from selling furniture but - but – Helen had been a lifeline. He must have thought Mom had sent her to him. Was there love? I doubt it, but he needed it and thought he had it, and I wasn't going to criticize him anymore.

No one was around. Arlington is very quiet away from the Kennedys and Unknowns, just where the unfamous people are. Unfamous. And volunteering their lives for their country.

He took my picture. I tried to smile. Sure, it would probably be odd to some people, taking a picture by the marker. But for most of my life, he'd always taken a picture of Mom with me. Going to church. Going out to dinner. All dressed up and ready to go somewhere. And here we were again, Mom and me, Dad taking a picture.

I remembered another picture. Mom at twenty-one in front of the log chapel at Notre Dame, where Dad trained for Naval service in World War 2. They'd just gotten engaged, so full of hope and young love that never ended. I'd been so lucky.

That had been their beginning.

Dad had been there at the end, desperately going back and forth as she choked and gagged on her last bits of air – he desperately calling Hospice and getting a machine – it was the Fourth of July – and finally someone called, and he ran to her, and she gasped and – stopped. He held her in his arms, but she was gone.

The memories that must have come to him – Peggy at Oliver's Bar in South Bend, walking toward him. Their letters back and forth overseas during the war, she flying to meet him when he landed back on US soil, getting married two weeks later, more than forty years of a pretty happy marriage with a few rough spots and one big fight and they fixed it with romance and kisses because it really was a strong marriage, weathering family, business, and yet – yet – always in love, always crazy about each other, and even passionate until she could not be – and she moved to a cot so she wouldn't die in their bed – and there she died, weighing almost nothing. A bitter endnote to the years she'd smoked to keep thin.

She who had been our chief organizer, cheerleader, nag, and proud wife lost almost everything but her skin and bones, and then she was just gone. In his arms. He broke down. Just broke down.

And the men came, and they took her away from him and no, it wasn't fair. How could God allow that? What kind of God would allow anything like that?

And I wanted something to do with that God?

The last time Dad had hugged me so hard was when I graduated from college. That hug had been a mixture of pride, then of loss, then of congratulations all in one. A sentimental, feeling man, a man who now seemed forever lost.

He'd had to get away of course– away from that apartment that had taken her away - away to another city, even to another woman – why, Helen was just that – why hadn't I seen that? That love when lost shoots itself afar, like a stone on a slingshot. Get me away from the pain. And anger, too, at God. Well, why the hell not? All that Christian gibberish about Jesus' resurrection conquering death was just that – gibberish of words made to seem like gospel and hope. Yes, I felt pain for my mother's death and certainly that pain had been exacerbated – multiplied – so much more – by Dad's anger at us – and he'd been angry before we'd said a word because we reminded him of her and – what – happier days? Days - of bitterness of lost dreams and hopes he'd convinced himself would come? He was closer to her death than we had been – he had been THERE - and grappling with time and loss and love, and I gripped him harder, and he gripped me, both of us holding on to whatever in us both was part of her.

I'm not saying all that fixed us up. Helen was still a problem. She wasn't good for him, that was evident, but I couldn't say anything. She didn't want us kids around. Her kids were better, more successful, richer – hell, after two months, they gifted the newlyweds with a cruise. Dad never said anything, but still, it hurt, for we three could not have afforded that. We were harshly kept away (except when treating them to dinner).

Still, in those moments when I felt and understood – he wasn't only Dad, he was my mother's lover, and she was gone – in those moments, I realized that the world is filled with this pain.

This is why I must be a priest. Not that I could help. I feel helpless about helping – my God, I can barely help myself – but I can listen and not judge – I can listen and feel. I can curse God and yet bring Her love to others. And a part of me, funnily, felt that the mere presence of my mother, his wife, was with us – could she have pushed me along? Did she, too, miss my Dad? Was she telling me, go gently? Oh, God, what tortuous mysteries you give us!

"I'm sorry," I said to him.

"I know," he said. "So am I."

And that was that. Then Helen took over, and I let her.

So, it turns out that I did learn something about the heart on that cardiology trip.

CHAPTER 21

I discussed some of what I had gleaned during that Arlington trip with Steven and Michael during a discernment meeting in the church garden. Steven was moved to tears. It turns out his mother had married again – and he'd had similar problems.

Parents.

After a few weeks, I was on the road again with Meg.

A few of our friends saw us to the airport. Paula gave me a hug.

"Steven talked to me. You must be a priest."

Well, that was nice.

Once in the air and heading for Los Angeles, Meg said, "What was Paula talking about?"

"Steven broke a bit of confidence from our discernment meeting."

"That's not fair. What was it about?"

"It was about visiting Dad."

"That must have been rough."

"Yeah."

I looked out the window.

"Well?"

She expected me to talk about the discernment meeting?

"If I tell it too much, it'll lose it – here." I pointed to my heart. "Maybe later."

She fiddled with her braid. "So, Paula knows, and I don't?"

"Meg. Your own rules. And I didn't tell Paula anything."

"Okay, sorry. Hey, guess what. Rick got the okay for me to get ordained in a few months."

"That's a fast three years."

"Isn't it? But I'm so mature."

"What are you going to do then?"

"I don't know. I love New York but every available job pays twenty thousand. I'll have to keep my teaching job if I stay here."

"A woman priest teaching Catholic boys. I like it."

"Ain't that a hoot?"

"Will they know?"

"Only if I walk in with vestments on and consecrate a host."

"Let me know when you do that."

"I really did believe in the Catholic church once."

"Me too."

We picked up a rental car in Los Angeles. Meg had ordered a small car, but the agent said, "This *is* a small car. Any smaller ones are gone."

We burst out laughing when we saw it.

"It's the Batmobile," I said.

We got in.

"I can't drive this," said Meg. "It's like driving my apartment."

"Your apartment's smaller."

"Look, it has stereo. Did you bring any cassettes? I brought Joseph Campbell."

"I brought Beethoven and Peter, Paul, and Mary and Marilyn Horne."

"We're set."

"And look here. A place for cups and a tray for food. Speakers up there. Power steering?"

"Uh huh. We'd better do a countdown before we blast off."

"We'd better name it."

"Name it?"

"So, it'll like us."

"It's an Oldsmobile. How about Ollie?"

"Original! Hello, Ollie!" I patted the dashboard.

"Here goes." Meg turned the key.

The motor purred.

"Yup, a full tank. Here we go."

I sang the merry Oldsmobile song, pulled out the map, and found where I'd circled the area from the airport to Irvine.

"We have to get on Route 405 East. Wherever that is."

"Must be after 404 East. Left or right?"

"Sign! Route 405. Nothing else."

"We'll take that. It should get us somewhere. Put on Peter, Paul, and Mary."

I dug out the cassette and soon we were singing along. I got a little caught up and we whipped past a sign for Route 404 East pointing to the ramp we swiftly passed.

"We've got to turn."

"Oh, shit! Why weren't you looking?"

Sun to storm.

"I was singing."

"I can't be looking everywhere. Pay attention. I have to do all the driving. Where am I going to turn?"

"Gas station exit coming up." I swallowed her accusation. Plenty of New Yorkers didn't drive.

We made it back to Route 2. I put on Joseph Campbell. I loved his books but my God, what a droner. I made sure to follow the map and watch the road and was relieved to see the sign for Irvine. After that, Meg had directions from her friend, and I just read them off. I was rattled by her consistent sharpness with me followed by a prolonged silence filled by stultifying Campbell. Things were reverting back to Rome. Not good. The blood on my hands after losing that scarf...

We pulled into a drive by a little white house. Nancy, a slim woman who would have been gray save for Clairol, and her lover Alice, rushed out along with their dog Pixie. Pixie wore an Elizabethan collar, having gotten scratched by a cat. I cooed over him, and he settled by me. Meanwhile, Meg, Alice, and Nancy spent the time recalling grad school antics. That discussion continued with ordered-in pizza. I felt invisible.

Well, at least Pixie liked me and chose to sleep next to my bed.

The next day, Meg and I rode north to Yosemite. I had looked forward to introducing Meg to that park, but her persistent silence filled me with dread that she would ruin the most glorious place in the world.

But once in sight of those granite cliffs, the sun reflecting on them, she said, "You just know God exists."

As we got out of the car, I glanced at Yosemite Falls, which had dried out from the early Spring. It was barely a trickle now.

We checked in.

"What to do?" she asked me.

"The open tram tour. I got us tickets."

"Can't we just walk around for a bit?"

"After. This is good. You'll like it."

"I'm tired of riding."

"Meg, you did ask me. It's only an hour, and we can walk before we eat."

"Yes, but we've been sitting on the plane and the car."

"Okay, I'm going, and I'll sell your ticket."

We took the open tram tour, and she ate up the Native stories, just like I always did.

After that, she wanted to see more of the park.

The next day, we drove up to Glacier Point and to the Tuolumne meadow. Meg sang out when she got out of the car, and she lay down on the grass, shrieking, "This is heaven!" I wandered around, spinning like Julie Andrews on the Alps. I had to drag Meg away to get her to see Tioga Lake, and when she got there, she didn't want to leave either.

"It's like heaven. Now I see why you love to come here."

"It's the most beautiful place on earth. And the most dangerous."

The next day, when we left the park, I let her go on about how beautiful it was. She acted as if she had discovered the place and was trying to sell me on it. Funny.

We drove to lonely Bodie, and we sang "America" with Marilyn Horne as we rode through the desert.

We enjoyed an elegant dinner in Denver.

Meg talked and talked at dinner. All about what she would do after she got ordained and had her own church. She would rule out Rite One – no more groveling before God. Women would be important. Nothing Catholic. Everything simple.

"I doubt you'll be able to get rid of Rite One if you're on staff."

She shrugged.

"What if the people like Rite One? Some people are like Donald."

"I'll show them that they're wrong."

Well, that was one way.

One more hotel in Denver.

"Quite a trip," I said. I did feel sad that it was over. And at the same time relieved. We did laundry, ordered room service, and Meg talked about what it would be like "when we were ordained."

"I'll get a job in some western city – and you can be an associate when you're done."

"I'll get the church on the other side of town, and we'll fight it out," I teased, but she gave me a sharp look.

"Oh, no, we're friends."

We traipsed the sidewalks of Virginia City.

I wanted to see the desert lake, Pyramid, so we got into Ollie and headed north on the only road in that desert. The lake didn't come, and it didn't come, and Meg said, "That's it. We're turning around."

I said, "No, it's not it. This is a lake of the Paiutes. There was a war here. The lady in the store sent us this way."

"She was joking with us. I'm turning around here. I don't want to die."

"It's here, it's coming up," I said, but it had been a half hour and no lake and less gas. Meg started cursing. I started to believe her but then I fought that urge to do whatever she said. You gotta be strong, Shannon.

"It's coming up."

"I'm turning around."

And there it was. Immense, blue, peaceful.

Meg said, "Oh, my God. Look at it."

I felt that I'd made a conversion. Once we got out of the car and walked and sat by the lake, she didn't want to leave. At one point, she took my hand and said, "You're lousy at maps, but you know where things are." "Oh, you of little faith," I said. She said, "Yup." And she started to dance, and I joined her, and it was the most special moment we were ever to have.

We said our farewells to Ollie at the Reno airport. Meg slept on the flight. I read the *New York Times*.

As she dropped me off at my building, she gave me a hug and kissed my cheek.

"See you tomorrow."

Really, except for a few moments, she had been so apart from me, as if little by little, she was pulling away.

Was that what getting a collar meant?

CHAPTER 22

If it was the first Tuesday of the month, it was a liturgy committee meeting.

"Welcome back, you two." Rick gave me a strong hug and his smile shot through my soul.

He did not hug Meg.

"Thank God," John said. "My soprano is back."

"We'll have pictures on Sunday after I've developed them all," said Meg. "What's the agenda?"

"We have a priest ordination coming up. Lily's."

"Hard to believe," said Lily.

"It's happening!" said Meg.

"And yours in a month," said Lily.

"Wow," I said. "What a pair."

But that Meg's ordination had been so sped up put a knot of worry into the back of my mind. Wasn't the process supposed to be something a little more than a racetrack? Well, she had been a nun. Anyway, why would I want to slow down her achievement? Wasn't this a good thing?

"We'll have cars going to Trenton on Saturday," said Rick. "We'll all meet here."

"You're all invited to the reception after," said Lily.

"Meg will need a party, too," said John.

"She'll have one," said Rick. "A big coffee hour."

"We'll plan a big anthem," said John.

"We have one other issue," said Rick. "Should we stop doing the eight o'clock service?"

"How did that come up?" asked John.

"It's come up," said Rick. "We need to open the church up at seven thirty in the morning, make sure the heat will be on by then if we need heat, have everything set up. And sometimes no one comes."

"We should stop it," said Meg.

"Why?" I asked. "The church is open. People come knowing it's not the main service. That it's quiet. Perhaps we should just advertise it more."

"It's Sunday. It's Manhattan. No one's coming to the eight."

I had a selfish reason for liking the eight o'clock. When I preached, I would preach at both services, and the eight o'clock was like a rehearsal. Plus, I liked the intimacy of it, the few people. Besides, the two or three people who came were part of the larger community but had jobs on Sunday. They'd gotten up early to come to church. It seemed unfair. I said so.

"It's too much like a Catholic private Mass," said Meg. "The Eucharist is to be said in a community."

I wasn't familiar with private Masses, although I knew that Catholic priests were required to say Mass every day, no matter where they were or who was present.

"I like the quiet. And how many people make up a community?"

"No one comes. What's the point?"

"A couple people," I said. "Isn't that a community? Donald comes to both. He should have a say. Maybe we should call him."

"He's out of town," said Rick. "He doesn't have an answering machine."

"He doesn't?" said Peter. "Doesn't he work for a newspaper?"

Rick smiled that serene way he had. Maybe it was the beard. "He says that if you call him and the phone rings and he doesn't pick up, you know he's not at home."

"It's how we all used to live," said John. "Do we need to decide now?"

Meg said, "This is the meeting. If you're not at the meeting, you don't have a voice in the vote."

"When did that become a rule?" I asked.

"It's our tradition," said Meg.

Peter said, "We have a tradition?"

John's eyes rolled heavenward. He only worked the ten o'clock, so he didn't care.

I guess I didn't much either. I'd be able to sleep in a little on sermon days. Not that I preached much.

Rick said nothing but looked down at his notebook.

I was puzzled. Meg had made a unilateral decision in a committee where we'd all agreed there was no one chairing, although Rick came with an agenda. Well, we all did, and he would add our items to his list. But that was it. And here was Meg saying we had a rule that we'd never discussed, and Rick wasn't saying anything. Stupid me, I didn't feel strong enough to fight, and I didn't care enough about this to fight, and I didn't want to cause trouble that would make Rick not want to recommend me for ordination.

Did that idea have to come up in my brain? Rick wouldn't mind if I dissented.

Or would he?

Lily didn't seem concerned about the issue. She was dreaming about Saturday.

"Maybe we should talk about it more?" I asked.

"No," said Meg.

"I don't think we need to," said Rick.

The next item was a Quiet Night before summer started. I volunteered to take it for a Teresa of Avila meditation, but Meg said, "I have a special feeling for this one. I'll be a priest then."

"I agree," said Rick.

"Your time will come," Meg said, and she winked at me.

After the meeting, John and I walked to Eighth Avenue.

John said, "Our almost priest is feeling her oats."

"It's odd that Rick hardly spoke."

"He doesn't like conflict, and she's quite a force."

He'd summed that up correctly. I wondered if that force would hit again.

CHAPTER 23

Back to work, and back to seminary.

"Preaching class is going to be interesting," I said to Meg on the phone. "This ex-Catholic Episcopalian among all those Baptists."

"You'll show 'em."

Besides classes, I had to work with the recording companies and the music program. That business had exploded. You'd think there wasn't a recording studio in New York.

Oh, yes, and there was my job. I'd been promoted to Managing Editor, and with the church committees, choir, and altar work and school – I felt as if I were working forty-hour days rather than weeks. But I was happy.

We took cars to Lily's ordination in Trenton's cathedral. It was fabulous. Music, even dancing, and we cheered when the bishop ordained her. That Sunday, she celebrated, and I was the subdeacon. When we came up the aisle, instead of a hymn, John led the applause. Lily began to cry.

I imagined what it would be like for me.

Coffee hour was filled with music and dancing, I had thought we could take Lily out to brunch, but Meg had vanished, so I went with Paula, Tom, and Steven – and a flushed and happy Lily, who had been invited to stay on working in the office until she got settled in another job. In the meantime, she was an associate priest in the parish.

Time flew. The liturgy committee met again. Bob, John, Donald, Lily, Rick, and Meg were already there.

"Sorry," I said. "I had to stay late to check the Poison Hotline. Don't ask."

"What's the Poison Hotline?" John asked.

I shook a fist at him.

"Let's go," said Meg.

"Yes. I'll start," said Donald. "Why did we drop the eight o'clock Eucharist?"

"We voted on it."

"I wasn't here. That was a pretty major decision."

"Well, tough." Meg looked directly at him. "If you're not here to vote, then you're not here."

"You weren't here for several weeks. What if we'd had the meeting then?"

Meg shrugged.

"That's quite a change," said Donald. "Dropping a whole service. I'm bringing it up again."

"No one comes."

"People come. They come because they have jobs or are going out of town or can't make it to the ten o'clock. Or they like it better than the noisier ten."

Meg shrugged. "We voted. Anyway, you'd still have lost."

"If we'd have discussed it, I could have made some points."

"We did discuss it."

"I wasn't here."

"And we couldn't call you. You don't have an answering machine. The decision stands."

I looked over at Rick. He was doodling on his note pad.

I said, "Maybe we could talk it over some more."

"No, we voted," said Meg. "We can't go back and forth. It's practically a private Mass. It's too Catholic."

"It is not a private Mass," said Donald. "There are people in the pews. Don't they matter?"

Finally, Rick spoke up. "Let's revisit this in a few months. For now, we'll stop having the service."

Donald did not look fooled by this wishy-washy decision.

"You need to be at the meetings," said Meg.

I wanted to kick her.

We had voted, after all, but I still felt troubled. I thought that Rick might have handled it better.

At my next discernment meeting, Michael, Steven, and I sat in the garden. I felt relaxed, enjoying the late summer flowers. They peppered me with questions. I answered.

"What sort of priest do you think you will be? Or that you are now?"

"Can you say that the Bible holds all the truths necessary for salvation? It's in your vow."

"How do you see yourself in a parish with a dogmatic priest?"

"Could you raise money?"

Remarkably, I stayed calm.

"I've held an administrative job for several years. I'm aware of the conflict between that and the pastoral side. I think I should take the extra classes now being introduced at General Seminary about parish administration and law. But I am essentially a poet of the gospel, for the gospel itself and the Old Testament lends itself to poetry. We do not have to depend so much on literal truth than on stories of hope, of surrender, of aspiration, or of human life related to God."

I'm not sure even I knew what I meant but I felt my soul did.

Michael, the pretend Jesuit, wiped his eyes. Steven nodded at me.

I had already shown that I could raise money. In addition to the music series and the recordings, and thanks to a letter of recommendation from the Community Church, they knew that I had done the press work when I had chaired that church, and I had raised a record amount of money based on that press. I had no idea how that had happened, but money talked.

As for that dogmatic priest, I said, "He wouldn't hire me."

"Sure it's a he?"

I smiled.

"I'm done," I said.

One more hurdle – the Vestry's vote. Given that I was pretty sure I'd be approved, my certainty naturally turned to doubt. Was this the right path? Was God calling me? What did that mean? How should I know? How much was my ego and how much was God? Was there a God?

That Saturday, I took the train to Spring Lake, the ocean. My family had vacationed here for a few summers when I was small. The beautiful hotel where we'd stayed had been torn down for cheap imitations of that grand old place. Still, the boardwalk was still just a boardwalk, no stores or built-up piers. The season was just over, and it was quiet, just a few people walking about.

Once, while lying on the beach with my mother, I'd asked, "Where is the Garden of Paradise?" – I must have been in the first grade and had my first communion to ask that. Mom pointed to the horizon line of sea and sky. I imagined that place as a doorway opening up to the Garden of Paradise. It was not that far.

Dirk and Jules didn't like to go into the water. None of us could swim, but we could walk in for a few feet and paddle about. I would say, "Don't be afraid" and head into the water. The Garden of Paradise was not far away. I felt safe.

Now, so many years later, so much lost in my family now, I walked onto the beach, took off my shoes, and walked up to the water – the surf sweeping over the wet sand and me going in up to my knees.

"Don't be afraid," I said aloud.

I waved at the Garden of Paradise.

And I was back for Sunday service.

Rick preached.

...The women and men of God are more often those who have encountered the deepest darkness in themselves and in the world. The gospel paradox is that in the same moment... that same light takes them into God's life and transforms them into uniquely powerful instruments of salvation.
Times of transition are difficult...But the stormy, painful time can also be times of real growth, real spiritual growth. In our transition we can, if we will, if we have faithful eyes, see beyond that whirlwind, to the gift that God is. Now."

It sounded nice. I didn't realize that I would soon be caught up by the whirlwind.

CHAPTER 24

As a guest at the next Vestry meeting, I didn't hear much of the usual tragic budget report. Eventually, Rick brought up – me. Michael and Steven presented their support and affirmative votes for my being a priest.

Then it was open for questions.

"It's a hard road."

"You have all the difficulties Meg had in addition to school and a job."

"You're in a parish Heine doesn't like."

"We're not like the churches you'd be serving in."

"How would you want to serve?"

"But we'd lose you!"

I sensed that "we're not like other churches" was something every church would say, but these were all good objections. And thanks to Spring Lake, I felt calm.

"Of course, it's tough. It should be." I smiled. "I love the work. My grades are good."

"What are your grades?"

"I have a 3.9 grade point -."

"3.9!" Meg shrieked. "Oh, man."

"What's yours, Meg?" asked Tom. He smiled. His smiles always looked sly.

"3.2."

"You copied off the wrong people."

We laughed.

"School isn't everything, but it feeds me. I hope to share the food.

Look, I know what you're saying, but here I am. I can't go anywhere else."

Rick said, "Jan, we need you to step outside for a bit while we…"

"Gossip about you," said Meg.

I had a bad feeling for a moment. What would Meg say about me?

I went out to the rectory's front stoop and sat on the steps, but they were cold, so I walked up and down them.

The door opened. Paula came out.

"Don't you have to vote on me?"

"I left them my vote. I needed a smoke."

She pulled out her cigarettes.

I leaned against the banister. "Oh, sure. YOU need a cigarette!"

She grinned. "Why are you worried?"

"Nothing's certain until it's certain. I remember Meg telling me how people argued over her."

"But I think you'd make a wonderful priest."

"Thanks, Paula. That means a lot. You have high standards."

"I made a scarf, I mean a stole for Lily, one of those things you wrap around your neck. Can I make one for you when you're ordained?"

That seemed so far away. I said, "Thank you."

The door opened. Tom appeared, his face noncommittal, even stern.

"You can come in now. We're done."

A little too fast.

Paula stomped on her cigarette and waved me to go in first. We walked down the hall past the pictures of previous rectors to the Vestry room where I was greeted by a storm of applause.

"It's unanimous!" Rick cried.

"Which way?" I grinned as Meg came to hug me and then Rick. I sat down, and I said, "Thank you."

"We'll have a real celebration when you say your first Eucharist," said Steven. "You'll sing it, and Rick and Meg and Lily will all support you at the altar."

I wasn't sure how realistic that was, but I smiled at Meg and Lily.

"Are you saying I can't sing?" Meg retorted, and we howled.

"You sound lovely on one note," said Paula.

It was a merry table, and after a few minutes, Rick ended the meeting with prayer.

As Meg, Paula, and I walked to the corner, Paula said, "Did you have any doubt?"

"Everyone thinks highly of you," said Meg, and she laughed. "Not like me."

"That was Sherry," said Paula. "Just her one vote, and she's no longer here."

"Thank God she's gone," said Meg.

"I'm grateful," I said.

"Unanimous. Hey, A 3.9 average?"

"Janene is obviously destined," said Paula.

We parted at the corner, me thinking, destined for what? Paula's worshipful attitude bothered me.

Back to school and a heavy schedule. Professor Forrest came down with some sort of pneumonia, so the two (two!) people – me and someone else - who had registered for Forrest's course in late biblical Judaism were to write papers covering certain topics and incorporate those into a personal research paper. There would be no regular classes.

Professor Forrest would be reading and personally commenting on my paper! That was a challenge I could not ignore!

I called Rick, asking to give up managing the recordings. Even though I'd done it from my office desk, it was still a burden.

"Of course," he said. "It so happens that someone in the neighborhood expressed an interest in helping out. Of course, you have too much on your plate. I give you your freedom!"

Meg called." I got you the responsive reading for my ordination. Okay? You'll be up by the organ and sing the chant and wait for us to sing the response."

"Whatever you want. Feel good?"

"I feel great! Oh, I wanted to see *The Last of the Mohicans*."

"Okay."

"I mentioned it to Rick. He wants to see it. Betty and Rick. Okay if we double date? Saturday night?"

An odd way to put it.

"Sure."

The movie didn't hold together for me. A predictable romance. Lots of violence.

After, we went to the Galaxy, Meg and I on one side of the booth and Rick and Betty on the other. Meg told funny stories about her classes. Betty talked about the house, complained about the Rectory, and she made us laugh with stories about their kids. I'd never seen Betty joke. In fact, I realized I hardly saw Betty at all. She was usually in Massachusetts, looking after her grandchildren. When I mentioned that, she said, "I've had too many years of being a rector's wife. I'm waiting for Rick to retire. It won't be long, will it?"

Rick patted her hand.

Meg and I said goodnight to Rick and Betty at the corner of Twentieth and walked to Seventh Avenue.

"In a week, you'll be a priest," I said.

"Yup."

"Then what?"

She shrugged. "I'll be an associate like Lily. At least until something comes up."

"Can the church afford that?"

"I'll be teaching. It doesn't matter. They'll pay me a token."

"Shouldn't the Vestry approve it?"

"Why?"

The steely eyes. What was so odd about my question? The Vestry oversaw the parish finances, so if Meg would be getting any salary, they should approve it.

"Because it's their job?" I said.

She flung back her braid, and I stepped back to avoid being hit.

"Tom and Chris are giving him trouble because if I get a job, I'm off, but Rick said it was his decision and not the Vestry's."

All right, but it bothered me.

"Have you been looking?"

"Yeah." She shrugged. "It'll be strange, not to be at Saint Philip's. And now it's your turn."

And she hopped on the bus, her braid flying as if free.

That Saturday, I dressed in my yellow suit and walked to the rectory where I met Lily, all decked out in a black suit with collar. We hugged and hurried up the steps and rang the buzzer just as Rick opened the door.

"Great," he said. "All on time."

We clattered down to the car.

Lily started to get in the front seat.

"Could you get in back with Jan? Meg will have her alb, and she won't want to wrinkle it."

"She can hang it up," I said.

Lily said, "Okay," and opened the back door, sliding in beside me.

It was a short ride to Meg's apartment on Eleventh Street.

"I'll go get her," I said.

But Rick had already opened his door.

"Apartment ten," I said, but he was already out of the car. I watched him cross the street to the front door.

Lily was saying, "I wonder where Meg will end up."

"I hope it's somewhere nearby."

"Me too."

"Then it's your turn," said Lily.

"I hope Rick can get me on the fast track like he did with Meg."

"They don't like to do that much."

'Yeah, but I'll be done with seminary next year."

"With a 3.9 average."

We laughed.

"Seriously, Jan, that's monumental. Did you know that the average for General students is 2.9? Most fail the GOEs. And they're in the *Episcopal* seminary. They should have an edge over NYTS, but NYTS students taking the GOEs always do better."

"Excluding you." Lily read Greek and Latin and was an early church expert.

Meg and Rick arrived, Meg carrying her alb. She looked pale.

"How are you feeling?" I asked as she settled into the front seat.

"I just know that Heine will pull me out of line and say, 'Not today.'"

"He already approved you. You and he chatted."

"When we talked about the Creed, he kept looking at his ring, playing with it, as if to impress me that he was a holy man. It reminded me of pastoral liturgy class, when the students obsessed over the collar and the clergy wardrobe."

"They still do. When I'm at the library, that's what I see – catalogs on the desks – vestments, clergy clothes – and the first minutes of liturgy class are all about the collar. When can we wear it? Can we wear it to the supermarket?"

"Why are we talking about this?" asked Rick.

"Priesthood is an inward sign," said Lily.

"I hope so," said Meg.

And so it happened.

We stood behind Meg, our hands on her shoulder, supporting her. Several people from the parish stood in the pews behind us.

Meg was ordained. Heine never betrayed a smile.

We surrounded her when it was over, hugging her and each other.

Paula hugged me hard. "We won! We won!"

We celebrated at an Italian restaurant across from the Cathedral. Rick left us there, and Meg, Lily, and I, the last to leave, each drank three glasses of wine, then crowded into a cab back to church to rehearse for Meg's first Eucharist as celebrant. I would be subdeacon and Lily deacon.

Meg was nervous. Or drunk. Maybe we all were.

I set up the altar. As we began, Meg kept getting lost in the Altar Book.

"I'm right here," I said. "My finger will always be where you need it."

At that, Lily burst out laughing,

"Ayee," Meg grinned.

"In the book," I said. But we giggled.

"God, forgive us."

"You two can do that now," I said.

Meg raised her arm and made the sign of the cross.

"Whew," I said.

Meg made it through the canon, then lifted the chalice and said, "This is my body."

Lily and I laughed. Meg looked puzzled. Then she giggled.

"Guys, this feels so weird."

"It'll be fine," Lily and I said together.

"You two were with me every step of the way," she said and hugged us both. "I love you."

"I'll be there for you tomorrow," I said. "And if you get stuck, just watch my finger."

That made us giggle again.

"You'll be fine," said Lily.

"Guys, thank you," said Meg.

CHAPTER 25

The next day, the congregation filled the pews. Up at the altar, we felt their support and joy, and that feeling infused us. From grieving widow to Catholic nun to Episcopal priest. I was proud of Meg's journey, envious of her strength.

Coffee hour proved festive. I stayed long, not willing to do the tons of homework that awaited. Meg stayed. She was going back to the church to be quiet for a while.

I was busy with classes through Thursday, and on Friday, I called Meg to see if she'd wanted to go to the movies. Her answering machine picked up.

I kept trying. Same result.

I joined the Garden group on Saturday. Betty showed me how to nudge the fading flowers, how much water was too much and too little, and sent me weeding on the long corridor of flowers between the rectory and the church.

"They never get enough sun," she said. "Why did they have to build the church so high? It's only caused trouble."

I laughed. She didn't.

"And the kitchen ceiling is leaking again. I swear that the devil comes in and pours water on it all night."

The thought of the devil pouring water up – or anywhere – made me laugh. Betty realized the joke and then said, "I feel so hemmed in here. Home is a wide-open space with a view of the sea. Everything works. Here, everything breaks down. If it's not the plumbing, it's the boiler. If it's not the boiler...and what does he care." She shrugged at me. "I've always been the practical one."

But when she talked about her kids, her face went bright, and her voice turned musical. Rick was the same, especially when he talked about his grandson. I enjoyed the work and her company. It was just the flowers. Such a nice break from everything else.

I later called Meg to ask if she had time for the garden. Just her machine.

Did ordination make you disappear?

During the peace on Sunday, Betty announced she had to resign from Buildings and Grounds. "I'm going to spend more time with my grandchildren."

During coffee hour, Rick said to us, "The trip back and forth weighed her down. I'll be going over a few times a month."

"It seems wrong," I said.

He peered at me for a moment.

"I'm sorry. I didn't mean to criticize." After all, he was nearing retirement age. This was probably just a short-term thing before he joined his family for good.

"Of course not," he said. "It works for us."

"It'll be hard on you. When are you retiring?"

He laughed. "I love that trip to the Vineyard. The breeze, the water, the feel of the boat…maybe a year or two."

Paula ran after me as I left and, as we walked toward Eighth, she talked about her wonderful trip to New Mexico. I didn't really listen. I was wondering if Rick would retire before my BACOM.

"Maybe you'd want to come with me when I go again?"

I was embarrassed that I hadn't been listening. What?

What the heck. It would never happen. Poor Paula. Trying to be friendly as we all ran off getting ordained.

"I'd love to go to New Mexico."

She looked so happy that I worried for a moment. I had no intention of going. Paula was gay, and I knew she was asking me to go with her on some romantic hope she had. I didn't know how to discourage her, but I put all that in the back of my mind. She'd soon forget.

All week long I tried to reach Meg. She never called back until the end of the week.

"I've been busy. What's up?"

"Let's meet after the liturgy meeting."

"Okay."

Yes, it had come around again. At the meeting, Donald suggested celebrating with Rite One on Sundays in Lent. John and Chuck agreed. I wasn't sure.

John said, "It's the heritage of the church."

I said, "You're saying something if we're only doing Rite One in Lent."

"And Advent," said Lily. "The first two Sundays."

"Maybe two Sundays in Lent and Advent."

"All agreed?" asked Rick.

We all agreed.

"It will be interesting," I said. "And if we don't like it, then we can stop doing it."

"That's right," said Rick.

We moved down the agenda. Meg came in and apologized for being late. Rick ran down what we'd done, including the Rite One decision.

"No. You can't vote on that. I wasn't here."

Donald smiled. "The vote happens no matter who is here, remember?"

"It affects me," said Meg. "And I won't do it."

"Eight o'clock services affected me," said Donald.

"Then you don't celebrate on those Sundays," I said.

"Maybe we were too hasty," said Rick.

What?

"This is what you say. Decisions are made by those who show up," said Donald.

"I'm a priest. I'm not saying Rite One. I don't want to be in a church that says Rite One. It's ancient English. It's all about groveling on the floor in penance. It's 'mea culpa, through my fault' all over. It's bad for women because we're always at fault for everything."

"You may not have a choice," said Lily. "Depending on the parish you go to. Many people like it because of the ancient language and feel good to acknowledge they are sinners and obtain forgiveness. I learned that when I was going to Grace Church to hear Fleming Rutledge preach. Before I started here."

"It's part of Episcopal tradition," said Donald.

"We should appreciate that," said John. "And talk about the language. Rite One expresses our humility before God. Maybe we should feel a little of that occasionally."

Trust John to be tactful and on subject.

"I can't say words I don't believe."

I expected Rick to say something, but he was looking down at the table.

Meg said, "I vote against."

Rick said, "Maybe we should give it some more thought."

I threw my hands up.

John gave a short laugh. He muttered, "Rick can only compromise."

Was he saying that Rick was a coward?

The meeting ended as Donald stalked away.

"Let him go to Grace Church," Meg muttered as we got up to leave.

I didn't say anything until we got to the corner.

"Sorry about Rite One."

"It's against women," she muttered.

I decided it wasn't worth talking about. She'd just get worked up and mad.

"I have three pre-interviews coming up."

"For the Commission? Oh, my God. So fast. We'll still be priests together."

Well, maybe. My process wouldn't be as fast as hers. I'd never been a nun. And Rick's pals on the Commission were all dropping off.

"How's the job hunt?" I asked.

"Nothing here. I may have to leave town. I don't want to be a part-time priest."

I wondered how I'd feel if she left town.

CHAPTER 26

One Sunday, we in the choir were practicing the anthem when Bishop Tutu and his wife walked in as if they had always been coming to church here.

Rick hurried out, greeted them, talked with them, gestured to a pew.

We tried not to stare.

Rick introduced them at the announcements. Bishop Tutu was visiting General Seminary, and he and his wife had come to the closest Episcopal Church.

I was scheduled to hold a little class on hospitality after church, and to my amazement, the Bishop and his wife joined us.

They sat with us in the rectory chapel, sipping coffee. As we talked about how to be welcoming and hospitable to strangers – both in church, on the streets, in our lives -- I realized that they were just folks, like the rest of us. Amazing. It meant I should have the same courage. Well…

Suggestions came from all over – Joseph said that "Here no one accosts me for being a gay man who has AIDS. I'm safe here. I can pray here. What would I do if someone came in to tell me I'm a sinner and losing my leg was God punishing me? How can I welcome them?"

"After you slug them with your crutch."

"Hover over them at coffee hour."

"Lead them to Father Rick."

"Coffee hour?"

"Should we make them comfortable?"

"Didn't Jesus make the Pharisees and Sadducees uncomfortable? Was that hospitality?"

"We need to be who we are but not close the door."

"It can take time," said Bishop Tutu. "But you can't be who you're not."

"To thine own self be true," said Paula.

"In some places, you could go to prison for that," said someone, and a few rolled their eyes. But Bishop Tutu said, "Yes, you could."

I didn't know what to say. Except, "Let's pray."

When they were leaving, Bishop Tutu held my hand and said, "You don't know how much we needed your prayers."

Rick introduced me and mentioned that I was on the road to the priesthood.

"Good," said the bishop. "And good luck."

His wife kissed me.

The two took some time making their way through the Rectory, shaking people's hands.

But Meg, after, said, "You should have pushed people harder."

I walked away. Then I regretted it and called her. No answer.

No answer for days.

CHAPTER 27

It took two weeks, but Meg finally answered my calls.
She wanted to go camping. In Canada. I convinced her it was winter. So, she said, "Florida."

I was out of excuses. I said, "I can't."

I wasn't going to travel with her again. I didn't need that constant tension about her moods.

"Why?"

"Because I can't. You're mean."

"You can't read a map."

"Then go with somebody who can.'

"If you don't like something I say, yell back at me."

"So, it's on me to tell you when you're abusive? Boy, it's nice to have your world on a string, isn't it."

"I'm going through a difficult time. Come with me. There's stuff I need to talk over with you."

"No I can't. Too much work. And my BACOM is coming up."

I think she asked a friend from her school.

It hurt to say no, but I don't think I could stand another trip with her. I did agree to celebrate Christmas with her and the gang on her floor, for there would be other people.

And it was fun.

I managed some after-Christmas shopping. Saks Fifth Avenue had a phenomenal sale, and right inside the front door, as if God put it there, I found a table of silk scarves. I burrowed through them and was thrilled to find one that if it didn't match, it almost matched, the scarf I'd lost in Rome. At least I could assuage that guilt and pay all debts.

A week later, when she'd returned and school was back in our lives, I called her. She never returned the call. I tried a couple of times.

When I saw her in church, I said something like, "I tried to call."

"I know, I'm so sorry. I've been so busy."

Yes, we're too busy for each other.

I went over to the choir to practice, but it was a short anthem, so we had time to sit and breathe before the service. The altos, Jessica and Cate, were talking up some television show I never had time to watch. I grabbed a Bible from one of the pews to review the Scripture lesson I was to read.

Dean Milson, short, stout, and deliberate about everything, was sacristan that day. He took his job seriously, and he was already arranging everything carefully and double checking it.

Meg, who was celebrant, came out of the sacristy to check the Altar Book. On her way back to the sacristy, she glanced at the table Dean was checking.

"What are you doing?"

Her tone was sharp. Even I jumped. Dean said, simply, "Finishing up."

"No," said Meg. "This setup is too Catholic. You have to change it."

"What are you talking about?" said Dean. Not very respectfully, but then again, why should he be respectful?

Meg, whipping her braid behind her, faced down the smaller, squat Dean. I imagined him reaching for the sword in his scabbard.

"Oh, for crying out loud," John muttered.

"Who should know? Me! I was a nun, remember?"

"I'm the sacristan," Dean said. "Rick said we can do what we think is right so long as all the necessary elements are present. That's always been the case. He's the rector, you know."

Fighting words.

Meg fought back.

"Within a certain boundary."

"I'm the sacristan, and I like what I've done. If you don't like it, tell Rick and take me off the rota."

"It's too Catholic. I can't say the Eucharist with this."

"Do you believe this?" John muttered. "Give the girl a collar, and she becomes the Pope."

"He's too Catholic," I muttered, and John guffawed.

"Change it! I'm the celebrant."

Rick walked in.

"What's wrong?"

"This setup, Rick. It's too Catholic."

Rick smiled at Dean.

"Is this what you did?" Rick asked Dean.

"Yes."

Dean faced him down as if this were the last question he'd be asked before he was convicted.

I finally had to say something. I walked over and called out, "You have always said that we can apply our own individual style so long as it's - well – right."

Meg glared at me.

"It's fine. Thank you," said Rick.

"He covered the chalice with a cloth!"

"What's with you?" I argued. "Dean is the sacristan. He hasn't done anything wrong. We are all free to do our style, and his is perfectly correct. This is what they taught in liturgy class at General. You must remember that."

"It's all right, Meg," said Rick.

I thought, okay, he's not totally lost.

Meg threw up her hands. "We can't budge an inch, or we lose who we are."

She walked into the sacristy.

Rick followed her.

Dean said, "Why did she do that?"

"Who knows?" I shrugged. "But this is fine, Dean. It looks lovely."

I found Meg in the garden.

"Are you mad or crazy?"

"No."

"Such a silly thing to get upset about."

"I give a damn. Dean just wants to wallow in his Catholicism."

"So let him. Some Episcopalians are high church. He's not going to a Catholic church. He's here. But that doesn't mean he can't miss some things about it. So let him drape chalices. Unless you want to drive him out."

She shrugged.

"I get it. So long as we worship at the Meg shrine, we're fine."

She walked away.

Well, I'd said it.

She called me later that day.

"I'm sorry. I don't know what got into me."

I took a deep breath. Don't scold her. "Look, once upon a time, you decided to be a nun in the Catholic Church. That took a lot of thought and preparation. Then, after some years, and when the church wouldn't change, you left, and that took a lot of thought and preparation, and somehow you can't stand anything that reminds you of those days. But nowhere in the Gospels do I find Jesus screaming at someone because they didn't cover the chalice properly."

There was a long silence.

Then, "Jan? So far as I'm concerned, you're a priest. I hope you know that." She said that quietly, and I heard some trembling in her voice.

"Just take it easy on yourself," I said. "And on the rest of us." I tried to laugh, but it came out choking.

"Thanks, Jan. See you later."

The next week, I was subdeacon, and I was in the sacristy, marking the Altar Book when I heard Tom and Chris talking about Lily's being so disorganized in the office that they had to do something about it.

Lily had been working in the office for two years. They just noticed that she was disorganized? Disorganized about what all of a sudden?

Tom came by on his way to the pews. He saw the expression on my face.

"You heard that?"

"Yeah."

"Lily's been falling down on the job."

"Since when?"

"The filing system is all a mess. Rick was putting the parochial report together and nothing was where it should be, and her desk is a mess."

"She's not being disorganized. She's being busy."

"I hear an 'I told you so' coming up."

"I'd said it was a bad idea to hire a friend to do that job and make the apartment part of the salary. She's getting her PhD. Her mind is somewhere else. But she's good. I haven't seen any more typos in the bulletin."

"We can't go on like this," said Tom. "We're not sure what to do. She's going to be out for a few days. I think Meg's going to work the office since she'll be on spring break."

"This is nasty."

"That's what churches do. Nasty stuff. You should know that, future priest."

Meg called me up, a surprise.

"Lily is a mess. Rick is up to here with her."

That didn't even sound like Rick.

"Has he talked to her?"

"Oh, many, many times."

I didn't say anything. It wasn't my decision. I knew nothing about the office, but it seemed strange that Meg would be talking about Lily right after I'd heard about it from Tom.

Then she said, "I have a good job interview coming up.'

"Great."

"In Portland."

"Maine? Oregon?"

"Oregon."

I had envisioned her in the tristate area, not a continent away.

"At their cathedral. Barbara Sutton is there. She knew Rick. He recommended me for her job as canon pastor."

Canon pastor at a cathedral? Newly ordained priests usually became assistants. Maybe her qualifications from nunhood had something to do with it. Still, that had been *Catholic* nunhood.

It did seem a long shot. They probably had plenty of candidates. Maybe someone was doing Rick a favor in getting her an interview.

CHAPTER 28

Easter was coming round again, and the choir was ramping up to the work. By unanimous vote of the liturgy committee, I was to sing the Exultet again.

"You sing it right," said John.

"But next year, someone else, okay?"

"Next year is a year from now."

I registered for the ordination exams, the dreaded GOEs. Lily handed me a massive three-ring binder with several past tests and outlines to study from. I gaped at the topics – all over the place – and several questions on the nature of Christ. Oh, more than several. Whole pages on the history of Christology. Was he human? Divine? In between? When did the human take over and the Divine end? Or did it?

Who the heck was this guy?

You'd think I'd know.

Ah, church.

Holy Week again came round again. Rick attacked my foot with a zesty, firm touch and planted a kiss on the toes with such gentleness that I thought instantly of Jesus – his fierceness of mission, his love, his gentleness to his friends. I felt converted, sinking into the haven of knowing God and wanting to be Her friend.

The altar party cleared the chancel with its same ferocious energy.

I kept Vigil, again at eleven at night, and I read prayers from my old Catholic missal, thinking more about my childhood faith than the imprimatur from the Catholics.

And Friday – behold the wood of the cross. Rick believed it with an intensity that carried into each of us.

We sang the Passion. I sang Pilate. Oh, wretched man, heeder of the mob. The Jews had consistently risen up against the Romans for decades. Really, this Passion gospel did not make sense, and it troubled me.

The bell rang thirty-three times, one strike for each year of Jesus' life. Thirty-three and then silence. We sat quietly, and we left quietly.

Paula caught up with me, her face all aglow. She wanted to know all that I was doing.

I told her.

"I've started making your stole."

I laughed. "I'm not ordained!"

"You will be."

"Gotta go study," I said at the corner.

"You will be," Paula repeated.

I gave her a hug.

Dad had left "Give me a call" on my answering machine.

I didn't call him back.

It struck me that the "after three days he rose again" was a lie. He was dead at three on Friday, was put in the tomb all of Saturday - so it was one and a half days. If it was three days in the tomb, he would have risen on Monday. So, it's "on the third day" as in the Creed but not "three days." It only took me this long to figure that out.

Saturday's service was at noon, just a few prayers, but I wanted to go. Jesus was in the tomb. I hadn't gone the year before. Few people did attend, resting up from the week.

I arrived ten minutes to noon and found the church locked. Puzzled, I went into the rectory. Nan, Paula, and Beth, the hospitality stalwart, were back in the kitchen. I heard raised voices outside in the garden.

"What's going on?"

Paula shrugged, rolled her eyes, and gestured to the back door.

"Our new priests are rustling their new feathers."

I opened the door and yes, they were going at each other.

Loudly.

"It's tradition!" Lily shouted.

Meg screamed back. "Tradition with the Catholics!"

"But before the church split up –"

"You don't know what you're talking about! I've been Catholic! I won't do it! I'm the celebrant. I'm not going to wear the cope."

"What's a cope?" asked Paula.

"It's a cape," I said, wondering if I sounded as disgusted as I felt. "It's worn during celebrations."

"It's tradition," Lily was arguing.

"How far back? You don't know! And I have the right to say what I'll do. The cope is Catholic tradition."

"We do a lot of Catholic things here. Our Rite Two is…"

"It's not the same thing! You think you know everything, with your Greek and Latin but you don't know this church!"

What a strange thing to say. Lily knew this church as well as any of us.

Lily kept trying to be calm, but Meg seemed to want to go for her jugular.

Rick walked into the kitchen slowly.

It was ten minutes after twelve.

"What about the service?" I asked.

He started to say something, paused, and then turned and walked away.

"Jesus," said Nan.

Jesus, I realized, was in the tomb.

I shut the back door.

We still heard them.

"Can't you stop them?" asked Paula.

"I don't think they're stoppable, arguing over a cope. Let's do a service in the chapel."

Beth hurried out to see if anyone was trying to get into the church.

I heard Rick go upstairs. Why didn't he stop them? These women worked for him.

I called up after him, "We're going to have a service here in the chapel."

No answer. He kept going upstairs.

In the chapel, I passed out the Common Prayer books and found the service for Holy Saturday.

Beth returned with two people – Tom and Steven. When Paula said, "The priestlings were fighting," they laughed.

I began, "In the name of the God, God's Son, and the Holy Spirit."

It was a simple service. I allowed for meditations on loss of love, of

Jesus' death, of disappointment and bitterness and prayed to relieve us of them, and I asked others to supply their petitions.

A door slammed. Someone stalked down the hall. I knew it was Meg. I looked up. She paused at the door to the chapel. I did not smile. She stalked down the hall and I heard her go up the stairs.

Lily came in quietly and joined us.

At the end, they all thanked me and clearly wanted to know what was going on. Lily just shrugged and said she was going for a walk.

"Thank you," Paula told me. "I can't believe they were fighting over a vestment."

"Meg's on edge. I guess Lily is too," I said.

"I heard her job's on the line. Is that true?"

"Oh, I don't know. I think it's strange that all of a sudden, she's disorganized. She works hard. The office, her doctorate, the kids' group."

"She has one of her own," said Paula.

"She's worked here for a long time. If there'd been anything wrong, they would have dealt with it long ago."

I put the prayer books back and grabbed my jacket.

"You acted like the priest. Rick chickened out."

"I don't understand that."

We walked to Eighth Avenue. She gave me a big hug.

"You'll be a great priest."

I wished she wouldn't say those things.

"I'll see you tomorrow," I said.

Back home I went, puzzled. Why had Meg charged into Lily that way? It had to be about something else. Or was it two newly ordained priests battling for knowitallness? I rather sided with Lily. After all, St. Philip's was mostly Catholic in liturgy – the liturgy committee was all lapsed Catholics or people the Catholics didn't want. except for Donald and Rick, who were cradle born Episcopalians. And who cared? Why did new priests care so much about the clothes? They were just symbols, and the service itself led us into the spirit of the Eucharist.

I called Meg.

"She's so stubborn," she said.

I wanted to laugh.

"I'm the one wearing the vestment. I can wear what I want, in the tradition. I'm wearing the chasuble, not the stupid cope."

"I refuse to argue about clothes."

"Of course not. Oh, Rick said thank you for doing the service. He had a job calming me down."

"You shouldn't be fighting like that with us around."

"I know. It got out of hand. Lily is up in arms because we're putting pressure on her."

"We're?"

There was a pause. Then she said, "Rick and the wardens. I'm the intermediary."

"Why do they need an intermediary?"

Some intermediary.

"You know what I mean. Look, I have to calm down and review what I'm doing. See you tomorrow – or, rather, tonight."

I bit my tongue.

I fell onto my couch like a limpid Victorian lady. Were they really going to fire Lily? Throw her and her son out of the rectory apartment? It seemed inhuman. And for what?

I pondered all this at the Vigil as we slowly processed through the dark church, stopping to light candles, a little light – an aura from small flames growing slightly brighter as we moved forward to the altar. I went to the lectern and looked down at the congregation, my friends, taking up about half the pews on either side, the stained-glass windows dark with only the outline visible. I smiled at the community and began to sing. I wanted to be happy, filling the chant with, well, exaltation.

The congregation bathed in the soft glow that grew with each reading. Finally, Meg stepped forward, opened her arms, and cried, as perhaps the first witnesses to the empty tomb, the women themselves, "Alleluia! The Lord is Risen!"

We yelled back, "The Lord is Risen Indeed! Alleluia!"

The church lights went up, everyone jangled bells, and I pulled out a tambourine.

As I danced, I thought of the great pines of the Sierra Nevada, tall, indestructible. They'd been through it all for centuries, and Half Dome and El Capitan, too.

I realized. The Resurrection is now now now. And again and again.

New life, new nourishment, new hope. Like Yosemite in the spring with the rushing waters, gift of the terrible winter.

Finally, the bell ringing stopped, we sang a hymn, and the Eucharist began.

Rick hugged everyone at the Peace.

Meg danced with me. I felt happy. I was glad to see that she danced with Lily.

I dashed down to the aisle, do se do'd with Paula and Norma, then ran up and clapped John's hands.

Gradually, the havoc died down, Meg continued the Eucharist, and I darted to the altar.

It all felt so good.

On Monday, Rick called to tell me I had to schedule three members of the Commission on Ministry – my pre-interviews.

"Jeez, that's fast," said Meg, when she called to say she was off to Portland for her interview. "Mine was so slow, and you're barreling up there."

Was she kidding? Her ordination process had taken ten minutes.

CHAPTER 29

A few days later, Meg, back from Portland, called me up and said, "Let's do dinner."

I could tell from her voice that the interview had gone well.

Despite the tension in our friendship, I wanted her to stay in New York or nearby. I would need support, too. I kept thinking, she has been like a sister but a part of me is relieved if she leaves but why is that? I need family…

I rehearsed arguments. She loved New York. She had friends here. She loved the city.

Meg only liked to eat on Eleventh Street, in a particular Indian restaurant. I can barely eat Indian food, but there she was, giving me a hug before I sat down. Her eyes were clear, and she was obviously happy.

"You got the job."

"Not yet. But I know they're going to offer it to me."

"And?"

"And I'll take it."

"Meg."

I ran down the arguments, wondering how she could be sure.

"No," she said. "Listen."

I kept on arguing.

She stopped me.

"Jan, I can't stay at Saint Philip's."

"Why not?"

"Because Rick and I are having a relationship."

I felt as if I'd stepped into another dimension. One where I thought, of course, that makes perfect sense. Rick's giving in to her, their special little hugs, his insistence that she be ordained, and his speedy entrance into her apartment building – why hadn't I seen this coming round the bend?

And there was that other dimension, like reality. The diocese had recently sent out regulations to guard from sexual harassment in the parish and a rector having a relationship with an associate or a seminarian or a parishioner was definitely not on the approved list. The penalty? Loss of job. Possibly loss of collar.

But I also felt…anger.

"So," I said, "this is why we're not going to have Rite One celebrated at Saint Philip's? Because Rick will do whatever the hell you want?"

"No!"

I leaned back and stared at her. Why had that been the first thing I'd said?

"We love each other. It just happened. He's not happy with Betty. Betty's not happy with him."

I tried to see it her way. I tried not to see how it affected me. If she was going to have a job on the other side of the country, Rick would be going there, too. Then I thought how it would affect the parish.

"Does anyone else know? And what, may I ask, do you mean by having a relationship?"

"No one else knows. Not even Betty. We have an advisor. She told us to tell you because – because we're friends. She told us to wait until you were into the process, that the Vestry voted on you."

And that my approval was tied to Rick's approval. Clever.

"And that I can't say anything about him having a relationship with an associate priest would be tossing out the one person recommending me for ordination."

I ordered a Manhattan.

"Janene, it's not like that. You're our friend. You have to know. And you should know that we didn't do anything until I was ordained a priest."

I had a vision of Meg in collar and black cassock closing the door to Rick's bedroom and flinging off her collar and ripping open her cassock to reveal her naked self with an, "I'm ordained! Take me!"

I had to laugh.

"Okay," I said.

"You can't tell anyone."

I got that.

"I'm going to leave New York at the end of August to start this job. Rick will come a few months later. Then when you get ordained, we'll help you get a job there, and we'll be together, like a family."

And I'm the stupid little kid.

I remembered how I could not get ahold of her after her ordination. How I'd thought Rick was teaching her the ropes and taking her on pastoral calls.

"Can't you be happy for us?"

I tried to smile. "Sorry – it's just – I should have seen it."

"We've been very careful." She lowered her voice. "The sexual harassment guidelines are really being looked at now. There have been so many scandals, and it brings real focus on the bishop. Hiney is after anyone who looks as if they're looking at a woman or man with lust and they're supervisors or pastors. And he'd love to have something on Rick. Rick could lose his collar."

"And you?"

"Possibly. Hiney wouldn't stand for such behavior."

"You'd have to leave Saint Philip's, but you could still stay in New York."

"There aren't any full-time associate jobs. This is a real job. I'll go out in September, and Rick will come out a few months later."

"Do the wardens know this?"

"Oh, no. We can't tell them yet."

Rick leaving Saint Philip's! And no one knew! Just Meg, Rick, and me! Not even, I assumed, Betty.

I realized that this had all been arranged. Rick had recommended her to the cathedral in Portland. Of course, he had contacts there. He had contacts everywhere. No former Catholic just out of seminary who didn't live in Portland would have gotten such a job without help.

Meg said, "And when you're ordained, you can join us. You love the west."

In that moment, I knew that I would not go with her. Them.

"I know I've been weird. I wanted to tell you, but Rick felt it had to be after the Vestry approved you and you were accepted into the process."

Because my future, my approval from the parish, would depend on him.

"Because then you'd be one of us."

That was why, I realized, I hadn't been able to reach her after her ordination. Well, so what? I realized, too, why she and Rick had to leave.

I had entertained a fantasy that we would all be at Saint Philip's, forever and ever. That I had a family to replace the one I'd lost. You silly woman. You are looking for your family all over again, and they won't be that.

"Now you can keep the secret. We trust you."

My silence or my priesthood.

Could I criticize them for falling in love? They were a great couple, that was absolutely the truth.

I had to change the subject.

"How was Portland?"

She talked. I thought.

I'd have to keep it quiet. I was tied to him. If I said anything to anyone, he could pull my recommendation.

And why would I talk? Wouldn't my promise to be silent have been enough before? Didn't they trust me? They were my friends.

Rick's marriage was bad. He and Meg were a marvelous couple. If the diocese found out, Rick could lose his collar.

I couldn't tell on them.

Maybe tell on them and Heine would love me.

If that's how you would be a priest, go suck an egg.

Meg was prattling.

I was a loyal friend. Not that it mattered. Those two were in their own world. They weren't thinking about anyone else.

I had one hope – that Meg wouldn't get the job in Portland. A slim hope, I feared.

Well, I had a life to live.

I had interviews coming up.

Get on with it, Janene Shannon. You're on your own now, I told myself on the cab ride home.

Those interviews - they were just conversations. One was a priest, and I felt that she was aligning me with herself, questioning me about how I felt about everything. I was careful. But with the other two, I felt comfortable – just chatting. With one, we went over our time. I guessed that was good.

Lily wrote me. "I've been fired. I have to move."

She didn't know where. General Seminary had no spare residential space. Plus, she was jobless.

"I need money for my last semester."

They couldn't put up with her for one more semester?

As soon as I sat down in my weekly meeting with Rick, I put it to him. "Why are you being so mean to Lily? Keep her for the semester."

He shook his head. "She made mistakes on the parochial report."

The treasurer put the parochial report together. Lily would have typed it. Was that the mistake? But certainly – why fire her? Did they proofread it?

"For that? She's done good work for the whole year. Plus, she has to move."

"I'd rather not talk about it, Janene. I wanted to ask you what sort of classes you'll be taking next year, and if we can work that into some time on Wednesdays."

Why? He wasn't going to be here. Why was he pretending?

I held my tongue.

Something was wrong.

There certainly was.

Dad called me at work.

"I just wanted to talk. Helen's not here. It's a good time."

It was?

"I cashed in some insurance that came to term and I'm dividing it with you kids. It'll be about three thousand dollars each."

"Thank you, Dad."

I spoke calmly. I was thrilled to get any money. School drained my savings, and I was starting to regularly dip into my line of credit. My trips home when Mom was sick – my bank account hadn't gotten over those yet. But why was Dad going to give us each three thousand dollars? What was going on?

"How are you?"

"I'm okay. A few aches and pains. I got sick on the last cruise we were on."

"I'm sorry."

"But I'm all right now."

I heard a door open.

"I love you, Dad." I said it quickly.

She was there.

A long silence followed.

"Good talking to you. Goodbye."

His tone had changed like that.

He wasn't going to say I love you to me with her there.

The easy answer, the right answer, was money. He didn't have enough to leave her. All his money had gone to take care of my mother for four years.

Helen had money.

He was trapped. Dear God, he didn't deserve this. For a moment, I was even angry at my mother for putting him in this position.

He started calling me at two o'clock on Thursdays, when Helen was not there.

I should have gotten on the train and gone to see him.

Something in me – something dark – wanted to punish him. I did not go. I should have realized he was being punished enough.

My excuse for not going? I had to study for the GOEs. They were a few weeks away, and I had made a plan for my preparation. I also had preaching class and independent study. And Advanced Theology. Ha. Couldn't go. Couldn't go. Couldn't go…

CHAPTER 30

"WHAT CANDIDATES OUGHT TO KNOW FOR THE GOEs"

- **The Holy Scriptures – the various approaches employed by scholars of biblical criticism – their values and limitations.**
- **Principles and practice of exegesis and hermeneutics. Chronology, history, important personalities in the Old Testament, New Testament, and Apocrypha.**
- **Geography of Biblical Lands.**
- **Knowledge of world events upon the development of the Judeo-Christian tradition.**
- **Gospel narratives in Johannine and Synoptic traditions, including Acts.**
- **Theme, contents, and historical context of each book, Old and New Testament.**
- **Major theological developments in the entire tradition.**
- **Biblical sources of creeds and historical doctrines."**

Those categories did not cover the wherewithal to decide Lily's severance.

At the meeting, I took a seat at the head of the table opposite Rick. Everyone but Meg was there.

Lily had dressed in her best professional uniform– a red jacket and skirt and white blouse. With collar. She looked confident but I knew Lily well enough to know she was scared and hurting. When she spoke, her voice trembled, but she'd always had a vibrato, so it was barely noticeable. Unless you listened for it.

No one was happy.

It all felt wrong.

I said, "Must this be a fait accompli?"

Rick sent me a sharp look.

I smiled at him. "Lily is a good priest – a good preacher. So, she's not a good office worker! But she's been working in the office for two years, and suddenly she's bad."

"It's not sudden," said Rick.

He did not look happy.

"There've been lots of mistakes," said Tom. "Of course, we like Lily."

Lily looked at me and shook her head.

Ellen muttered an uncharacteristic, "Geez."

"What sort of mistakes?" I asked. "Typos? Theft? What?"

Tom looked over at Rick.

"Nothing dishonest, certainly," said Rick. "Losing things, typos in letters, not mailing letters in a timely way, the files out of order, and we all know about the typos in the bulletin."

"I haven't seen any lately," I said.

Rick sighed.

"And she forgot to lock up a couple of nights," said Tom. "Someone could have broken in."

Lily looked down at her fingers.

"We're here to decide on her severance," said Tom.

I didn't like his tone. I felt we'd been left out of all the important discussions.

Paula's voice was sharp. "We have to give her a living allowance. We can't toss a mother and child out on the street."

"Must you be so dramatic?" asked Tom.

"Yes," she retorted.

Meg rushed in, took the empty seat next to me, ripped off a page in her notebook, and wrote on it. Her excited look told me what the note said before she handed it to me.

"I got Portland. Starting late August. I haven't told Rick."

We were firing Lily, Meg would be gone in August, and Rick soon after.

Ellen said, "Why not keep Lily on as a priest for a few months while she looks for another job and place to live? And say she's just not an office worker?"

170

Lily spoke. "No, I couldn't do that. I want to find another place."

Why? I tried to catch her eye. I felt I was swimming in an unknown sea.

"I want to start over someplace else," Lily said. "Really. I'm fine with that. But I didn't get much notice, and I need a better severance package than the one the Wardens offered."

She seemed definite. Not that I blamed her.

We were losing all three priests and the Vestry didn't know. Even when Meg gave them the news, Rick would not tell them that he was headed for Portland right after Meg said she was going. It would imply…

The truth!

And I couldn't speak. If I did, I'd have ended my trek to ordination, ended my friendship with Meg and Rick and my life at Saint Philip's. Plus, the parish would be torn. I still loved Meg and Rick. But what about Lily?

I said, "Why fire Lily, though? Meg is –" I struggled to say it correctly – "going to get another job somewhere soon. We'd need Lily."

"We need someone in the office more," said Tom.

"I want to go," said Lily. "It's all right, Jan. I want to talk about my severance."

Why was Lily all right with leaving? There was something I didn't understand.

Why couldn't I just speak out the truth that I knew? But it seemed that there was some other truth diving in under the table and leaping up all around.

While I was tossing thoughts back and forth, the discussion had turned heated. Tom and Steven had proposed severance of barely a thousand dollars.

"That's not severance!" Paula shouted.

I said, softly, "It needs to be more than that."

"She got five hundred a month," said Tom. "And housing."

"And housing!" yelled Darryl at my side. "What housing is she going to get in New York for that?"

"She doesn't have to live in New York."

Paula sputtered. "She has a kid here in school."

"We can't give her three months' rent and severance," said Tom.

"Why not?" asked Paula. "At least three thousand."

The table rocked with people talking.

Rick called a break. "Everyone, calm down. We want to do what is right. Let's take a break and give it careful thought."

Everyone got up – but me. People went to the kitchen or the restrooms. Meg hurried out to the parlor and said something to Rick, and they both started laughing.

How could they laugh?

I put my head down on the table.

Paula came over. "Miserable stuff, isn't it? I can't believe Tom is so cold."

I sat up. "There's so much I can't believe, Paula."

She gave me a hug and went back to her chair.

I got up to get to the bathroom. I found Lily coming out, and in the hallway, I said to her, "Why not fight this?"

"I want to go. It's – it's changed here."

"Do you know things?" I asked quietly.

"I know a lot. I have a tip on a job. I'll be fine."

If she knew what I knew – were they afraid she'd talk, and Rick would be penalized somehow?

When I got back to my seat, Meg and Rick followed me in. Meg sat and squeezed my hand.

Well, I could play a little. I looked straight at Rick. "Two thousand."

He looked at me calmly for a few moments. I did not smile. He did.

Lily was granted one thousand dollars in severance and another thousand for housing costs. A serious discussion between Paula and Ellen versus Tom argued that Lily could work at her job with full pay for two months, but Lily herself refused that.

"I don't think that would be right if you aren't happy with me working here."

I felt awful. I still didn't understand how she had been so suddenly disorganized. A few typos didn't merit firing, but everyone else seemed to accept the reason for Lily's dismissal. So, there must have been some other facts behind this.

Then came the killer.

Meg said, "I want to let you know that I've gotten a job."

Everyone applauded.

Except me.

"I've been appointed canon pastor for the Portland, Oregon cathedral."

The applause continued, but it petered out.

"In Oregon?" asked Paula.

"Yes. I'm leaving in August."

"Then we're losing two priests," said Tom.

Little did he know.

Rick said, "I should add something else."

Dear God.

"Betty and I have been separated for some weeks," he said, slowly. "She and I have agreed to a legal separation, and this will – I'm sure – lead to a divorce."

After a silence, Ellen said, "I'm sorry."

All I had to do was say something.

I looked over at Lily. She smiled at me, gave a shrug, and raised her eyebrows. I thought, she knows. That's why she's being thrown out. So she doesn't tell anyone here.

Why didn't I say that? It was the truth.

It was like a collar around my neck, and I wasn't going to give my chance at a collar up.

I was as bad as anyone else.

What would have happened if I had told the truth?

I would have lost Meg, and I would have lost Rick's support.

For that I lied by not speaking up. Not only would we be out three priests but two of them would have to be charged with sexual harassment, or at least Rick would be. And I loved Rick too much to want to do that.

"I'll see about getting a deacon in," said Rick. "We'll need one, and Janene isn't ready yet."

"Janene can take the rota," said Lily. "She's helped with it the last two months."

Paula caught up with me as I left. "Do you want to set a date for Santa Fe?"

Swell, she was energized.

"No, no," I said. "Not for a while. School and stuff."

CHAPTER 31

A few weeks, yes weeks, later, Meg called. We'd both been busy, and I'd been – unwilling to talk to her.

"Let's go to Spring Lake on Saturday."

I was touched. She knew that was a special place to me, that quiet place on the Jersey shore.

"Just to say goodbye," she said.

She showed up in her new car. I got in.

"Like it? It's an Audi coupe. After California, I really wanted one. Isn't it cute? I'm going to drive across the country and have myself a time."

And on she bubbled all about her job and Portland and as I listened, I got sick of hearing about it.

I said, "I had my interviews, you know."

"Oh, yeah. How'd they go?"

"Rick left a message on my machine last night. All three okayed me to move on."

"Three?" She laughed. "I only got two approvals. Okay. You're going to be a deacon in no time."

"They'll have to accelerate me."

"Just ask your interim."

"She or he won't know me."

"Janene, don't worry! You're a church person. Anyone can see that. I have no doubts."

At Spring Lake, she left me, while she wandered over to Asbury Park, which was important to her own childhood, while I went onto the beach, crowded with the summer people. I walked onto the breakwaters and peered out at the Garden of Paradise.

Couldn't Rick stay a bit longer until I was settled?

No. Nothing mattered but Meg. I got that and felt miserably isolated and alone.

Meg returned and we had a quick supper in town before starting back. Meg talked on and on about Portland, adding to my feelings of isolation.

At the next coffee hour, I found Tom and said, "Did Rick want Lily fired or did you?"

He shrugged. "He complained about her. We did the rest."

"Of course, you would."

"But you know what? If we fired people for being disorganized, Rick would have been out pretty fast."

I laughed. But he went on, "He leaves piles of papers, all of them completely different – sermon extracts, budget reports, letters, diocesan reports …"

"Did you warn Lily?"

Tom shrugged. "I think there was another reason, but he didn't want to say, so we weren't going to push it. I like Lily. I didn't want to know what she did."

I didn't like what I was thinking.

CHAPTER 32

Meanwhile, I had another sermon to conquer and tons of work. This time I would talk about the Holy Spirit. Yes, Rick assigned me Pentecost. I was certainly going to emphasize Her femininity. I wrote that up fast. And rethought it all twice. And again.

"I like this," Rick said of my sermon. "Keep saying She – Don't alternate He and She. The Bible says, in my image. Humans are male and female in my image. Cut about two pages, and it'll be wonderful."

"Okay."

"I'm almost done with my recommendation to the bishop for you. I take my time to do it well. But once you're on that path, then nothing can stop you."

"You won't be here."

"Once the Commission approves you, it'll move fast. Just don't commit a murder."

On Sunday, I albed up, put my sermon on the pulpit, and went to rehearse in the choir. I had brought a box, which I put beneath my choir chair.

After rehearsal, I went to the pulpit to look at my first words so that I could look out at the congregation while saying them. Just as I did, Chris plugged in the fan, and my pages flew out over his head and fluttered to the floor.

"No!' I yelped. "The pages aren't numbered!"

Then I laughed.

"The Holy Spirit is editing my sermon."

Tom and John helped me gather my pages. John looked at one piece and shouted, "Heresy! Heresy!"

"You should see the next page," I said.

It really wasn't hard to sort the pages, but we were laughing so, and Meg came out in her deacon robes and said, "What's with the noise? It should be quiet out here. Give people a space to pray."

"Yes, Father," I said.

John and I exchanged amused looks.

Tom said, "The Holy Spirit just flew away."

Meg went back to the sacristy.

I thought, I can unmask you in a second.

But that would mean wounding Rick.

Men falling in love with controlling women. Where had I heard that song before?

"The young cleric has ideas," said Tom. "Hurry up and get through."

I groaned and followed Meg into the sacristy after placing a hymnal on the sermon to keep it in place.

Giving the sermon felt as if I was discovering a wondrous God in the faces of the people, my friends. She as God, as healer, as a spirit of wisdom, understanding, counsel. I read the wonderful passage from Wisdom:

For she is a breath of the power of God; and a pure emanation of the glory of the Almighty; therefore, nothing defiled gains entrance into her. For she is a reflection of eternal light, a spotless mirror of the working of God, and an image of God's goodness. Though she is but one, she can do all things, and while remaining in herself, she renews all things; in every generation she passes into holy souls and makes them friends of God and prophets; for God loves nothing so much as the person who lives with wisdom. For she is more beautiful than the sun, and excels every constellation of the stars. Compared with the light she is found to be superior, for it is succeeded by the night, but against wisdom evil does not prevail. She reaches mightily from one end of the earth to the other, and she orders all things well.

Not God, but God's companion, and a trifle gnostic, but injecting the female pronoun in church in relationship to God is something I feel compelled to do, and it is in the Bible.

I sat down, feeling – I don't know. Humble sounds silly, but it's the closest I can come to it. Or a feeling of being a small part of something – filled with light – that envelops all of us in walls stronger and more profound than the church walls. I wanted to kneel, to open my arms.

Rick finally stood, his voice filled with emotion.

"We have all just traveled to another place. All of us."

I joined the choir for the anthem. John blew me a kiss.

Right from his pew, Joseph yelled, "It felt fucking incredible!"

I bowed to him. It probably wouldn't have passed the bishop's muster, but here, they all laughed and applauded.

Norma called, "Hallelujah!"

At coffee, I waved Meg over to the steps.

"I hate you." But she was smiling. "You can preach like nobody else. You connect it all to Christ, but it's like a big dance." She twirled her braid like a lariat.

"I'm not sure what that means. Here. You're getting old. Happy Birthday."

I handed her the box.

She sat on the step leading up to Rick's apartment.

"Oh, you shouldn't have!" She ripped off the paper and opened the box, undid the tissue, and burst out, "Oh, my God."

She lifted up the scarf.

"I call it the Saint Peter's scarf."

"Oh, God, I'm so…"

So?

"Embarrassed!" She bent over laughing. "Did you really buy this for me?"

"Yes." I poked her. "Do you really like it?"

I didn't tell her that I'd bought it long before this, but I just hadn't wanted to give it to her. Mixed feelings. Holding back. Still, I had lost her precious scarf.

She laughed. And laughed. She rocked back and forth. Then she jumped up and she hugged me. "You are a doll. Rick gave me the other one."

I guess I'd realized that.

"I'm not sure he'll notice the difference. It'll be our secret. Thank you."

Norma popped her head out of the parlor.

"You two look so happy. Are you getting married?"

We laughed.

Meg put the box in her bag and when we stood, she hugged me hard.

"I thought you hated me."

"But I do."

We sauntered into the parlor, arm in arm.

"They're getting married!" Norma called out.

I couldn't figure out if she was joking but to my surprise, people believed.

"Are you?" cried Chris.

"Yes!" said Meg.

Rick called out, "Congratulations! When?"

"Oh, after I get my degree," I joked.

Rick called out, "Congratulations to Meg and Janene!"

Tom said to me, "I kind of figured that was happening. I wish we could have the wedding here."

"Are you kidding?"

Somehow Norma's innocent joke had become a reality that Meg and Rick somehow decided to endorse.

Could I say the truth? If I did, I'd be saying that Rick and Meg were liars.

"So, you're not going with me to New Mexico?" Paula looked shaken.

"Paula, I meant what I said to you. It's just that – I can't explain."

"It's all right. Really."

"But Paula…"

She got up and went to a table where others were laughing. I headed for the corridor and my jacket.

I could have yelled, "Stop! Stop! Lots of lies going on here!"

And then I would say, "He's leaving." And point to Rick. "And so's she." And point to Meg. "And they are having a relationship." Oh, yeah, go Jan. "And he's divorcing Betty. Got that?"

Sure, and then I'd wreck the church, everyone would hate me, and I sure wouldn't get to be a priest. Not without starting over at another church, and there was no church like this one, or was that just propaganda or – why did I ever want to be a priest?

Because I thought I'd be better, that's why.

When was I going to start that trick?

Anyway, I didn't say anything.

Meg caught up with me as I headed toward Eighth.

"I'm so sorry. Norma's thing caught me by surprise, but it'll sure keep everyone off the track."

"It sure will. Nice of you. I didn't even give you a ring. Should we move in together? Your place or mine?"

She laughed and twisted her braid around me. God, that had been the business all along. Meg couldn't be running off with Rick because she was running off with me. Ours had been a friendship of convenience.

"Don't be silly. It's just for a few weeks before I go. Look, Rick could lose his collar. Hiney would love to do that at the drop of anything seeming to breach the sexual harassment guidelines – that's hot news – and he could take down Rick and look like he's cleaning up the diocese. Norma gave us a nice red herring. You understand."

"Why would we need a red herring? Oh, yes, Bishop Heine sent a diocesan letter back a few months saying that any infraction of the sexual harassment guidelines, such as a pastor making love to an associate or a parishioner, would be strictly punished. As in removal of one's collar. That's why anything justifies your ends."

"We'll make it up to you and boost you through the process. Will you stand up for me at our wedding?"

"Did we just get a divorce? Things are happening so fast, dear."

Paula and John came into the hall.

Meg kissed me lightly on the lips.

"See you later!" she called and hurried out the door.

And all I had to do was speak the truth.

I didn't. I had this silly idea we were still friends.

"Walk you to the corner?" said John, coming up to me.

"I need to do one thing," I said, and I hurried back to the parlor. Rick was pouring himself a fresh cup.

I wanted to knock it out of his hand.

"Thank you for the congratulations," I said, hoping to sound sarcastic.

He didn't even wince. He put his cup down and took me in his arms. His eyes seemed warm and loving and for a brief instance, I realized why Meg had fallen in love with him. I could be in love with him, too. What a plot twist that could be, right? Don't leave us, Rick, stay with me. I wanted to yell," It's not Meg I love. It's you! You!"

Of course, I didn't.

Outside, John was waiting.

"I had no idea you're gay."

"Well," I said, "Men are so tiresome."

"I don't think so."

"It's better to be honest," he said, as we walked to the corner. "You know, I was married to a woman once. Of course, it ended badly. It's better to be honest with yourself and others. When I was a Lutheran minister. I knew I was gay. I was living a lie. I had to get out of my marriage. I did and my parish threw me out. Lutherans won't – well – I didn't get a church, so I took up church music and I love the Episcopal liturgy."

Better to be honest. But churches are stupid. You had to lie.

"I had no idea. I'm sorry."

"The truth in us will always out."

Well, that should prove exciting.

"By the way," he added, "that was an incredible sermon. You are incredibly poetic and at the same time, you preach the Gospel flat out. You remind me of Martin Luther."

"Martin Luther would not refer to the Holy Spirit as a woman."

He laughed. "But you really have a gift."

A gift for lying. A gift for cowardice.

It had been quite a couple of hours.

CHAPTER 33

Go to church, I could tell people. It's like a mini-series. When I got home, there was a message from Dad. "Call me between three and four."

When she wouldn't be there, I suspected.

The words I'd prayed for and yet dreaded. He said those words.

First, he said, "How are you?"

I rattled on for a bit, trying to be cheery.

Then, "How are you, Dad?"

"I have to talk to someone."

"Okay. What's wrong?"

"I can't stand her."

"Helen?"

Oh, precious words I thought I would never hear.

"I can't stand her. Nothing I do is right. She criticizes you kids. I'm tired of that. And I do look at other women. Don't do anything, but I look."

"Mom used to joke about that," I said quietly. "She was never threatened. Besides, she had a great figure and took care of herself." Well, except for smoking.

"Peg was great. She knew I wasn't going to do anything, that I was half teasing. Helen gets all worked up and starts yelling."

"Well, give it time."

"Time? She wants everything her way. And she's paranoid. She won't let me out of her sight because she's afraid I'll be running after other women. She won't let me get another car because she says I can't drive in this city. That's what she says. What does she think? That I'm a philanderer or that I'm too old to drive? I'm sorry."

"It's okay, Dad."

He ranted on. I'm thinking at first, this is the call I wanted him to make. Except everything he said about her – not that I didn't already know all that he said about her – started to hurt me. This was Dad, the guy who held my hand to help me learn to cross the street. This was Dad, the guy who went with me to buy a Christmas tree. This was Dad, who had been there all the time until he lost Peggy. He had cared for her, he had been with her every moment, and they had shared a good life together, and she had died.

"Why didn't I stop her smoking?"

"No one could, Dad. We all tried."

"Helen is no lady. She's no fun. She has no sense of humor. She hates my brother and sister. She won't let me out of her sight when she's here. She's paranoid. She's vindictive about you kids. I don't know why."

"Okay, Dad, what do you want?"

"A clean break. I don't believe in divorce, I just want to get away from her."

As he talked, I felt the anger leave, a physical feeling. I stretched out my arm and I forgave him. It was just there, and it was physical. As if I'd just lost fifty pounds. He'd been lost. He'd been grieving. He messed up. Oh, he messed up big. But like our old dog who used to run off through cow pastures and muddy fields, he was coming home. And when someone comes home, you take him in.

The other funny thing? His voice, all that time since he'd gone to Helen, had become high pitched and softish. Now I heard my father's strong bass-baritone again.

"Okay," I said, tears stinging my eyes. "Do you think you could live with Dirk temporarily? He has a house. I only have a postage stamp apartment."

There was silence. Then he said, "Yes. I'd have to apologize."

"Dad, he'll be better than you think."

"Would he do it?"

"I'll ask him, but I think he would. He has an extra room. You can look around for something else."

"I could get a part-time job."

"It'll be all right, Dad. I'll talk to Dirk. We'll get you home."

"I want to come home," he said. "I'm sorry. I'm so sorry."

I wanted to hug him. I felt, he's come home. Mom had pushed him along, and here he was at last.

I called Dirk. He was astounded, hesitant, but when he said, "Of course, he can come here," I knew that our family would be all right again.

CHAPTER 34

Meg left.

We didn't actually say a final goodbye. She drove off one early morning, leaving a message that she wanted me to visit.

I remained busy with my job, studying for the GOEs, and church work. The GOEs were coming right after Christmas.

Rick called me in to say, "I can only tell you that I'm leaving soon – I won't give notice for a few weeks – January – so I hope you can help with my legal correspondence about Betty. Our legal separation. If you'd type the letters and mail them. They shouldn't be in the regular mail."

"Sure."

Sure, sure. Anything to get ordained, right? Me and my poetic sermons and presence on the altar. All that. Right.

I typed the letters. Cold. I mean the letters and the office. The boiler was on the fritz. It fritzed every autumn. The letters showed none of the feeling that I associated with Rick. They were filled with legal sentences about long separations affecting the relationship, growing apart, a distance of minds. Some forty years of marriage with three children.

The end.

He read them. "No errors! Thank you!" and signed them. I mailed them.

I called Dad at "our time." This time, Helen answered.

"Why don't you care?"

"What?"

"Why don't you call? Months and months and you don't call."

"You know that's not true. Well, believe what you want, but it's not true. Dad always called me when you weren't there. Because you're a bitch."

No answer.

"You had better come before it's too late."

"What do you mean?"

She hung up.

I called Jules and Dirk.

"Something's wrong. I'm going down there.,"

I made a reservation on Amtrak for the weekend. Dirk was going to fly in and we'd meet at the station.

On Friday, Helen called. "He is in the hospital. Arlington Hospital. Room 305."

I let Dirk know.

"Geez, if it's that bad, why didn't we know?"

I got off the train and saw Dirk. He had rented a car and he drove to the hospital.

Dad was barely conscious.

"What happened?"

Helen sat there, looking at her hands.

He was much thinner, he had lost most of his hair, and he was hooked up to several machines.

I sat down. I took his hand. Nothing mattered but him.

"Hi, Dad."

"He can't hear you."

Helen stood up. "I don't want to be in the same room with you. You didn't love him. You didn't even come to our wedding."

She walked out of the room.

Dirk bent over him. "If you can hear me, blink twice."

"Too many TV shows, Dirk."

But lo and behold, Dad blinked twice. He squeezed my hand. A nurse came in, roly poly and blonde.

"Mrs. Shannon does not want to be in the same room with you."

I had to think who Mrs. Shannon was.

She put her hand on my shoulder.

"I'll come get you."

I got up and saw the name on her chest.

Margaret.

Mom's name.

Dirk and I left the room and walked toward the waiting area not knowing where the hell we were.

A doctor came to speak with us. "His doctor is on vacation, but he did not expect Mr. Shannon's illness to become serious so quickly."

I wondered, what disease?

Margaret called, "Come quickly!"

And we ran back into the room.

Helen sat there, looking at him.

I took his hand.

"I love you, Daddy."

That machine thing flattened out.

Dirk leaned over Dad and then he looked over at Helen. "I'm sorry."

"It's too late for that now," she snapped.

Whatever she meant by that, I didn't like that emotion as being the last words over my father's body. No, I held onto his hand, the one I'd clasped around a pine tree as we analyzed its worth. The hand that saved my life, that held mine when crossing the street. The hand that opened up my first jewels, that fixed my bike, that clapped at the shows I was in, that taught me to dance those dances that none of the kids would do, that held my mother's hand through their life together, that held her when he watched her die, the hand of a young Navy ensign slipping his class ring onto my mother's hand eight years before she would be my mother and a few weeks before he went off to duck the Japanese kamikazes in the South Pacific.

That was when I realized this was their wedding anniversary.

Margaret escorted us out.

I said, "What was wrong with him?"

She said, "Myelodysplastic syndrome."

"And what's that?"

"The blood," she said. "His doctor is on vacation, but he didn't expect your father to die for years. It seems that he fell. But he also – he didn't seem to care."

My throat tightened around the tears I tried to swallow. My mother had died with his arms around her. He died desperate to escape the stupid mistake he'd made out of anger and loneliness. He'd deserved a new beginning. He hadn't deserved Helen.

I had to believe in heaven.

Dirk and I walked – stunned – to the car. It was a long walk. I struggled for good memories, and they came, and we chained them together. Whiffle ball games in the backyard. A new car every two years. Traveling all over town to pick out the "just right" Christmas tree. Loving to be with his family. Making holiday fun. Dad jokes. He'd *invented* Dad jokes! Hard work for a family business without much support or appreciation of the profits he made for them that made New York Coca-Cola want to buy the business ransacked by Mom's family. Going out to dinner. He and Mom dancing, hugging, kissing…

We got a motel room and made calls. Our aunt, his sister, would be devastated. She was. Jules who would bring drama and a tape recorder and care more about that. Dirk's wife. Dad's brother.

I felt numb. I didn't sleep.

Dirk dropped me off at the Amtrak station the next day and went on to the airport. We were both still in shock.

Dad hadn't told anyone he was so ill – back pain and stuff but "I don't have cancer. I'm fine." But he did have cancer of the blood.

Why hadn't he said anything? Did he feel he deserved to die? That he had no place else to go?

He had tried to come home. And his voice had changed. He had become himself again – almost. He hadn't had that cheery heartiness for so long. He'd come back. But – did he think that he had no place to go? Just Dirk's – and after all that had happened, had he felt he couldn't go back?

I fell to my knees on that one. As much as I could on the train, bending low, my head in the seat in front of me, in my arms.

CHAPTER 35

When I got home, *her* voice was on my machine. There would be a service at a funeral home and after that, a service at Arlington where his ashes would be placed with Mom's.

No Mass for a man who once wished I would go to Mass every morning.

Aunt Mary was beside herself. "I didn't know he was sick. He could have come here. Gotten away from that bitch."

I cried along with her.

I thought of all my parents' friends, but I'd lost touch, and I didn't know where they were or how I could find them.

I was worthless.

I made another set of Amtrak reservations – a motel room at that Comfort Inn, which would be our family center. It was the same Comfort Inn where I had phoned Dad the night before his wedding.

And all he'd had was Helen to go home to. He'd been trapped, all the money saved through his life had gone for Peggy, practical Peggy, who smoked all her life, and the medical bills had drained them. He had married Helen because he thought he'd have a new life. Instead, it had brought him death.

I would never forgive her.

Some priest I was. I had let my anger and sadness take over when in fact he'd needed me. That's what those last phone calls had been about, and I'd been thinking about letting him suffer. My anger had taken over my love.

Damn it.

I couldn't call him back.

He'd died alone and sad.

I picked up the phone again and called the hospital in Arlington.

"I wanted to leave a message for a nurse on the ninth floor."

"A message?"

"I want to thank her for helping my family."

"Which nurse?"

"I don't know her full name. Her badge said 'Margaret.' She helped us when my father died – Edward Shannon."

"Of course. Just a minute. I'll connect you to the ninth floor."

A woman answered, and I repeated my message. "Margaret? There's no Margaret."

"She was a little plump and had silver hair."

"For Mr. Shannon? No, the nurse was Susan Mintern, and she has red hair."

"But I remember her. Margaret. She was helpful."

"I'm sorry, but there's no nurse on this floor and no nurse on duty when Mr. Shannon died whose name was Margaret."

I hadn't been confused. She'd had the same name as my mother. I remembered her smile, her quick sizing up of the situation, the tact, her haste when she knew the end was near to get Dirk and me into the room. Her light touch on my shoulder.

Margaret.

A nurse with my mother's name who didn't exist, but who did.

Margaret.

Mom, was that you?

Call me crazy. I believe it was.

If you helped him through death, eased his pain, took him into your arms with forgiveness and your love – Mom, I'm going to believe that. I believe in your love of him for after all, isn't your love the reason I am here?

Charley tapped my shoulder.

Oh, right. I was at work.

"Are you okay?"

I'd been crying, head in my arms.

I looked up and smiled. "Yeah."

"Do you need to go home?"

"No, I'm fine."

I picked up a folder and nodded to him. Someone called his name, and he went down the hall.

And I felt – silly as it sounds – the feel of a touch on both my shoulders. Oh, I never believe those stories except I felt those touches but also *them*. Standing near me. Loving me no matter what.

CHAPTER 36

It was a puzzled and tearful family gathering at the sadly named Comfort Inn. Dad's sister could not stop crying.

"He was our baby brother," Aunt Mary kept saying.

Uncle Donald, looking ashen, put his arm around his sister. Cousin Pete stood alert in his Navy uniform next to his what-am-I-doing-with-these-people wife. And there was Dirk and me. His wife could not come, but Jules came with her daughter Laurie, now in the eighth grade.

Uncharacteristically, Jules didn't say much. Innocent of tragedy, Laurie chattered, intent on being noticed as the cute grandchild. Dirk and I didn't talk much. We were spent out. But his wife, Elaine, came and did the talking for him.

"Why did he marry her?" Aunt Mary looked so crushed. "She was hateful. She couldn't smile. She wasn't fun. What did he see in her?"

"Escape," I said.

"To what? He was going to come down to Sarasota and we were going to find a place for him. He said he wanted to and then this."

I thought, he didn't have enough money for a place she would have found for him.

That's why he'd been so angry at us, really, when we'd argued with him. He'd had no other place to go.

Aunt Mary had expensive habits. Cruises, restaurants.

And Mom's family had left him out of my grandmother's will, which she had told them to leave him in, but what did Mom matter? Her brothers and sisters drained our grandmother's bank account until there was little left, so her will didn't matter.

A stark, generic service in the funeral home. The urn containing my father's remains. So few people. Our family. Helen and her stupid daughter.

I thought of all the friends my father had made over the years. I guess they hadn't been told. They would have been filled with stories and fun. Helen didn't care for stories and fun.

We arrived at Arlington Cemetery and received stickers for our cars. We all stopped somewhere and parked. I saw three military men, a trumpet. A hearse.

One man in black slacks, clergy shirt, and collar tapped at our window.

"Mrs. Shannon does not want anyone to speak at the service."

"Why the hell not?" I blurted.

The minister didn't blink.

"That is her special request."

"The hell," said Aunt Mary. "She's just afraid we'll say rotten things about her. I want to talk about my brother."

"I understand."

The minister went down to Uncle Donald's car and to Dirk's. Then he went back to Helen's. Then back to ours.

No go.

"This is ridiculous," said Aunt Mary.

I was beginning to hope for a knock down drag out at Arlington Cemetery.

Dad had lived a wonderful life, been a wonderful man. He'd just tripped up. He should be remembered with laughter and music and his family and friends. But it was just numbed us.

The minister came back. I felt sorry for him, but he was calm and soothing. He really was trying to keep peace. I felt grateful to him.

"Here's what we'll do. We'll have the main service and then move over to the resting place and once Mrs. Shannon leaves, we'll have a small prayer service, and you may say what you want."

Who the hell was Mrs. Shannon?

Oh, right.

Our cars, led by the one with the minister moved slowly through the Arlington Road, past the white markers of our service men and women. Green, quiet, the tourists mobbed up on the hill path to the Kennedy graves, quiet and peace beyond, a few people laying flowers at graves. I wondered why the crowds didn't honor the unfamous soldiers. When I returned, and I intended to each year, I would visit some of their graves.

The columbarium is a field of stately marble walls, each with resting places for urns. Beyond these walls, surrounding a courtyard and fountain, was an area for the funeral services. A soldier directed us to where to park.

We walked up to the canopied area, and I felt conscious of my mother's presence.

Was she really here?

I had expected a cold service, given how many funerals are held at Arlington, but that was not the case. The priest, that sweet man, spoke about Dad's service in the South Pacific. The military guard stood at attention.

Well, they didn't know my Dad. They didn't talk about the years of his being a loving father and husband and a diligent and responsible worker even if his job was thankless – well, no, it wasn't – he had the respect of everyone who knew him. The Arlington priest did his best, but his contact had been Helen, and she was ignorant of all my father had been.

Prayers.

The three soldiers took the flag and folded it with strict precision, impressive to watch. One took the folded flag and knelt before Helen, who with impassive face, held out her hands to receive it.

One thing I could not do was speak. I had no words, only a flood of happy memories trying to muscle in and had no place.

Dad had found his escape. That was the one thing that made me happy.

We moved to the wall where Mom's remains lay. The door was already open, and without asking, I reached up and touched my mother's urn. My cousin Alice, Aunt Mary's daughter, brought roses, and she slipped two in.

The priest spoke the funeral prayers. A soldier placed the urn in the opening, next to Mom's. I wondered what that was like, dealing with death all the time both at Arlington and in the service. And yet, looking out at the expanse of the grounds and the white tombstones as far as you could see, it didn't feel like death. It felt like life, like a profound generosity of sacrifice, of fighting for our country, which could have – if

I'd felt political – depressed me, but it didn't. I felt love all around – the love of country, of families coming to visit love, and I didn't feel alone – for a moment. It helped. This was not death here. It was vibrant life.

Shocking me out of my calm – shattering gunfire. The gun salute. I couldn't talk. I couldn't even feel.

Helen and her family left without saying goodbye, but the priest who had accompanied them, returned with the shells from the gun salute and went over to Laurie.

"Mrs. Shannon wanted you to have this," he said.

I wanted the flag. I amused myself by plotting Helen's murder as I stole the flag back.

The priest said, gently, "Let us say the Lord's Prayer."

Thy will be done like hell. I stared up into that perfect sky with hardly any clouds and asked why my father, a faithful and good man all his life, had had to suffer, and why didn't some angel or Son of God or someone knock me down with a bolt of lightning to make me realize he'd been suffering?

Then the thought came, ever so gently into my heart, that Dad knew I'd forgiven him, loved him, believed him, that all that love had been hiding underneath the surface all the time, and it was what – human pride, stubbornness, what – that had kept us from coming together again – somehow Dad had come home, that is, as much as he could have.

If only we'd had more time.

We would meet again. We would have to. We had so much to say to each other.

"Please feel free to say what is in your heart," said the chaplain.

I wanted to say something – so much in my chest – love, anger, bitterness, disbelief.

Alice read a poem she'd written. Dad had been her godfather. It was sweet, and she read with a broken voice.

All I could muster was a whisper, "I love you, Dad. I'll miss you forever."

The chaplain blessed us and said, "Please stay as long as you like. A guard will wait until you leave to take care of things."

Aunt Mary and Uncle Donald sat on the bench. The rest of us tried to find words. We did. Gentle ones.

We walked slowly toward the parking lot and to our cars. We drove back to the Comfort Inn. We ordered pizza. We huddled in one of the rooms. We tried to talk it out. I felt sad that we could not bring up happy memories, and there were many. Aunt Mary went on and on about how could he have married that bitch.

"Well, he's free now," said Uncle Don.

"He could have come to Sarasota," said Aunt Mary.

He wouldn't have gone anywhere. Too proud. Too ashamed of the awful mistake he had made. In death, he found relief and forgiveness. I hoped finally that he and Peggy were together again. Did I believe that? I had to. It was the only way I could live with his death. I had to believe in resurrection.

I dropped to my knees on the Comfort Inn's carpet. Forgive me. Oh, forgive me.

CHAPTER 37

I returned to the penance of the GOEs. I spent hours studying that autumn. I had meetings with Rick. But our conversations were about him. I tried talking about my father, but Rick listened in silence and then spoke about beginning a new life at his age, about interim priesthood, about new possibilities for Saint Philip's. I let him talk. On and on.

What was he saying?

He'd had a long conversation with Portland's bishop about his options.

He would be an interim pastor at one of the city's churches.

He would rent an office, and that would be the address he would give to Saint Philip's.

Finally, after two meetings all about him, I said, "When are you telling the Vestry?"

He just laughed. "Not for a few weeks. It needs to be the right time. I've hired a deacon to come in and let some friends – other priests know, so they'll be ready to supply. The Vestry will have time to select an interim priest and begin the process to find the right rector." He patted my hand. I drew back. "These are fruitful days for all of us. You of course are welcome to visit us. In fact, Meg will invite you to our first Thanksgiving, and of course, you'll be at our wedding. And, once the diocese approves you for the process, I'll recommend you for the process there."

Oregon? Was he crazy? I loved New York.

I should have betrayed them. I should have gone to the wardens or another priest or even damn Bishop Heine for help. But Heine had been so often represented as the enemy that I couldn't even get past just a wandering thought about doing that.

I would be a loyal friend.

I politely declined Meg's invitation to their Thanksgiving. I ordered in a turkey dinner from the local diner and watched *The Best Years of Our Lives*. It had been my parents' favorite movie. I sobbed through it.

Then I got mad.

I took a train back to DC and the Metro to Arlington. I found Mom and Dad's resting place. I sat on a bench with paper and pen. I wrote to my father. I wrote my gratitude for his taking care of all of us, for his joy and humor, for his love of my mother, and how he had cared for her and how she had died in his arms. Then I wrote how he had to escape, and he took the first escape route. But he was sorry. He had told me that he hated her and that he wanted to get away from her. That she was paranoid and cruel and had no sense of humor – a real sin in my father's book. I folded the paper, and I taped it with a short stemmed yellow rose to the plaque with my parents' name. It wouldn't last there. The sign said that anything left would be picked up by the staff. But I had said my say. I kissed my fingers and touched my parents' names. I promised to come by every year.

And I took the train back to New York.

A week later, I got a card with a New York return address that did not disguise the sender. I opened it and it said, "You say you are Christian. You are not."

I knew the handwriting. Did I hurt her? Yes. Hurt her for the rest of her life. She had tortured him enough just by being herself. Was I sorry that I'd done that to her at Arlington? No. I had struck a blow for my father. And I'll bet she worried that I would strike again.

Let's leave it at that.

CHAPTER 38

I spent Christmas at Dirk's. I felt out of place, like a stranger. The kids were small and thank God they took up time and had us laughing. Plus setting tables, cleaning up after one of Dirk's elaborate meals, and yeah, going over and over what had happened with Dad. When I told Dirk and his wife what I'd done at Arlington, they laughed their heads off. I'd hurt someone on purpose. And I didn't give a damn.

Back in New York, I started selecting the books I could take with me to General Seminary, where I'd reserved a room for the GOEs. Peter sold me his computer – little more than a word processor, which was all I needed. I also rented a small printer from the seminary.

Rick finally met with the Vestry and gave his resignation.

Tom was baffled. "Portland!"

He turned to me.

"And then you'll be going to Portland, right? When you get ordained?"

"Will I?"

"You'd rather be going than Rick now."

Did I know what he was saying?

God, I'm stupid.

"He didn't give much notice." I tried to give Tom a nudge after the meeting.

"He hates Heine, he's at the end of his career, and here's a Bishop who respects him. But it leaves us in a bind for sure. The search process is hell. Who will want us? Our finances aren't wonderful, and our building is old and in trouble."

Rick was leaving January 6, the feast of the Epiphany and last day of the GOEs.

For a couple of days, I delivered reference books I knew I'd need to my room at General. Then, on the first day of the test, I walked to my "office," with my laptop, put down my coffee, and went to get the first part of the exam.

Back in my room, I opened the manila envelope and pulled out the sheet.

"Set 1. Open Book"
"You are the new rector of a parish with about two hundred members. The previous rector had a long tenure, during which his liturgical preferences had become well-established. You would like to make some changes, especially as to the participation of lay persons in liturgical roles."

It was as if they'd designed the question for me.
By eleven, I was done.
I went to get a sandwich at Frank's.
He recognized me right away.
"You are taking the big test?"
"So far, so good."
He bagged my turkey sandwich and water.
"You will do well. All my seminarians do well."
Like a blessing!
More victims came in with complaints and hopes, and I gave Frank a wave and left to eat in my room. At ten minutes to one, I went to get the next question, also open book, and focusing on ethics and moral theology.

"Individuals and interest groups in the Church have been calling on dioceses to speak out and provide prophetic witness on a range of contemporary issues. Write an essay in which you define the task of the Church as it faces contemporary moral issues."

I picked racism – the resentment of people who "got something for nothing." This was tougher to outline as I could go back to Reconstruction. Instead, I focused on the Biblical commands of God to the Israelites and of Jesus to his followers. I also had to address the limits and problems inherent in speaking in a pluralistic society to the issue I picked. I perused my books, picked a few passages to reflect, writings of black theologians. James Cone. Mercy Amlie Oduyoye, Audre Lorde…

I invented a congregation much like Saint Philip's – mostly white, some having other than European backgrounds, with consistently white and male leadership, and in its early history, its members had owned slaves.

I wrote and wrote and typed and proofed and handed in.

The first day was done.

I felt exhilarated. This was fun.

The next day's question took all day.

It was on Scripture, Church History, and Contemporary Society. And it was a doozy.

"You are the Rector of a middle-sized parish in a diocese that has experienced much conflict during the last fifteen years. Issues confronting the whole Episcopal Church have sharply divided your diocese and its parishes. There has been considerable conflict over such matters as: the ordination of women, changing attitudes toward human sexuality, divestiture of diocesan and parish assets in South Africa, programs for the poor and homeless, and so on.

"Your bishop has asked you to design a presentation on 'Conflict in the Church' for the next clergy conference. You decide that a kind of case study approach will facilitate discussion and foster applicable learnings for the clergy. Write an essay that includes the substance of your presentation for that conference."

First, I was to focus on a conflict from Scripture and a conflict in church history. And then,

"Choose a contemporary conflict in the Church and indicate how you would advise your diocesan family to approach it."

Sure.

The examiners must be looking for help for themselves.

I picked the dissension in the Corinthian church and the abolitionist controversies in the nineteenth century. I spent an hour reviewing my books, grateful I'd brought a good supply. I outlined. I wrote.

Part Two was to deal with a contemporary conflict. Picking women's ordination was too easy. I started writing about a priest who fell in love with his associate, but I realized I was too sympathetic, so I dumped that paper and instead focused on the need for inclusive language despite a congregation's resistance.

It took all day.

I felt brain dead when I'd finished. I barely slept.

Then came the next day's question.

"One of your parishioners, who is suffering from cancer, had been participating in faith healing services and for a time had seemed to improve. Now she has learned that the disease has spread, and she faces increasing pain and death. She says to you, 'I guess I just didn't have enough faith or the right attitudes. Otherwise, I would have licked this disease.'

"How would you respond to this woman?"

I thought about that, thought about my mother.

God is getting me through this.

When I went to lunch, feeling sober, it was snowing heavily. Several inches had already piled up as I was working.

Frank said, "I was waiting for all of you. I will probably close up in an hour."

"Thank you, Frank," I said. "Get home safely."

The wind picked up, the snow still fell, and I wrote. I breezed through the short answers and smiled through the coffee hour questions, trying hard not to write, "No one asks questions like this at coffee hour."

And then I was done.

CHAPTER 39

I crossed Ninth Avenue, pushing through the wind, and decided to take a rest break at the rectory. I had keys, but I rang the bell just in case someone was in the office. Rick wouldn't be there – he'd left that morning before the storm was bad, and at the worst, he'd be stranded at the airport. I didn't care.

Guess again. Rick opened the door.

"You're still here?"

He had papers in his hands and didn't seem to recognize me.

"Everything's canceled. I'm doing the financial report."

Shouldn't he have already done that?

He didn't ask about the GOEs. He went back into the office. I went down the hall to find a mini-Vestry meeting about finding priests until we hired an interim.

I made coffee and sat down with Tom, Chris, and Donald, who congratulated me on finishing the GOEs and being able to speak in coherent sentences. I didn't speak much, but I listened. There wasn't much left to do. As we prepared to go out into the still raging storm, I muttered, "Shouldn't he have finished that report? He's still doing it?"

"Yeah," said Tom, matter of factly. "He left it for us. I told him he had to do it, thanks to the storm. He's just not here anymore."

I realized I hadn't said goodbye to him.

I walked east, into the whiteness, a blank slate, I thought.

I watched *Star Trek*. It was "The Corbomite Maneuver," the one where the attacking ship's captain looked like a monster but was really a tiny boy. I wondered if *Star Trek* was trying to tell me something.

The weather cleared, I heard the sound of snowplows in the land,

and Rick flew out at nine in the morning, so Tom informed me in a morning phone call.

"He left a mess. I'm in the downstairs office. Chris is snowed in. You're closest. Can I ask you to come in to help?"

"My office is closed. I'll get breakfast and be there in an hour."

"You're a goddess. Rick left a bunch of papers in the upstairs bathroom."

The bathroom?

"I won't ask."

I braved the high drifts on the curbs, courtesy of the snowplows, and leaped across mounds of dirty snow on the crosswalks. It took half an hour to get to the rectory, but I liked the walk. It was challenging, and the city was silent save for the sound of shovels and, in the distance, snowplows. It felt magical.

I found Chris in the office.

"We haven't gotten a priest yet for tomorrow, so I'm calling around. Rick barely made any calls. He just stopped. Don't you go to Portland now."

"I don't drive. I need the subway."

I headed upstairs.

"Leave the underwear!" Chris yelled. "Just attack the pile."

Underwear?

The upstairs office had been stripped of everything – book, pictures, desk – even the couch was gone. But the chair where Rick had sat remained.

God, the place felt empty.

In the bathroom, I found eight pairs of Rick's underwear hanging by the toilet. He'd forgotten to pack his underwear? He'd been here an extra day.

A tall pile of papers sat on an empty bookshelf, over a foot high, some papers this way, some that. I took the papers into the office, sat at the desk, and started sorting.

Several were financial reports.

Some were letters.

Some were memos Rick typed to himself.

A thick notebook, half opened, stuck out. I pulled it out. Handwriting. A diary?

"… Meg yelling at me for way I dressed the chalice."

What?

I flipped to the notebook's cover and saw the name, "Dean Meadows" and "Spiritual Journal" written on the front cover. Good God. He'd probably talked its contents over with Rick and here it had not been returned, left for anyone to find.

I shut the book, pushed it aside.

I had no idea how to deal with it. I figured he'd just have to believe that no one other than Rick read it. And, as tempted as I was to read the rest of that passage, I resisted.

I kept sorting.

I had to laugh at Rick's two sentence memos on whole sheets. Why not simply make a list? Well, to each his…

Then I found it.

"Lily confronted me today and asked if I was having a relationship with Meg. Must discuss with Meg." I looked at the date.

Lily had been fired a few days later.

Oh, Christ.

A few pages down, I found another memo.

"Recommend firing Lily. Make clear: No recommendation if she breaks silence. Trouble if she breaks silence after she is hired somewhere else. Will contact Bishop Spong in Trenton."

Damn.

I couldn't fathom this. Rick had fired her for – not for being disorganized – had he started that rumor?

He was good at starting rumors. Hey, I was gay.

And Lily had cooperated.

We walk in silence like the night.

Lily had kept her silence and gotten another job.

And been humiliated in front of the whole parish. A part of me admired her. For if she'd spoken, the parish would have descended into factions. And she'd gotten a job away from here.

"Will recommend her in any other diocese."

Silence, silence.

And that fight on Easter Saturday. This had been the real cause, that Lily had found out and could have destroyed Rick and Meg – and at least Rick's collar.

Nothing more important but Meg and Rick.

Shouldn't I be sympathetic? Two people in love?

And why had I stayed silent?

Because I didn't want to destroy the safe haven I'd found and needed. Because I'd wanted yes, to be ordained, but more, I'd wanted to be loved, with my parents gone. Needing to be loved had been my big weakness, like my father's, and I had let it win over me. I should have gone to someone I could trust to say, what should I do. Who would that have been? Not Hiney of course. I had let Rick and Meg make the rules because I'd needed to trust them. Like a little kid needing approval.

I had responsibility for this, too.

That desire had distorted many things. The business of this parish. Lily.

A truth I did not want to see and should have.

What had been wrong? Two people in love?

But they'd had to be secretive. They could have, and actually did, threaten the balance of the parish, its spiritual health. They could have said something. We would have taken it in stride. We were grownups. Now, once they found out, they'd feel betrayed.

Rick had helped Meg get the cathedral job. I was sure of that.

Lily had kept her silence and gotten a good job in New Jersey.

I sorted the papers. I put them in folders. I tossed the memos except the few that would remind me. If anyone wanted to look through that folder.

Had Meg gone along with it all?

Must discuss with Meg.

Rick had power. He was a strong figure in the liberal wing of the diocesan priests at least against the conservative Heine.

He was a nice person, an extraordinary priest, a powerful preacher, and he'd created a lively intelligent parish.

And he'd fallen in love.

But why hadn't they shared their news with the church? Or at least Tom and Chris, the wardens?

Because they had broken the sexual harassment guidelines.

Because they didn't trust letting go of their secret.

Because they were hiding out from Heine.

They'd spread the rumor that Meg and I were a couple. Which had inadvertently hurt Paula.

Rick, how silly. Leaving these things around.

He was safe in another diocese.

I put all the papers back, straightened them, put the folders in appropriate folders in the file drawers.

I went downstairs.

Chris was just off the phone.

"Okay, we have priests for six weeks."

"Good job. I straightened out the folder mess."

Another folder, with Dean's journal, I put in his mailbox protected by a manila envelope. He could assume that Rick had left it there.

I went home, mentally done in. I needed to talk to someone. Who?

CHAPTER 40

I kept busy. Preparing the altar. Keeping up the rota now that Lily was gone. I had tried to get up a party for her, but even Paula said, "She let us down."

I assigned myself to a sermon when the priest imminently scheduled said he had no time to prepare one.

Going through the mail, I found the weekly mailing to priests with sermon hints, and I scrabbled something together and then discarded it for something about Judith.

Meg called, filled with happiness about her job.

"The BACOM," I said.

"I forgot. When is it?"

"Three weeks from now."

"Hold your position."

Whatever that meant.

Church attendance went way down after Rick left, and we had a flock of unfamiliar priests coming through. Also a few people moved out of the city. Now the pews were barely half filled. Our brunches went down to four people, Peter, Robert, Paula, and me. They just weren't as scintillating. The brunches faded away.

Paula kept at my side. After one service, she waited for me and walked east with me on 20th Street. I never knew what to say to her.

"I know you're sad about Meg."

"Happy for her, too," I said.

Right.

"Of course. Still, I'm surprised you didn't go with her."

Oh, boy.

"So, did you two decide to break up?"

"Break up?"

"Oh, you know. We all knew."

"Knew what?"

"Janene, it's me."

Now she was looking straight at me. "I won't mince words."

God, please do.

"What are you asking me?"

"You know. I love you. You're strong, and you're going to make one hell of a priest."

"I love you too, but…"

"You've always hinted at it. I know you're upset about Meg. I know that Rick went after her. I think it was a power grab, and he wanted to get away from Betty. I guess their marriage was over."

"Paula…"

"I want to tell you that I promise I'll support you. I definitely support your ministry, and I believe in you."

She touched my hand.

"Paula, I'm sorry. I don't know what gave you this idea."

"You and Meg were lovers."

Thank you, Rick.

"And someone asked during some meeting of the grounds group. And he said yes then, too. We all know. You two were always together."

I decided to be direct. "How better to avoid any suspicion about your own love affair? Do you understand? Meg and I were never lovers."

She stared at me.

"You're calling Rick a liar?"

"Paula, I'm straight. Rick was wrong."

"Was he?" She pulled away when I touched her. "Don't upset my intelligence. It's because I'm black, isn't it?"

"That has nothing to do with it."

"Yes, it does. I know you're broken up about Meg and Rick, I mean of all things, but at least consider this, could you? You know how much I love you?"

"You're a friend."

"You are impossible. You don't know one thing about yourself. And you're lying to me and to you. When you can be honest with yourself, give me a call."

She walked away.

Nice going. Another parishioner lost.

Could I blame her? At Saint Philip's, I'd never said anything about my love affairs or that I'd had any.

They felt like a long time ago.

Scott in college, the science nerd, a bit cuckoo but polite, well mannered, who brought his ukulele to parties, and we sang Broadway show tunes. But he wanted to stay in Chicago, and I didn't.

There'd been David in high school. Renaissance guy. Brilliant. Came to sit on my porch on many a night. My prom date.

And Jimmy in New York who invited me to the ballet and the opera. I forget what we fought about.

And oh, yes, Parker from that office job on Lexington Avenue. We'd shared an office, and after the Christmas party, he'd invited me to his apartment, and we'd gone to bed.

They were all smart, sensitive, fun, and affectionate.

How had I ended up alone?

I didn't know what to do about Paula, my resentment of Rick whom I'd admired or of Meg, or of damn church. The best thing to do was to leave, but I couldn't leave Saint Philip's now when they were so weak and when my future was tied to it.

Then I remembered. Tomorrow I'd get my GOE scores.

If I'd flunked, that would be that, and I could walk out of church and become a star on Broadway.

I suspected that was easier.

CHAPTER 41

Of course, there was a long line outside the office at General. Seminarians came out, ripped open their envelopes, and pretty much stared in horror. Several yelled, "Shit!" Latin for "I screwed up bigtime."

Finally, it was my turn.

The dean's secretary looked at my number, checked a list, and gave me a smile. She went through a box of envelopes and handed me one.

"Congratulations. You have the top score in the entire city."

I hurried into the courtyard, sat on a bench, and opened the envelope.

Several pages were stapled together. On top lay the results.

I had passed everything.

I had four outstanding marks: in Holy Scripture, Church History, Contemporary Society, and Theory and Practice of Ministry. Theology, Ethics, and Liturgics and Church Music were marked "adequate."

Best score of those taking the test here?

Well.

The "adequate" for liturgics rankled, even if getting that score amounted to having solid knowledge and being able to use it.

I skipped to the overall evaluation and read "outstanding integration of the canonical process," "breadth and depth," "considerable power in exegesis and hermeneutics," "graceful treatment of liturgical theology and practice," "clear sense of the ordering of ministry."

Seminarians passing by and a few teachers gave me sympathetic looks, probably thinking that my tears meant I had done poorly.

Nope. I was the top scoring seminarian in New York City.

Now all I had to do was get my divinity degree and pass the damn BACOM.

Then I'd be at Step One.

There were very few people I could share my scores with. I called Rick. Although Rick had left a separate address and number, he was living with Meg. I was one of The Few Who Knew.

Rick answered. Meg was at work.

I gave him my news.

There was silence.

"Janene, I'm deeply moved."

"Or surprised?"

"No, no. I'm proud. Meg will be thrilled."

She was. She laughed. "I failed Ethics. They let me in anyway. They don't bother much with the scores obviously."

Thanks. She'd had Rick's pals on the Commission.

"Hurry up, get ordained, and move here."

Who was she kidding? I had been a pawn.

I should have – should have – gone straight to the wardens and told them all. Why didn't I? Part of me clung to the idea that I was loyal to Meg and Rick because they loved me.

I had already met with Alice Edwards, a blonde, slim woman who wore correct suits and had a soft voice. She was the guidance counselor of all of us wannabes and had given me several forms.

At my next meeting with her, she asked, "How did the GOEs go? I know they were tough this year. The National Convention insisted on more complex tests, not the short answers and multiple-choice questions with a few short essays. They wanted almost exclusively essays that covered all the canonical areas. You should know that scores dropped. No one knows how to prepare for something like that. General Seminary's scores were embarrassing, but all this will be balanced out by other factors."

I handed her a copy of my scores.

She stared at it with her big blue eyes.

"But...but...really?"

"I enjoyed the test." I said that clearly. She seemed confused as she stood up to file the paper.

"Those are wonderful scores. You're at the top if not the top." She smiled even as she appeared nervous. "So, good for you. As for your pre-interviews..." She scanned a sheet. "You had two yesses...no, three. Good!"

The door opened, and a plump little man walked in.

"Are you ready? I made a reservation at the Boathouse."

It took me a second to recognize Bishop Heine – without his miter, staff, and that pointed hat, and in color in contrast to the newspaper, he looked like someone's clumsy father who didn't know how to meet his daughter's girlfriends.

"Excuse me," he said, offering his hand. So, I had to kiss his ring.

"This is Janene Shannon from Saint Philip's. She's the top scorer from General's GOE takers."

His eyes narrowed, but he smiled. "You lost a rector."

"Yes." What else could I say?

"Scores aren't everything," he said, almost under his breath. Then he said, "Awful thing, abandoning you on short notice. Tough parish. All those Catholic gay men. You should do field service somewhere else."

"I've done my field service." I would have to ignore his "all those Catholic gay men" reference.

"Really? And what would that have been?" He laughed, a short but threatening laugh. "No, you should go somewhere else. Or – I'll be sending someone good over, and you can do service at Saint Philip's and learn from him."

"She has nearly a 4.0 cum at New York Theological Seminary, Your Grace."

Why did he look annoyed?

"All the more reason for you to be trained right."

Alice Edwards quickly said, "I'll be ready in ten minutes. We're finishing up."

Heine turned toward the door. "I've recommended an interim for Saint Philip's. Reverend Kennedy. A good, solid man. He should be helpful to you."

I'd thought the Vestry picked the interim pastor, but I said, "I'll enjoy helping him."

"He'll get the parish where it needs to be."

What could that mean.

"I'd better go," I said to the Reverend Edwards. "Have a nice dinner."

"Good luck," she said, her tone curt. "Congratulations on your test. Good work. Are you finished?"

"Graduating in May. Master of Divinity."

"I'll see you at the next BACOM. You'll get an invitation."

CHAPTER 42

K ennedy looked like a ferret. At our next Vestry meeting, he
listened to the reports, sitting up straight, and didn't say much
until the end.

"I see you have a lot of cleanup to do." He smiled right at me. "All
you need is structure."

Tom and Chris wanted structure and looked happy.

I called Meg and Rick, but they were more thrilled that the divorce
was going to be smooth sailing and rapid, and they were planning a
spring wedding.

"You'll come and stand up for me?"

She was surprised when I said, "Let me think about it."

I graduated. No one came. Possibly because I hadn't told anyone.
After all my work, I wasn't sure it meant anything.

When I told Tom about the BACOM, he said, "You'll wow them."

"Not necessarily."

"But you aced all the tests."

"This is different."

Meg had had rehearsals – people praying for her!

Well, I hadn't had any problem with my interviews. Maybe things
would be all right.

On Monday, Kennedy called me up at work. "Tom mentioned you're
in seminary. I spoke with Alice at the cathedral, and she told me about
you. Good for you. I should have noticed – your questions and remarks
are typical." He laughed. I had no idea what he meant. "You stand up for
your rector, which of course you should do, but there are certain questions
I have, and I'd like to hear about the parish from you. Why don't we meet
at the pastry shop across from the seminary? Saturday? Ten o'clock?"

So much for sleeping in.

And there he was, complete with collar, sitting in the corner. He waved. Slight of build, graying hair, big smile. He stood up as I came over and sat across from him.

"How long have you been with Saint Philip's?"

I explained about my membership at Community Church and my field service at Saint Philip's.

"Tough church."

"We've had a lively parish."

"It seems so."

I took his meanings.

"How do you feel about Father Rick?"

I felt betrayed and angry. Was I going to tell this guy that? No. I hardly knew him. My time at Saint Philip's had been good. I could not forget that. I was grieving so many things, and one more thing I grieved was that the good times were definitely over in the parish. Mental note: When a rector leaves a parish, everyone else goes, too.

"Father Rick believed in process," I said. "He believed that liturgy is the work of the people. I learned a lot here."

"Come on, "said Kennedy.

"Sorry?"

"You know what happened."

I bit into a delightful croissant.

"You wanted to know about Saint Philip's. It's a lively community."

"That's what I hear. Come on, Janice."

"Janene."

"I've heard a lot. Gay marriages where one person agrees to torture the other? A priest who jewels up his body and has obscene tattoos?"

I shrugged. "I came in after Father Tom was gone. As for that wedding, I wasn't here then, and I've heard a lot of different things. They weren't parishioners. They'd rented the church. If the diocese were more helpful, maybe they wouldn't have had to raise the money that way."

He didn't like that. I could tell because he grinned.

"What do you specifically do for the church?"

"I'm on the Vestry. I'm in the choir. I started a recording project in the church to raise money, and it's a success – the other restoration projects haven't been going as well."

"Good for you. What sort of recordings?"

"Mostly classical music, pianists, small orchestras. And just recently an opera by Amy Beach. It was too much after a while, so I handed the project over to a musician who used to be in the parish. And I serve at the altar, manage the rota, and chair the liturgy committee, though I'd like to give that up."

He smiled. "Yes, that's too much with school and final exams. I'll take liturgy. You're not gay, are you? I don't get that vibe."

I must have looked startled.

"He laughed. "We're aware that Saint Philip's is out there. People who left and went to Holy Apostles told some wild stories. Saint Philip's needs to include more than just gays and women."

We were "out there?"

"Father, if by out there, you mean that we take our liturgy seriously with a light touch, that we believe that we receive the body and blood of Jesus, that we love a good sermon, and that we love our community, then yes, we take it seriously. Oh, not that it matters, but I am not gay." One thing I noticed was that he didn't mention that we had very few Black people.

"Married?"

"No." I hesitated. "My boyfriend died."

He patted my hand. I could tell he considered me a naïve ally.

"It's the same with all seminarians. They have school, process, church work, most have jobs – it's a lot – and they miss what's going on."

That was true enough!

"Rick was involved with other women going way back. If you ever read his thesis – it's hot stuff – erotic in every line. Any determined woman could have landed him."

"Really?"

"There's a man whose only thought was sex. You knew his wife. That was not her only thought. That priest he pushed through – that offended Heine the most. He pushed her through for his own lustful feelings. She must have been a looker. Plus, she must have given you the wrong impression."

I was tempted to please Kennedy because I was mad at Rick. But that didn't take away Rick's good points – his love for liturgy and justice. I couldn't forget that, no matter what.

"Betty was the girl no one asked to the dance. Still others say that Betty and Bishop Bulla were more than just friends in the fifties and that she was in love with Mrs. Bulla. Yes, really." He smiled at my startled face. "You'll get used to stories like this."

"They spread a rumor that I was gay." Why had I said that?

He looked disgusted. "That's exactly what he would do. He's more comfortable with gay people for the obvious reasons. Or maybe he wanted you to start believing you were one of them. All that's over now. I'll be at church on Sunday, in the pews, and I'll get a sense of what's going on. Don't point me out. Who's your celebrant?"

"Father Harrison."

"Good guy. Well, lots of work to do, right? I have to get back to Saint John's. I'm paying, so put down your purse. You are off to where?"

"Library. One more research paper."

"Good for you. I've heard about your superlative record. Don't worry. We'll fix Saint Philip's. You'll feel more comfortable."

And the bishop had picked him specially for us. Play along with him, Shannon, and you're in.

I looked up Rick's thesis at the library.

They had it.

Seeing your lover the way God sees you. Christ in us, we in Christ. The poetry was breathtaking. I'd of course read Tolkien and heard of Charles Williams, but they were several mental bookshelves away. Rick wrote about them with intensity and breathtaking immediacy.

I wish I'd read this before he'd left. I felt as if I hadn't tapped his rich thoughts, oh, yes, I had, but I would have loved to have talked to him about this.

The BACOM loomed. I went over the responses with myself. No prayer group. I didn't tell Paula; she might have started one. Actually, I hadn't talked to Paula about anything. We'd only given each other polite greetings at coffee hour.

I picked out my suit and checked it for last minute problems – all set. A few pairs of pantyhose, one for my purse in case I snagged a run. One more day.

Peter called.

"You know I'd love to be in any parish where you were a priest. Your respect for people, for the Eucharist, for your sermons and work. But it's not going to happen. You won't get through."

What? Before I opened my mouth?

"The BACOM's tomorrow," I reminded him. "How do you know I won't get through and you're just telling me this now?"

"Because I work in New York Episcopal Ground Zero. Two of the members came by and chatted not a few feet away and said that Heine will have a fit if Rick's candidate goes through. He won't approve whoever it is. You could be the Virgin Mary, and he wouldn't let you in. Most of Bulla's people are gone now, and the Commission is made up mostly of his people. You'd have to do it again after working with his hand-picked interim."

"Why does he think that way?"

"Because Rick ran off with that bimbo."

"Bimbo? Meg is forty."

"Saint Philip's is closed in his mind. I suggest working with Kennedy."

Damn, no. "I want to get it over with. I have a good record. I should stand on that. And I don't like Kennedy."

"No one does. Heine didn't even bother looking at the recommendation letter Rick wrote."

And so, no prayer meeting, no good luck from a rapidly diminishing congregation – I took the number one subway line up to the cathedral and signed in for the BACOM.

How could I convince the Commission on Ministry, now without any friends of Rick, that I was called to be a priest? Would I have to say what they wanted to hear? Or should I be myself?

I had to go with the person who felt called.

CHAPTER 43

How it worked: You met four or five members in each room. I was polite and firm. I answered questions. One question was an exact question from the GOEs - about how I would conduct a funeral of an unwed mother.

Somehow that wandered into homosexuality.

"You do not believe homosexuality is a sin?"

"I'll leave it up to God."

"You are a priest for this question. You need to decide."

"Then I'll follow Jesus even if it goes against church policy."

Well, that was dumb.

What would I do if this or that. I tried to keep my wits. They wanted to nail me, but I kept going back to Jesus, and in some cases Paul, to hold up my case. When it came to the Old Testament, I relied on my knowledge of hermeneutics, which it would seem was stronger than some of the priests who were questioning me as I named several passages that had them rifling through their Bibles.

The next group had me describe Saint Philip's, and after I did, one person asked, incredulously, "You all hug each other at the peace?"

"Yes."

This seemed unbelievable to them.

"We fill the aisles and greet each other. We hug or we shake hands and ask if everything's okay and we wish them the peace of God. The Eucharist is a party, it's a celebration of God."

"It commemorates the death of Jesus."

"I would say it commemorates the life of Jesus and his friendship."

These "commissioners" had been saying, over and over, "Not every parish is like Saint Philip's." Apparently, it wasn't praise.

I shot back. "What do you think Saint Philip's is like? Did you ever visit?"

"You do your own thing over there."

"We do the Eucharist. It's a high service. We follow Rite 2 of the Prayer Book. We use the hymnal. I don't know what you mean by our own thing."

"We know," said the man in the corner. "That's all. We're done."

I sat and watched them file out of the room. When they had gone, I followed them, and I know I saw a few fist bumps exchanged.

I grabbed lunch from a deli and sat on a bench, trying to enjoy the spring day and the peacocks strutting about as if they knew something I didn't. Which certainly could be true.

Other aspirants sat together. I felt alone. I felt angry at Rick and Meg who had put me here.

Why did I defend their church?

Because I had loved it, and once, them.

I went home, furious the Commission was attacking Saint Philip's. This once happy, lively place, filled with enthusiasm – and now shattered and fleeing. I would defend it. I would.

The first group the next day seemed bored with me.

"What's your favorite psalm?"

I thought, oh, let's give them something where God is pissed off. Instead, I chickened out and said, "Psalm 23. It was my mother's favorite when she was dying." Then I recited it, slowly, taking up some time.

Then came the fun room. It was tiny. I sat against the wall across from the door. The small room held twenty people. I counted. They sat two rows deep, even across the door. I checked. They didn't have stones.

Five people in that crush did most of the talking. They attacked Saint Philip's as a parish that needed salvation. They asked why I didn't go to Saint Peter's, a "real church" that served the same neighborhood.

A big man in a corner yelled, "Repent! Repent!" at me. Repent of what? I asked him and he waved his hands with disgust.

I couldn't walk out. I should have. I barely had a chance to speak and yet, if you asked me what they'd wanted of me, other than to abuse me, I would not be able to answer.

"We know all about Saint Philip's," said the man, whom I later found out was awarded a "peacemaker" award in the diocese.

Their outrage, probably fanned by "Hiney," was all directed at me, and I hadn't the faintest idea how to handle it. I thought of saying, would you all like to step outside, and I so wish I had.

I couldn't flee without running over a few priests blocking the door, which I should have. But I saw it to the bitter end and, knowing it was all for naught, I nevertheless went into my next room, which was bathed in warm sunlight from the windows. The leader, a young priest with dark hair, welcomed me with a smile.

"What do you like best about the Eucharist?"

I talked of re-creation, of symbols that led to God, of imagination and the Holy Spirit. I described friends embracing, men who'd been kicked out of a church because of whom they loved, joining in planning Sunday Eucharists and loving the Book of Common Prayer – with some revisions. I spoke of the acoustics, connecting the building with a space that resonated and that "This is my body" took in the joy, the pain, the despair, the transformation, all of it.

They let me talk. The woman, Mother Jenny, thanked me and wished me luck.

I almost said, "I see you didn't get the memo."

I got a hamburger to take home.

The call came at eight o'clock. I knew, from Meg's account, that they were all there at some table and that they were all listening to the call and to me.

Mother Jenny said, "Janene, I am sorry, but the opinion is the Commission will not recommend you to postulancy at this time."

I said, and boy, what a wimp, "Thank you for considering me."

A pause. Another voice.

"The vote was nine to one. I voted for you. I don't understand why you didn't get more support. You are wonderfully qualified."

I was a sacrificial lamb.

"Frankly," she said, "I'm stunned."

That was one of us.

I said, "They know why they voted against me."

Someone said, "We don't think your parish trained you adequately."

"Saint Philip's is unique."

"Perhaps you could tone down your mode of expression when working with another parish," said someone. "You just need some better guidance."

"I don't want to be anyone but myself."

I heard Alice say, "Good for you." Then she addressed the others. "The interim rector there will be Father Kennedy, and he's already met with Janene, and he said it was a fruitful meeting. This may simply be a matter of proper supervision and guidance."

"Her academic record is excellent," said someone else. "And I see she raised a lot of money by coming up with an idea and executing it. That's not something we can dismiss."

"Let's see how it goes with Father Kennedy," said Alice.

I said, "Thank you all."

They'd rejected Rick. Not me. I just ended up in the crossfire.

I hung up without them ending the call.

I cried.

Who wanted to cast a lot with those sinners?

I also got that if I went along with Kennedy or even if I switched to an "acceptable" church, I might have a chance. But did I want their approval?

That, alas, was the answer. No.

CHAPTER 44

Meg called. She sounded excited. "Tell! Tell!"
"The vote was nine to one, Meg."
"Who was the fool?"
"Me."

Nothing. She said nothing. For like a minute.

"It's no," I said.

"How could they not…?"

"Just give it a little thought, Meg."

"Let me get Rick."

Rick – I heard him say – "Oh, my God."

"Pick up the other phone."

He came on an extension. "I don't believe this. You are such a strong candidate."

My fury broke. Finally.

"You? You don't believe it? What were you ever thinking of? Not anyone. Not me. Not your wife or your children. Just of you. Of your precious little time left on earth. How you and Meg had to be together. That was the only point to your priesthood these last years. Don't think I don't understand. But that's all you cared about. Not the parish, not anything. You – you and Meg. You lied to people about me, telling them Meg and I were in love. To cover up – to lead them off the scent – to hurt me and hurt people who might approach me. You tell us, over and over, that we're all adults in our parish and then you don't even share your important news with us – as adults – or even with the wardens – and when Lily found you out, you fired her. Damn it – Rick – so what if you loved Meg? Do you think we wouldn't understand? Did you think we would run and tell Heine? Well, he took his revenge on me! It wasn't me they were talking about, it was you. They wouldn't have approved Jesus if he'd gone through. And I heard that from Peter. They weren't going to vote for me because of you. You had to sneak off and make me keep your secret. I did. And much good my honor did me. Your secrets destroyed Saint Philip's and my friendship. You don't care. You never did. I hope you're both very happy. Congratulations on your marriage. But go to Hell."

I went walking that night, thinking of the wasted years. Not really wasted – just what was the point of friendship, of love, if we were – even the best of us – just out for ourselves? I walked, not sure if I was weeping because I had cursed Rick or because "they" had said no, or because I wasn't even sure of my own motives for loving Saint Philip's or the people in it.

When I got back home, I found three messages from Meg. Just "Call me."

Three times.

The phone rang. I picked it up, ready to fight. But it was Mother Jenny.

"Are you okay?"

"I'm not jumping off a roof."

"I called my bishop and left a message. You'd have to move to New Jersey and do some of the process over. It might take two years. But he would consider you."

"Oh, dear God."

"The thing is – to deny you – because your priest was disobeying the harassment rules – well, he just laughed when I told him. The hypocrisy of it."

"Yeah."

"I *mean* hypocrisy. Heine is having an affair with Alice Evans, who reports to him. That's not gossip, that's the truth. I'm friends with some of Bulla's Commission members, who say those two have a little love nest in New Jersey. It's probably why he was hard on you. To cover up his own crap."

If I'd felt tired before, I was ready to sink into a grave at that. What was I doing hanging out with these people?

"Thank you. I just can't think now."

"I understand. You've had a shock and been treated unfairly. I wanted you to know the road is not closed. Okay?"

"Okay."

"I'm the rector of Saint Joseph's Church in Belvidere. Starting tomorrow. Call me when you're ready."

"Thank you."

I meant that. At least, she had a conscience.

The phone rang.

I let it ring.

Meg's voice. "Janene, call me dearest. We love you."

Sure you do.

I hated everything – my job, my apartment, my life. What was my point? Why had I spent so much time in God help me – church?

I wondered if I should even go to church.

Oh, I did.

I was early for choir practice.

The good thing is that no one knew about the BACOM – even that I was going or what it was. I sat, alone, in the choir, going through the music.

Ah, there was Kennedy. He came over, sat next to me, and said, "I didn't know you had the BACOM this weekend. I could have helped you. Alice is a good friend of mine, and she said that you didn't get the support you needed."

"I couldn't say," I said.

The thing is – the collar – I looked at his. It symbolized being set apart and oh, the temptation was to feel as if set apart meant set above. Had I wanted that? Had I wandered onto that path because I'd needed that extra proof – not that it was – that I was lovable? My father had pushed me away. Was that what all this was about? Lily – good as she had been – clinging to that collar in hot weather. Rick hiding his truth in order not to lose his collar – or Meg's.

Or Meg.

As I sang, I looked up at the small congregation of what was barely thirty people. Where had everyone gone? I heard Kennedy say, "Rick lied about attendance."

Well, hey, I'd lied to myself for years.

I canceled my reservation to Portland. I wasn't going to stand up for them. I was going to Yosemite. I got a tent cabin in the Valley. It was a miracle because you had to make reservations a year in advance, but someone had canceled. How nice of them.

Yosemite. One of the few places where I could breathe.

In the meantime, I continued to go to Saint Philip's. No, I didn't walk out and go somewhere else. I needed to see that things didn't get any worse. And I loved the choir and John and all the people who were hanging on no matter what. If they could, I could.

The inevitable happened.

For two weeks, Kennedy muttered about how bad of a rector Rick had been – condoning sodomy, letting anyone preach, not maintaining the church building, and of course, having an affair with a parishioner and a subordinate and pushing that parishioner through the process to suit his needs.

Then came the inevitable, that one Saturday when he took me into his confidence. Oh, that one Saturday. I remember defending Rick, but after two attempts, I gave it up. I liked hearing Kennedy go after him.

"I've gone over your records," Kennedy said to me, with a gentle voice. "Alice sent them to me. You scored a 3.96 cumulative average in seminary, and you scored the highest on the GOEs in the diocese. It occurred to Alice that you were not prepared for the BACOM, that Rick just abandoned you."

"That's true," I said. I let myself be bitter. "Meg had several rehearsals. And a prayer group! Rick called us in to pray for her when she went through BACOM. I just went in."

"Of course. You must be angry."

I didn't say anything.

"It's going to be okay. The next BACOM is in six months. Alice put you on the list. We'll have some talks while I'm here, and you can meet with Alice. I told her how you were poorly prepared. That all Rick did was support his girlfriend. Don't worry. She will tell Heine. I'll help you with sermons, you can continue to serve on the altar. You can help me whip this parish into shape.

I thought of trees with apples and serpents.

"Thank you," I finally said, but it was a listless gratitude. When Kennedy hugged me, I could see that I was going to be a project to prove how lousy Rick was as a human being and as a priest. More in love with an associate priest, pushing her through, and ignoring someone who obviously had a better right to be a priest than Meg.

Would I have disagreed with that? To be honest with myself, no.

CHAPTER 45

Kennedy did things differently. He stopped our circling the altar at communion. Instead, we went up the aisle and received two by two. He held his own books, which I didn't mind, and he only let me be a subdeacon, since I had seminary training, so I was on the altar all the time. I had no idea why seminary training was needed. I suspected that it was just one of those "we have a collar, and we are better" things, but I didn't protest. At least I could be on the altar.

At coffee hour, though, I heard what people thought.

"He's cold. You talk to him, and he looks straight through you. I asked him why we changed communion, and he doesn't answer. Doesn't even look at me."

"I thought interims weren't supposed to change things."

The hardest thing was his changing the peace.

"This is not a party," he told the liturgy committee, which now consisted of Peter, Donald, and myself. "We commemorate the death of Christ."

"Early Christians were joyful," said Peter.

"There are many ways to be joyful," said Kennedy.

Peter left that day.

Inside I was simmering. Kennedy criticized Rick at the Vestry meeting. Tom loved it because "he's organized." Chris just went with it.

Kennedy dismissed the liturgy committee as being unnecessary.

That got John mad.

He would roll his eyes heavenward because Kennedy wanted to know the hymns in advance. Rick never had. He had trusted John, and

John got used to it, and although the hymns were technically the priest's responsibility, Rick trusted John. They'd had a great rapport.

People kept coming to me saying they had to leave.

"He's so cold," I kept hearing about Kennedy.

"I heard him say that Rick ruined this parish, but people are leaving because of him."

"He won't look me in the eye. I ask a simple question. Why did you change the way we do communion? Why don't you use the inclusive language version of Scripture that we compiled? How does this prepare us for a new rector? We want a new rector for us not for him."

John said to me, "I'm going to sit him out. He can't last forever. The search committee has narrowed down possible Rectors to five. There's only hope there. And people will come back."

John and Joe agreed that Kennedy was cold and unresponsive to the community – a word Kennedy didn't like.

I weighed having a meeting with Tom and Chris about this and decided that the community was important to me. That of all the institutions in the church, the community was what needed to be cared for.

We met with Tom and Chris and while I spoke about misunderstandings, I was horrified when my friends spoke of Kennedy's outright lying of what his job entailed. John protested that Kennedy had removed the community's voice. Joseph said that Kennedy never answered his questions and would just walk away.

I felt saddened and dismayed by this hour. Tom and Chris thanked us, and I went home, troubled but thinking that some simple discussion would smooth the path. We were all grownups.

Well, forget that. I had no idea what the wardens told Kennedy, but Kennedy called me in a rage.

And this, this was my real refusal from the BACOM – and the Episcopal Church – being screamed at because I supported my community and that upset an overreacting, insecure man with a collar.

"You're leading a rebellion against me – after I tried to help you?"

"What?" I wanted to laugh. "I'll be right over. That's not true at all."

For an hour, I tried to soothe this poor, injured little boy with an oversensitive ego to try to say that people needed to ask him questions. Rick would have opened the service to these questions because he wasn't afraid and was certain in his own skin. But Kennedy acted like a martyr.

"I asked Alice, how can I support this person when she leads a revolt against me?"

I was calm. I kept repeating that people just had questions. He continued to rant. I wandered into "liturgy means the work of the people" but he had none of it. Eventually, he said, "Maybe I did misunderstand," and he was calmer when I left, but I was exhausted. What a baby.

The next day was Trinity Sunday. As the choir sat in the first pews, I had to stop my jaw from dropping when Kennedy began with the Trinity and then moved into "triangulation." That is, people going to someone else when they were in fact upset with some other person. I could hardly believe my ears – turning the mystery of the Trinity into a pathetic snort filled with self-pity.

John's face was pale. I looked back and saw that that serene ex-Jesuit's face was red with rage.

After church, John was ready to quit. Joe wanted to knock Kennedy flat. I ran right into Himself who forced a smile and said, "Why, Janene, do you think I was preaching about you?"

"Yes," I said, walking past him. I wanted to slug him.

And I laughed. I knew that ended my chances for ordination in New York, but who wanted to join a pack of fools?

He called a meeting, and he had asked some ordained friend to mediate. I stated simply, the facts. That it was all a complete misunderstanding. There was no rebellion, only people wanting to ask questions about changes in practice, that was all.

Kennedy said, "I'm a priest sent here to heal the parish after its trauma with Rick."

John burst out. "People loved Rick We had a full church until you came. You call that healing? You're the trauma."

Kennedy said, "This parish is out of sync with the diocese. You need help. That's what I'm here to offer."

I decided to chop my head off. "It hardly seems like the job of an interim to attack a much-loved priest who left and who people are grieving."

"It's a shame that you think that way," he said. "I'd think you'd want this church to be on track with what the Episcopal Church is."

We were calm as he continued to insult us. He ranted. He screamed. He pretended to weep, but no tears came. John and Joseph were the ones weeping. I felt for Joseph who had found in Saint Philip's a genuine welcome, but now there was no love for a man who'd so visibly suffered from AIDS.

"How can this man be insulted by our asking questions?" I asked. "Liturgy is flexible, is beautiful, and if we understand why a change is made, we can understand Father Kennedy more, and we get closer."

"You're a frustrated priest wannabe," said Kennedy. "That's all you will be."

I stood up. "We didn't intend to hurt you, but many of us had polite questions for you, and I'd think that you would want a chance to talk to all of us, to teach, to bring us together in understanding. But I see all you want to do is to rule by fiat, and that is not what a community is. We had hoped to learn from you. What I learned is that you are a frightened little boy who does not love the church but that you are in the church where you hide, trembling, from life. I would never want to be like you."

I was shaking. The community I loved was over.

John thought he had lost his job.

Joseph decided never to go back so long as Kennedy was there, which meant he would not be going to church. And he was crying.

I walked the streets, my foot stepping up then down then up then down. All right, God, what am I supposed to do here?

Anyway, I wanted nothing to do with Kennedy's church. If this was the gang I had to please to get ordained, who the hell wanted it? Thin skinned, insecure, power mad babies.

But still. I wept. Why hadn't Rick helped me to move to a friendly parish? Why was I so alone? Why couldn't anyone love me to make me the sole point of their existence? Well, okay, that's going some.

I had tried – blown years of my life and I had nothing.

CHAPTER 46

Well, I had Yosemite.

No liturgy is like the spiritual experience of seeing Yosemite. I had of course seen pictures of the granite cliffs but in real life oh, in real life – with the low afternoon sun pouring light onto the rock – all the world seems aglow in magic. God is here. No doubt about that.

I didn't feel the least bit afraid, even if the road seemed narrow for the bus and it was a long way down to the earth.

I usually stayed at the Lodge, but not this year as I'd reserved too late. My tent cabin was spacious, with a cot and a table and a lamp – also electricity. There were hooks on the wall, but I tossed my two knapsacks down and headed for Yosemite Falls.

It was May, and the falls were in full power! I hopped on a tram and got off at the path to the falls – it's more like a driveway, very short and paved. The tall ponderosas – oh, I stood for a moment, looking up at them and the blue sky through their eyes. I imagined them spreading their branches and heaving a deep sigh – welcome back, Janene! Here is reality! Forget the damn church!

I leaned against one of these great trees and breathed in the scent of its branches, feeling its puzzle bark, looking up as it stretched toward the sky along with its companion trees. The crisp air enticed.

Early May was a great time to visit! The water roared as it poured down and leaped over granite rocks – snowmelt crashing down and hurtling into the Merced River with terrifying force – creating great white foam and delightful mist as it poured on through the park. I took a deep breath, letting the cold from above fill my being, cleansing it of all the crap people called religion. This was where God's spirit lived.

A few kids in the small crowd leaped into the water. Rangers ordered them out. Signs were all over – Keep out! The current can kill you! Indeed, deaths happened at Yosemite if you were stupid, and it seemed many were. There are no protections. You're in wilderness.

You must respect the power of this place.

I walked onto the bridge over the Merced, enjoying the cold spray. I felt washed clean.

Dear God, this is your church. Soul filling and cruel, wild, and beautiful.

And, oh, God, I have a confession to make.

I've been stupid.

I went to that other church.

I don't mean the little community church, simple and hard working. I mean the church that claims to speak for You – tempting me with love and belonging.

Now I have a question. Did I pursue the priesthood because I needed to feel I belonged when my family crashed? Or because I felt that I had a gift from You that I need to share? Was it ego or did You really call me or is that just shorthand for the church wanting You in their clutches? How do I know?

Are You sending me to New Jersey?

I walked down the road to the great meadows, now green and waving tall grasses, pausing for a few moments at the memorial to John Muir. Then I crossed into the meadow to stand and gaze more closely at Half Dome. To stand in her presence is to know there is a God – not because there is this magnificent product of creation but because creation implies a creator and I needed to call out to you, my creator, who must not leave us so alone. We can't handle it.

I kept walking and my eyes caught the little wooden chapel across the road. Oh, church everywhere. Still, its presence gave me some peace. It was, certainly, picturesque.

I walked back to Camp Curry. I bought a hamburger, fries, and a Coke, and I sat by myself at a table, just enjoying where I was – the peace of it.

Then it happened.

"Hello there!"

That voice? No. I was imagining.

No, I wasn't.

There was Rick, grinning down at me. And right behind him Meg, also grinning.

I thought I had yelled them out of existence.

Damn, why had I told them I was coming here? Why had they remembered?

"What are you doing here?"

"May we join you?"

I wanted nothing to do with them.

"We have come to ask forgiveness," Rick said.

Of all the devilish tricks, God. And I'd just paid you homage.

I shrugged.

"I'll get some food, Meg. You girls sit here."

Girls.

Meg slid in across from me.

Meg said, "You really reamed into us."

"Yes, I did."

"I remembered you were coming here. We checked with the park."

"Here I am."

"We're staying here, too. Janene, we couldn't leave it like – we couldn't."

"I wish you had."

"It wouldn't be fair to us or to you."

I put my burger down, picked up a fry and aimed it at her. "You used me. There's no getting around that. You never liked me. Ever. How could you, the way you used me."

"We had to do it that way, Janene. I would have told you, but we couldn't. Would you want Rick to lose his collar? Heine hates Rick because – well, he thinks – Rick has no moral scruples and he's using us to prove it. Even Rick's New York friends won't talk to him for fear Heine will find out."

"Find out what? Heine knows it all. And what's so great about a collar? Your vanity is attached to it?"

"Heine can't hurt us now, and we know who Rick's friends are."

"I hope you don't count me in that group."

She gasped. It seemed inconceivable to her that I would begrudge being used for such a noble task.

"He must love his collar more than anything or anyone," I said, shooting that arrow right at her. "And the same to you. The number of people you hurt by your selfishness. Not to mention me."

Rick returned with fish sandwiches, apples, and a bottle of wine and plastic cups.

"I'm sorry," I said. "I can't feel bad for any consequences you've felt. Ha, what consequences. You used me, and you never loved me."

"That's not true," said Rick. "I will say that I hadn't counted on you wanting to be a priest."

"Meg nagged me. I should be mad about that, too."

"I was honest. You have gifts, believe me. We didn't think Heine would turn you down because of us."

"Because of what he thinks of Saint Philip's, and that was a sore that took years to build up. You knew about that – you were always nervous, Rick, when the bishop came to visit. You were being secretive because of Heine, because you knew he despised you and would have loved to find a crack in your goodness. Well, I could give it to him."

"I love Meg," said Rick.

"You love your collar more."

"Janene, stop that!"

"You wouldn't give up your collar – or Meg's. You didn't care about the wreck you left – a parish caught off guard by your lack of decent notice. We got a terrible interim because of that, Heine's right-hand man. What did you care? Nothing for us. Nothing for your own family. And nothing from me whom you abandoned to the dust."

"Come to Portland."

"Are you kidding? Shut up. If I had a call, you and Kennedy doused it. I've already been accused of a rebellion against the bishop."

"Why?" Rick cried.

"I cared for the community," I said. "And you spoiled me by being welcoming of dialogue. That's my sin. But you taught me that."

"Janene, if I had to do it over again, I'd do it differently. Everyone assumed you and Meg were lovers so – we just let it be assumed."

"Yeah, close women friends are obviously lesbians," I shot back. "You hated traveling with me. God, I loved you – my mother and father – I had lost my family. I was weak."

"I'm sorry," said Meg. "I loved traveling with you."

"You lie. You two fell in love, but that was all that mattered. You destroyed a church, you hurt your friends, but you're happy. What an example you are."

I got up, threw my uneaten burger into the garbage, and went to buy my own food. Then I walked to the Merced and followed it, the river of Our Lady of Mercy. It was a strong rush of high water, and a few people were riding down the river on rubber tubes, laughing, being free. I sat on the bank, wishing I could do that.

I wanted to be alone. I did not want them here, pretending to be friends, assuaging their guilt. No way. I couldn't even look at them.

As I sat, I felt something, a presence, something patient and comforting.

I turned my head.

A coyote sat, barely three inches from me, and it was watching the fun on the river.

I didn't speak, just looked back at the water, and the coyote and I sat there, side by side, enjoying the day. I even hummed a little. The Merced rushed below us, the lowering sun now casting shadows on the ground. Day was ending. I should get back. But what if I moved?

I looked at the coyote.

The coyote looked at me, shook her head a little, got up, and trotted away.

Was that a sign? I mean, God, if you're going to send a sign, could you like, put a sign on it?

I walked back to Camp Curry, hit the bathroom, and went to my tent cabin. Alas, guess who sat on a log across from the cabin. Trying to impress themselves that they loved me.

"Just go."

"We can't. We're staying here," said Meg. "We're down the row."

"How nice."

"We need you to understand."

"I understand!" I yelled. "You fell in love. You're tired of your wife. You had to avert suspicion because you could be afraid if anyone caught wind – including your wife, I guess. You had to defend yourself from suspicion. Meg and I were friends. So why not coax out a deeper friendship and let the parish suspect we were lovers? And then use your influence on Bulla's remaining commission to push Meg's ordination steps before they left? And contact your pal, the Bishop of Portland, to find work for Meg. Meg got a job. A nice one. You prepared to settle there, and in the meantime, Lily confronted you, and you had to take care of her while not damaging her career. You did that nicely. And you rushed Meg's process too. So off you go after Meg, and you are straight with the bishop here – and it's fine because you don't work together, and he's always been your friend. You couldn't tell Saint Phil's or me or the wardens."

"Our adviser told us not to."

"Your adviser didn't know Saint Philip's. Your adviser didn't know, and Rick, you could have told us, if not us, the wardens. They would have kept your stupid secret. No, you listened to some stupid adviser. She says keep it quiet. Tell them when they're ready. Ready? We wouldn't have told the bishop. You know that. No, bottom line, always bottom line, the priest is daddy, and we are merely little children to be kept in the dark. Keep your collars tight round your necks, you two. That's all that matters to you. Now good night."

"Janene, that's all true," said Rick, "but it's not the truth."

"You are my best friend," said Meg. "It's just that so much was happening."

"Sure."

"I have feelings, too. I have worries. I'd be thrown out, too. Yes, we were sneaky and selfish. We snuck out on dates."

"And double dated with me and Betty. Geez."

"We want to help," said Rick.

"Let's forget all this for a bit," said Meg. "Let's just play. We're here in Yosemite. Rick and I can stay for the weekend, and then you can have the run of the place. Let's do a big hike tomorrow."

"I was going on the Mist Trail."

"Which is that?"

"Up the side of Vernal Falls. I've done it before. It's a hike to the falls uphill, and then more than six hundred steps up to the top of the falls."

"We've been hiking all over Mount Rainier."

Well, we wouldn't have to talk to each other climbing – that trail up the falls was purely single file.

"Sure, okay, why not?" I said. "Breakfast at seven? We can start up by eight. We can eat lunch at the top of the falls. The forecast is good. It should be warm."

"Okay," said Meg.

"We can meet at that food shack. Now can you leave me alone?"

"Yes," said Rick. He hugged me hard. I should have slugged him.

"We'll fix this, Janene," he said.

Meg hugged me, too, God help me. "It'll be all right. Promise."

I went into my tent. It was cool, even cold. I changed into my pajama bottoms and pulled on a wool sweater I'd picked for a pajama top and went to the john. As I made my way back to the cabin, I looked up, and they were – the stars – glimmering all across that dark sky, seeming to be almost touching the tall pines. I felt I could touch them. You couldn't see stars in New York anymore. I missed stars – points of light, tellers of tales, source of our myths, even of Christianity.

I settled into my cot and tried not to wonder what sort of bedding Meg and Rick had. Were the cots pushed together? Whatever. Meg had found her man. I wondered if that was really what bothered me. That I was so alone.

And felt more so now.

I slept.

I woke. I heard people shuffling around, and light came through the slats in the wall. Damn, I'd wanted to see the sunrise. I checked my travel clock and shut off the alarm. It was not quite six. I grabbed a towel and my kit and slipped into sandals.

Outside, without my contacts, I thought I saw Rick in sweatshirt and jeans with a towel over his shoulder walking to a cabin down the row.

A few women stood at sinks in the women's restroom. We were all ages. One with striking gray hair all down her back. She was beautiful.

I showered and dressed quickly and met Meg and Rick coming out of their cabin.

Rick insisted on paying for our scrambled eggs and bacon, coffee, and juice. We ate, packed up our rolls, and bought water. Meg and Rick talked. I concentrated on eating.

We caught the tram. Meg sat with me, a move I thought was deliberate. She pointed out deer in the woods and Rick blessed the blue sky.

And our journey began.

CHAPTER 47

"Happy Isles! Mist Trail!" called the tram driver.

"Yay, here we go!" called Meg.

It was the last tram stop, and several people hopped off.

"Happy Isles," I sang to Mozart's Alleluia.

Rick's smile broadened as he raised his eyes to the tops of the great pines. He turned in a wide circle, his arms stretched out, taking a deep breath of Yosemite's air.

"It's heaven," he said quietly.

Meg dropped her backpack and ran over and gave me a big hug.

"It's so good to be here with you!"

I tried to smile.

Rick put his big arms around me for one of his bear hugs.

I pulled back fast.

I wasn't ready.

I suddenly thought of my father. How I'd wished I'd hugged him many more times before I lost him.

"A glorious day!" Rick took a deep breath, taking it all in.

"Hey, everyone's getting ahead of us!" Meg called out.

"Last warning," I said. "This is a tough hike." I became conscious that Rick was over sixty-five and Meg was fifty-two. I'd forgotten ages. I was thirty-five. But after being deskbound for so many months, I worried about my own stamina.

"It doesn't look so tough," said Meg.

"Just wait. It looks steady now, but after we get to the Vernal Falls Bridge, it's going to get tough."

"You've done this before."

"I do it every time I come up. This will be my dozenth time. Now look, once on the Mist Trail, there's no turning back."

I dodged as Meg tossed a fading brown braid behind her as she shrugged.

"We're not new at this, you know. We're tough. We hike all over Mount Rainier."

Yeah, you're perfect.

They were trying to make amends. I didn't care.

Meg interrupted my dismal thoughts by grabbing my elbow and leading me over the bridge leading to the trail. Once on the trail, she started skipping.

"We're off to see the wizard," she sang.

I started right in with her.

Just enjoy it now. It's Yosemite.

We skipped up the path, Rick laughing behind us. Bad feelings grew tired and fell away as the path grew steep.

Another sign.

Meg stopped.

"Uh oh."

The sign said, "Warning! You are entering bear country!"

"Lions and tigers and bears," I said, helpfully.

"For real?"

"I've never seen any. It's April. They could still be hibernating."

"Or they're done and they're hungry."

Several people walked right past, paying no attention to the warning sign.

"Of course you haven't seen any bears," Meg said with an eye roll. She told Rick about the moose I didn't see on our drive in the west. "It was huge! Right there, walking alongside our car! If it had crossed in front of us, it would have crushed the car and killed us!"

Yes, her smug cruelty.

"Maybe I didn't see the animals I didn't want to see," I said quietly. "But my eyesight is getting better."

She heard me. She took several giant steps forward.

I wondered where the coyote was.

Meg was no coyote. She could support you with all her might only

241

to pull out with a harsh, cutting word after weeks of silence. I realized I didn't care what she said anymore.

The path grew steeper. In some places, it grew quite narrow, and to misstep would be to soar among the pines. We just breathed, then huffed, each breath getting more difficult. Rick led the way, and he would stop, look around in wonder, catch his breath, and keep going. Vigorous man. Yes, he had hiked on Mount Rainier.

When the trail widened again, Meg took my hand.

"You'll join us. We'll get you ordained."

I don't need your help. You've helped so much already.

Rick called out, reading a sign, "Three miles to the bridge, three miles to the top of Vernal Falls. Ready?"

I shifted my small pack of water and ham sandwich. "Up we go."

The trail grew even steeper. We walked single file, for the path narrowed even more perilously, leaning to one side – the wrong side, Rick leading the way, me bringing up the rear watching Meg's bouncing braid. We took our time, pausing to admire the vista of Yosemite Valley and its sunlit cliffs dropping slowly below. Even as the immense cliffs shaped by glaciers grew smaller, I felt them filling my soul. And still my soul had things to say.

Don't you know how I suffered?

Well, hadn't they suffered? Meg had struggled through nunhood and a husband who died. Rick had struggled with a marriage he found unsatisfying, and that can't be easy, with kids.

But enough about them. They could have been happy without tossing me into the garbage.

The sound of the falls grew louder, the air cooled, the trail evened off, sloped a little down into the mud – as if the trickiest part of the hike was right here.

We turned round a curve, and the trail was growing muddy. And happily, downhill. The river rushed so loudly that I could barely hear Meg yell, "Look at that!"

We'd reached the bridge. There, just up the river, plunged Vernal Falls. It looked small from the bridge, a distant loveliness, beautiful and deadly, an icy white with small shades of blue, pouring down from high above, full white foam landing in the river.

"Let's go!"

But we did pause at the riverbank, the rush of water drowning us and all the playful families screeching around us. It was a heaven of a playground.

We drank some water, visited the porta potties, and met again, ready to climb.

"Let's go!" called Rick.

I led the way under the trees, the Merced pouring - laughing – beside us. Some people leaped from rock to rock and lay on a huge flat rock bed – picnicking. I had a moment of feeling that I wanted to stay and join the laughter.

But we continued climbing and soon came to the narrow steps erratically cut into the granite.

"Six hundred steps!" I yelled over the roaring waters.

"Like to a holy temple," Meg yelled back.

"There isn't always a rail," I yelled. "So be careful!"

The steps weren't steep, but they were slippery, and we stepped carefully, yet our eyes were fixed on that violent, beautiful, white foam of a powerful waterfall growing closer, more threatening and more indifferent than any bear. The mist from its plunging waters struck the granite boulders, the granite wall at our side, and made puddles on the steps.

Don't look down.

I grabbed the rail that finally showed up. At least it would be here for a while.

All the hikers went up slowly, single file, occasionally stopping and pressing against the granite rocks on our right as people came down the steps. I didn't think I could go down this way. I'd done it before, but maybe the falls hadn't been so powerful then.

No one spoke. We had to concentrate on the steps, which weren't even. One at a time. Occasionally, I gripped the side of the thick granite wall. It gave some assurance of security, even if mostly fictional. I could hear Meg breathing behind me.

Once I stopped to look – the cliffs, the deep blue of the sky, just a few clouds – wisps of God's breath. What did those clouds know of church and politics? This was reality. This life of nature, the warming sun heating the rocks, the melting snow, the coming to life of spring in gentle flowers and powerful waters that kissed my face. These things were the real Easter and always had been.

Who wouldn't come back to life with that powerful water?

I came to the curve in the path – here was a large circular flat space, shaded by an overhanging rock, where we could catch our breath for a few seconds. We slowed down as others ahead took advantage of that space, but finally we could gather there and take some breaths.

We held hands.

"There it is!" I called.

"It" was the top of Vernal Falls, sparkling in the sun, foaming with snow melt, glorious to see.

"How beautiful," said Meg.

Rick just looked, a calm smile on his face and what appeared to be tears in his eyes.

Meg opened her pack. She pulled out her camera and took a picture. She made a move to step off the narrow granite path to the steep grass hill at the side.

"No!" I shouted. "People have died here. See the sign? Don't go there."

"It looks okay."

A man stepped up just below us. "No!" he shouted. "She's right! People die here! You're in the wilderness."

He pushed his way up onto the rock, and we made room for him.

"I know it's the wilderness. I'm not stupid," said Meg. But she put her camera away.

"You got a good enough picture," said Rick.

"Can you move on?" a woman shouted at us.

"Sorry!" I called. "Come on, guys."

The spray grew fierce, the steps more slippery, our ascent achingly slow. Now I became aware of my body's muscles that hurt more after we stopped, for my body could think about what I was doing to it. My calves screamed at me in their own special way. The sun beat harder on the rocks, and I was sweating hard. I could hear people breathing behind me – and me with them – in rhythm with the falls. I worried about Rick. He'd been doing fine up until this point, and he looked fine as he climbed up, but still, I had this sense of dread as I stepped up and stepped up again and again.

Around another corner. I looked back. Meg had paused to look past the falls, up into the sky, the cliffs, the majesty.

"It makes me want to cry," she said.

"Me too."

We passed through a bit of welcoming trees and to another guard rail. Some steps led down – down! – to the top of the falls. My legs trembled as I grabbed a strong double rail and arrived high enough to touch the sky.

Here was a wide cement floor, large enough to hold lots of people with room to spare. I hobbled to the rail, and Rick and Meg joined me. We stared at the violent, swirling waters tumbling over boulders and crashing down below. A couple of park rangers moved among us hikers, answering questions and giving advice for the next part of the hike to Nevada Falls.

Some guy started to climb the rails, and a ranger hauled him back. "People have fallen into the river doing that! And died!"

"Damn," said Meg.

We looked out – way below was where we had started our climb – way below where we had looked up here. Proud at our accomplishment, we watched the great waters pour down into that disarmingly named river of mercy.

"Let's eat," I said.

There was a place to sit – on a granite shelf where we could watch the swirling waters. We ate quietly until Rick spoke. "It's getting cloudy up there."

"At least the sun won't be beating down on us," I said.

"How long is it to Nevada Falls?" asked Meg.

"You want to go? It's another three miles – some of it easy, some not from what I hear. I've never hiked it because I wouldn't do it by myself."

"We have to talk about what to do for you," said Rick.

A part of me was touched. He'd picked up on the ordination thing just by my saying I wouldn't go on the Muir trail by myself.

Still, I said, "Oh, no talk of the process now. It's so meaningless up here."

I noticed the rangers going from group to group and people quickly picking up their trash. One ranger came over to us and said,

"I'm sorry, folks, but you need to get your things together and start down."

A bolt of lightning flashed over the falls where the rainbow had been.

"Wow!" I cried. "Where did that come from?"

"The storm is moving faster than we had thought it would. It could be here in an hour or half that. You'd best get down this way to the Valley. Taking the trail will take too long. You'd be safer by the bridge and safest on the Valley floor."

Another ranger announced through a megaphone, "Please go down to the Valley. Don't run. You'll be a little wet but otherwise fine."

A rumble of thunder.

People cried out.

"Can't we stay up here?" a woman cried.

"No," said the megaphone voice. "It's not safe here. Lots of lightning strikes here. My partner and I are heading to warn people on the trail to find shelter. You go on down. Tell anyone coming up to go down and that's an order. Don't rush. You'll be fine. You have some time before it gets bad. Thank you."

"Okay," said Rick.

But no one moved. We all looked scared.

Rick grabbed his pack and strode toward the steps.

"Let's go," I said.

"I love adventure," said Meg.

"I'm glad I'm not alone," I said.

The steps were even slicker – there were puddles on many of them now. We all moved slowly. Step. Secure. Down. My legs were already shaking. No one laughed. No one called out about the beauty of it all. Roaring Vernal poured onto us, and the rain started lightly, but along with the spray, the granite steps were slick.

Another flash of lightning.

I could hear women crying. I wanted to. God, no, I want to live. Please no more lightning bolts or harder rain. At least, not until the Valley floor. Or the river of mercy. Soon – soon I will be in my snug tent cabin.

At one point, gripping the rail, I looked back, and a woman was going down very, very slowly, gripping the wall, the rail, whatever could be gripped.

I paused, deciding to leave a few steps between me and Meg. I didn't want to slide into her. She and Rick were just a step apart. I wanted to call out to them, but they wouldn't hear me.

My cabin. Two wool blankets. A heater. I would rip off my clothes, get into my flannel jammies –

Meg slipped and fell on her butt. She laughed. I gripped the rail – thank God it was there – and stepped down to grab Meg. My left foot slipped and pushed against her back, and she slid, rolling down into Rick, who fell with a howl. I stood there, gripping the rail, and watched Meg grab for Rick, heard their heads slam into granite, watched them roll off the narrow steps, their bodies crashing into boulders and then falling straight down, their heads, their whole bodies colliding with the granite boulders that would not stop them as they tumbled straight down the mountain, straight down toward the wild Merced.

I don't remember screaming. They tell me I did. I remember the people behind me screaming. I don't remember trying to jump off the steps, but they told me I had lunged as if to do that but that the woman behind me grabbed me and pushed me against the granite wall. I do remember pressing my lips against the wet granite and shaking.

Someone yelled, "Get the rangers! Get help!"

What help? They were dead, and *I* had killed them. I started shrieking again.

The rain, relentless. My tears.

People started to edge past me, slowly, gingerly, all crying.

"All right, we've got her," someone said.

I was pulled up to the wider step.

"No! They're down there!" I yelled.

A ranger held onto me. "Someone will get them. Come on up with me. A helicopter is coming for you."

"Down there!" I couldn't stop shrieking.

"I'll help you. Come on."

He gripped my arm and hauled me up the steps. I had to move, or I'd be scraped. I tried to stop crying. If only my legs could stop shaking, I could climb better, but my body didn't seem to care.

Maybe they were still alive, clinging to some rock in the swirl of waters. They were both strong. They could do it. Maybe the fall wouldn't have been as bad as it looked. When I got down to the bridge, they would both be sitting on the bank of the river. They would be battered, but they would be okay.

Now I was at the top of the falls, and a helicopter roared over us, whipping my hair as it hovered. I had to hold onto a ladder to get up, the ranger right behind me. He pushed me up, someone above pulled the rope. I thought of letting go, but the ranger held my legs. Another ranger pulled me in. I fell into a seat. A coat wrapped around me. I realized I'd lost my pack – no, it was at my feet.

Loud talking back and forth. A voice in the air, crackling over the helicopter roar. I heard it say, "We found 'em. Their skulls cracked open. Ribs – it doesn't matter. They're gone."

"You're okay," said the ranger holding me. "You're going to be fine."

CHAPTER 48

"You're going to be fine."

A nurse stood there, a woman in blue garb and brown skin. I felt old. The earth changing into something I'd rather leave behind.

Then I remembered. My foot. Meg falling. Rick calling out. Both yelling, falling. Someone grabbing me.

"I gave you something to sleep," said the nurse. "You needed it after what you went through."

Me? I wondered at their terror in those few seconds before they died. Did they die as soon as their heads hit the granite rocks or were they still alive when they fell into that wild river?

Now there was a man in black, also with brown skin. He had a strong build, thick black hair laced with gray, a fat face, and his eyes showed care that I had not seen in years.

"I'm Father Ben Poletti," he said, sitting beside me.

A collar. Right. Time to pretend to care.

"I'm a chaplain here at Yosemite. Do you mind if I'm Catholic?"

"I crowned the Blessed Virgin Mary on my first communion day."

"Ah. Lapsed?"

"Very."

"That tells me you care about your spiritual life."

Well, there was a perspective.

I turned away.

"I am sorry. Do you know the two people who died?"

Know. Present tense.

They were going to pump me for information I sat up, needing to feel professional.

Meg's yelp. Rick's scream. People around me screaming. Had I yelled? Meg! Rick! I didn't remember. My friends, my enemies, my companions, my traitors.

"You don't have to talk."

My shoes and socks were off, and my jacket was somewhere. I felt panic about my money, which had been in my backpack. And my ID.

I rubbed my feet together. More like they rubbed themselves together, I had nothing to do with it. It was that damn foot.

My tears were already falling. This priest took my hand. A collar guy. From a church that refused my right to be a priest.

I wanted to argue with him.

I sank down and cried instead.

He tightened his hold on my hand.

Someone else came in. I sat up tall. It was a ranger.

"Can you tell us what happened?" asked the ranger. "We heard that your friend slipped. She rolled into the man."

"Did it happen? Are you telling me it happened?"

"Yes."

I wiped my eyes.

The blue nurse handed me a cup.

"It's chamomile tea, dear."

I sipped. It went down warm. My tears kept falling.

The ranger sat down. "I don't know why we keep those steps open. Especially on a day when it could rain. But the worst thing is people looking to take pictures and do stupid things."

"We weren't doing any of that."

"That's what I hear. It only makes me feel worse. They wanted people in the Valley. The Muir Trail would have been better – but the storm came up too fast, and it was going to be bad, and the trail would take longer."

"There was a rainbow." Silly, but I said it for some reason.

I put the cup down. I swung my legs over and put my feet on the floor.

"I'll tell you who they are."

The ranger pulled out a notebook.

Father Poletti kept holding my hand.

"She is Meg Madigan. She is the Canon Pastor at the Portland Episcopal Cathedral."

The ranger looked startled.

"A priest?" Father Poletti looked startled.

"Yes, Father. Women can be priests in the Episcopal Church. And the man was also a priest. He is Rick – Richard – Campbell, recently the Rector of Saint Philip's parish in New York City. He recently moved to Portland. Oh, they are – were -are - married. They can do that in the Episcopal church. Publicly."

God, I was mean.

"Can I contact those churches? I'll need family information."

"Yes."

"Are you a priest?"

"Oh, no." I think I laughed. "I'm just a Master of Divinity."

"What is your name?" asked the ranger.

I had to think. "Janene Shannon. I live in New York."

"These were friends?"

I was afraid to answer that. "We were careful. We did as we were told. Rick led the climb down. No one wanted to do it. Maybe we should have stayed where we were. Then Meg slipped."

"And fell into her husband. Nasty business. It was a tough call for the rangers. There was no lightning striking on the steps and people got down quickly, although the accident scared them." The ranger folded his notebook. "The worst thing is when people die here. Usually it's something stupid, but every so often it's no one's fault."

A rational part of my mind argued that my foot had simply slipped on the granite and that Meg had fallen, her shoulder landing where it had not been just a moment before. She had slipped and fallen. That might have been the cause. Or had it been my foot that propelled them down that terrible descent? And had my foot meant to do that?

The ranger was still talking. "And two priests. Geez. Ma'am, I'm so sorry. The rangers will be heartsick. But at least you are okay."

I didn't answer.

The ranger left.

Father Poletti held onto my hand.

The nurse said, "Dear, you can stay here for the night. Where were you staying?"

"Camp Curry."

"Did you have any other friends here?"

"No."

"You shouldn't be alone tonight," said Father Poletti. "There's a house of ministry workers. Young women and men. You should stay there. Which is your tent? Someone could pack your things."

I couldn't remember. I started bawling.

The nurse must have gone through my bag and found the key. I heard her call the Lodge.

"Father Poletti will take you to the chaplains' house. You can spend the night there. Someone will get your things. Do you have anyone who can help you leave the park?"

"I came on Amtrak. San Francisco. I flew from New York."

New York seemed terribly far away. And terribly safe.

I forget how I ended up at the chaplain's house – it was a long log building – with a parlor/kitchen in the middle and circumspect dorm rooms for men and women on either side. There were crucifixes, Buddhas, a prayer rug, a statue of Mary, holy pictures.

I sat at a table with two young women who served chicken and salad. The guys came in later, subdued. After the meal, they started a prayer service.

The hell with that.

I went to my bed.

As I lay on the cot, I felt hate rising. I no longer loved Yosemite. The very heart of my heart had been ripped from me – by my friends. Once again – but- then I remembered my foot touching Meg's shoulder. Had I felt any joy when I did it? When she started to slide? Had I wished her to die? Had my horror begun when both tumbled onto the rocks? When had they died? When had they drawn their last breaths? Was there enough time for them to feel terror? To hate me? My grief, after all, had brought them there. They had wanted to make amends. I hadn't asked them to come. They'd died because they'd cared about me.

So came the regret – powerful stuff that bent me over. They had formed the center of my life for a few years and had taught me much. Yet, what did I learn? How to set up an altar? What rubrics were?

Mysteries are not as mysterious.

Except death.

Rick had at least ten years, Meg at least twenty. I'd stolen them.

My foot.

Stepping off a curb.

Priest.

I should cut that foot off. It only led me to Hell.

I bolted up. It was almost midnight when I ran out the door in my underwear and looked up at the stars – glowing, radiant white, covering us, so close. People told tales from the shapes those stars took. Tales that became mythology. Gods. Then three masquerading as one.

"You are a liar!" I yelled at the stars. They weren't anything but huge balls of gas.

Two of the women ran out, covered me in a blanket, and I just wept. There is no God. There never was. Male or female. Oh, yes, my work coming back to haunt me. Just making me feel good was all it was. Just making me want to be noticed. There was no life after death. There was just death. And so cruel of any church to keep that hope in us.

They put me to bed and had the sense not to pray over me.

The next day - I must have slept late – one of the women remained in the cabin. Her name was Susan. She had short brown hair, like I used to have when I was a child. She was slightly plump, and I liked her. Or I would have liked her. Before.

"Are you up to breakfast? Pancakes?"

I shrugged. I found my bag, a clean pair of everything, my "God is a girl" tee shirt – I tossed it then picked it up. I would wear it inside out. That seemed right.

I ate their pancakes fast.

Susan didn't talk. I didn't either. She swept, did dishes, dusted. I cleaned up after myself.

Father Poletti came by – I realized he didn't live there - and said that he had called the Portland cathedral and had gotten next of kin information for both Meg and Rick. He had called the New York diocese and said that the bishop had not taken the call but had dictated a stiff regret. A secretary called later and read it to him.

"We just have to see about getting you home. Unless you want to stay?"

"It doesn't matter."

"Janene, what you want matters. Come on, now."

I walked away, out to the trees, breathing them in. I wandered the great meadow before Half Dome – people had died there, too. They had climbed, dreaming, hoping, laughing, and they had died.

I remembered a picture. Two women in 1890s garb standing on a thin overhanging rock at Glacier Point, a mere finger of a rock over Yosemite, and God help anyone trying to imitate them doing that. They held each other. They kicked up their legs.

I don't know what happened to them after they did that and a photographer far away, safe on stable ground, took their picture.

That was our friendship, Meg and I, both of us on the precipice. Can I love you and hate you at the same time? Can I? Would I walk out on that precipice with you?

Too late to find out now.

CHAPTER 49

On the third day, yeah, yeah, on the third day, Father Poletti joined me and walked alongside me. He didn't say anything, but the trees sang in the wind, and that was voice enough, though I wished even the trees would stop trying to heal my soul. When I sat on a rock by the still indifferently powerful Merced, Father Poletti sat by me as well. I didn't have any sense that he expected me to speak. I don't know how he signaled that because he didn't signal anything.

I sat, the water rushing by, pounding on rocks. Before, it had just been a beautiful sight. Now that wonderful stream had murdered my friends.

I heard a rustling of pine needles and sticks, soft treading on the ground. I turned my head. A coyote sat on my other side. Was it the same one? She gazed at the waters of the river, and I – I started to talk.

"It's my foot. One day, I stepped off a curb crossing West Twentieth Street by Ninth Avenue, and I realized I wanted to be a priest. I was already in seminary, where I'd started by auditing a class taught by Doctor Norman Forrest, and I fell in love with the Bible. I loved it for what it is – ancient documents handed down through time in many languages with many translations and edits and awful things like changing the Greek word for human into man - betraying the emotions and prejudices of the times and politics and everyone passing it on and on, people of faith, changing things, adding things, dumping things, our link to an ancient time, perhaps to the beginning of times. Showing cultures different from our own. It is a gift if we respect it and don't worship it too much. It's fantastic."

I didn't speak in a great rush. I spoke slowly and quietly.

"I wanted to be a priest because I wanted to share those ideas, mainly that we continue the word of God by how we are. I wanted to be an Episcopal priest because I loved the liturgy, so close to my Catholic one, but I can do it."

I lifted my right foot.

"I stopped off the curb. I knew. Or my foot knew."

Neither Father Poletti nor the coyote responded. They just watched the river.

I told them how I met Meg and then Rick and how I felt them rally around me as a family until I learned about their relationship and realized what a pawn I'd been.

I got to the hard part. "The day before I went before the Commission - a friend who worked in the diocesan office said that the bishop said he would not approve anyone Rick had recommended because Rick had run off with that bimbo, and he had run a parish steeped in immorality. At my Commission interview, I was greeted with hostility and disdain."

"You had been abandoned."

"No one cares enough for me to fight for me." It sounded pathetic, but it was how I felt.

"What about you fighting for you?"

Now there was an idea. I resented him bringing it up.

"I don't know how. I'm not familiar with the system, and I don't know anybody. Rick rounded up his friends who'd been on the Commission to vote for Meg, but he wasn't there for me, and those people had left anyway. They'd hated Heine, couldn't support him."

"You could speak your piece."

"To whom?"

"What are your options?"

"I feel alone."

"What are your options?"

"Go to New Jersey. No to that."

"That's not an option?"

"The truth is - I don't want a collar just to get one. I don't want a collar if it means becoming like them."

"I don't like wearing it that much. Puts people on a different step. But it also brings in people who need help."

"Sure, Father."

"What can you do?"

"Two things. I can somehow fight New York, or I can just throw up my hands. But I just don't see how fighting is possible. No one gives a damn about me. Even Meg and Rick didn't much care. They got what they wanted. And our interim is a close friend of the bishop's who, if you even seem to be challenging him, blows his temper. A close friend of the bishop's, mind you. And my father died – oh, never mind that."

"I see. But you remained friends with Rick and Meg?"

"They betrayed me, but ultimately, I don't think they sinned. They just didn't think. The parish is a mess now, and so am I. The real kicker is that Bishop Heine is having an affair with his subordinate, the one who supervises all of us underlings. Blond, blue eyed, suited with skirts landing just at the knee, you know the type, and oh yes, married."

"Well, there you have it. He had to condemn your friends and everything they touched so that no one would suspect him. He probably didn't have the nerve to turn your friend down, but you were vulnerable."

"They invited themselves to Yosemite. I didn't want them to come here."

"But they did, and you went hiking with them. You didn't walk away."

"We were starting to make progress when we were told to go down the steps. Meg slipped up and this foot, this very foot came against her back, and she fell into Rick. And Father, I don't know if I did it on purpose or wanted to do it on purpose. A part of me is glad they're dead, glad they suffered. I can't bear that part of me. What kind of a horrible person am I?"

I felt a rustling, a brush of fur.

The coyote was gone. Heard my confession.

"Janene, your friends betrayed you. The more you love someone, the more you hate them when they hurt you. And the harder to forgive."

"And the harder to forgive yourself."

"But you were trying to work things out. You did *not* kill them."

Another long silence except people were running around and laughing and calling out to each other. The silence was in my heart. Life was going on without me.

"I don't think Rick gave a damn about anything after he fell in love with Meg except Meg and making a new life with her. That's what my dad kept talking about. A new life. A new life."

"Is your dad part of this?"

I shot him a shrewd glance. "I know he is. People just out for themselves."

"And their loves. Are you feeling lonely because no one thinks of you in that way? How about you being out for yourself?"

Bullseye again.

"They were two wonderful people. Were." I looked out at the river. "I miss them. I miss what might have been."

I hated them, too.

I hated my foot.

"I have to go," he said. "Tomorrow is Sunday, and I have to write a sermon. Would you read the Epistle at our ten o'clock?"

"In the little church?"

"Yes."

I shrugged, although I didn't want to go to church ever again. "Sure."

"Come at quarter to. All the chaplains will be there. It's a nondenominational service and gets some attendance."

"Okay."

Back at the house, the young chaplains were playing Uno. They invited me to join them, but I took some of the vegetable soup and just watched them play for a bit. When they laughed, I remembered laughing. When I finished the soup, I went outside to look at the stars and to breathe in the pines.

I wanted to wish Meg and Rick the best. I wanted to say I loved them.

But I couldn't.

God, are you going to get me through this?

CHAPTER 50

It was a nondenominational service, simple and short. I read the Epistle.

Interesting selection. Paul, second letter to the Corinthians.

Therefore, we do not lose heart. Though outwardly we are wasting away, yet inwardly we are being renewed day by day. For our light and momentary troubles are achieving for us an eternal glory that far outweighs them all. So we fix our eyes not on what is seen, but on what is unseen, since what is seen is temporary, but what is unseen is eternal.

I listened to Father Poletti's sermon. He spoke softly, but I could hear every word. He spoke about the pain of growth and learning how to tend it, and he mixed it with the words of Jesus citing the Lord's Prayer. It sounds odd, but he made it work. I felt akin to the trees and when I left, I felt the rough bark of the ponderosas. I put my arms around the tree, which looked silly, I'm sure.

I spent most of the day walking in the sun-drenched meadow beneath Half Dome and watching the birds and butterflies. Just standing in the presence. I felt no urge to climb them. Feeling their strength is enough.

The chaplains were working all over the park. I knew I had to leave, and I did not want to. I wanted to sit and listen to the wind in the trees and the roaring of the waters.

But I did have to go.

Several Yosemite employees saw me onto the bus, including Father Poletti and the chaplains. While we passengers waited by the

Lodge, a little squirrel hopped onto the cement wall bordering the building and chirped loudly, breaking our hearts.

What hurt you, little squirrel?

Father Poletti handed me a book about women in the Bible, which I assumed would be noxious, but I appreciated his thoughts and his help.

I kept my eyes at the window as we left the valley and the kingdoms of El Capitan and Half Dome and the Three Brothers and those great pines and then followed the Merced – no, it still followed me for a while. Finally, I turned away, wondering if I would return.

The book was not noxious. It taunted me. And made me smile because I knew that was what he was doing, taunting me to find my place.

I landed in a mess.

I hadn't realized that Meg's and Rick's deaths had made the national news. My name was left out of it. I was just "a friend." Saint Philip's knew I was at Yosemite, though, and my answering machine was filled with repeated calls of consolation.

Aside from one from Father Kennedy.

"Janene, I was sorry to hear about your accident. A priest from Yosemite called Bishop Heine, and he seems to have a false impression of why you did not get accepted by the Commission on Ministry. The bishop would never refuse an aspirant because of someone else's behavior. You must have been upset. A reporter for the diocesan paper called me. How could you – was it a menage e trois?"

Nothing like a consolation from your priest.

I hadn't realized how much Rick was beloved in New York until I got my mail and a copy of the diocesan paper. Rick and Meg were front page news along with several tributes for Rick from all over the country. Buried in the accounts was the fact that Rick had flouted the sexual guidelines. Heine's comment was that "Father Campbell was a weak priest; the bishop sent him to what I'd guess you'd call a loser parish. It didn't matter since we have another, better church, close by."

A paragraph caught my eye – that "Heine rejected a marvelous candidate for the priesthood because Rick recommended her."

That would be my one yes vote.

Another message was from Beth, a new Warden, who seemed genuinely upset.

"How awful all this has been for you! I can't believe it! Call me anytime. We are all praying for you. Heine's in a mess. I heard from Peter – Heine is scrambling all over. I'm not sure you heard…"

Then she launched into a tale. Not about me. About another lovely thing he did. Heine had accused a priest in the city with embezzling funds from the church treasury, this just before Heine himself had divorced his wife and embarked on a cruise with Alice Evans. On hearing about the missing funds, our bishop blamed a young priest who had just joined the Cathedral. This young priest, alas for Heine, had an uncle who was a Bishop of California, who defended his niece. Loudly. Meanwhile, Heine appointed Alice Evans to replace the accused priest, a better position than overseeing aspirants to the priesthood. The California Bishop told reporters that Heine and Evans were lovers. At least, "They both slept in the same bed when they stayed in my rectory."

Aha. And that was while she was still working at the Cathedral.

The accused priest, with the help of her uncle, sued Heine.

Heine's wife sued Heine.

Another of Heine's girlfriends went public.

The hypocrisy was laughable.

I tried laughing. Couldn't.

CHAPTER 51

I told Beth on the phone, "Kennedy was going after me. He said I was leading a revolt against him."

"But he's out. We fired him two days ago. Unanimous Vestry. Heine and Kennedy can't say that because you had nothing to do with it. We have a new interim. We'll get a priest-in-charge and then a new rector. We already have more than twenty resumes. You've put Saint Philip's on the map."

I put my hands in front of my eyes as if to ward off a shock. "Don't tell me that."

"I didn't mean that, honey. You've had a rotten time. I'm sorry."

I hung up.

The phone rang. I let it go onto the machine.

"Janene? It's Ben Poletti. Are you home? I wanted to make sure you're all right."

I couldn't bear having Yosemite here. I know he meant well.

I did call my boss.

Not being a reader of the diocesan paper, Charley didn't know that I had been the witness to the terrible Yosemite tragedy.

"Good grief, I am so sorry. Take the next few days. The last thing you need is work. I'll arrange for the company to pay you but not take away from your remaining vacation and sick days. I think that will fly. Mike will certainly sign for that."

Mike, our emotional, Italian, free trip to DC publisher. At least I worked for human people.

How the press got my number, I couldn't say, but the networks were calling me to comment on Heine.

"Please," I said. "I'm in mourning."

I kept the machine on and turned the volume down.

I went to my diner to eat a salad, and I listened to the machine when I got back. Several newspapers. Father Ben.

And oh, yes, my one BACOM vote called from New Jersey.

"I'm sticking up for you. And Bishop Spong says you can be a postulant in New Jersey."

"He's never met me."

"He wants to. I should say yes, he'll interview you. The rest is easy. You're big news. On top of that embezzlement fiasco, Hiney's denying you. He's clinging to his throne, hoping it will die down, and he has good support, and his successor defends him loudly, but I must say, anti-Hiney priests are suddenly popping up.

"But how is that part of the story?"

"It's timed with the terrible tragedy at Yosemite."

"But they're two different things. I'm not sorry Heine is in trouble, but to combine it with me doesn't seem right."

"His denying you is another abuse. Don't you see?"

Yeah, but I didn't like it. Much as I despised the man, I didn't want to be dancing on his grave or anything. I wanted to be seen for who I was.

John called. "How about choir practice? Are you up for it?"

God, yes.

I wanted to pretend it was back to normal. No Kennedy. Well, no Rick or Meg either. We just practiced. And no one mentioned Meg or Rick.

I walked in Central Park. I tried to let my emotions catch up. I looked up other Episcopal churches. I thought I would try Grace Cathedral because I knew the choir director and I had heard Fleming Rutledge preach. I didn't always agree with her, but she had one powerful voice.

I would say farewell to Saint Philip's first.

As I walked up the aisle, heading for choir practice, a man kneeling at the altar, in a white alb, was standing up from prayer, and when he turned, he saw me.

"Welcome back. I'm Father Stephen."

He was short, thin, and had a nice smile. I approached tentatively.

"Nice to meet you," he said. "Welcome to Saint Philip's. How are you doing?"

"I'm doing."

"Pretty rough what you went through."

I sang in the choir to a church with barely twenty people in the pews. So many people had left. And after communion, John told me that he was taking another organist job at a church in Queens.

It certainly was time to go. And it certainly hurt to be here.

But just as I left, Father Stephen stopped me. "You're the parish representative to the diocesan convention."

"Me?"

"Everyone else is gone. You were the alternate in the last election."

I'd forgotten that.

"Really, I'd rather not."

"I understand," he said. "I know you'll be stared at. But what is your interest in continuing with the Episcopal church? Shouldn't you have a larger view of what's going on in the diocese before you decide? And what other churches are out there for you?"

He had a point, didn't he.

CHAPTER 52

Ijoined Stephen and his station wagon at the church. On the way to picking up other priests sharing the ride, he spoke familiarly and humbly.

"I'm in for the politics," he said, "and the justice. I want to marry my lover. He's a priest in New Jersey. We are working to make gay marriage legal in New Jersey. That's the fight. Heine isn't exactly on board, but so long as he's bishop, I need him to seem to be leaning toward my side."

"How did you get with us?" I asked.

"There weren't many applicants. Saint Philip's is a church in trouble, and everyone knows Heine doesn't like it. You guys screwed Kennedy, and Heine ranted about it. I applied because, frankly, I wanted a Manhattan church. He okayed me because he despises me but knows I'll be good and do as he says."

"Congratulations," I said.

He laughed.

"I know I'm lousy. I know I don't pay attention to things. No one wanted to come here. I'm a lousy preacher. But I'm a political animal when it comes to justice for gays. I have a lot of friends in the diocese. This may be an interesting convention. Heine isn't coming. Schick is presiding."

"Interesting name."

"What can I say. Heine is followed by Schick."

I had to giggle.

The ride to Poughkeepsie felt short because after Stephen picked up his pals, the three priests in the car gossiped all the way – nostalgia for Bishop Bulla, about Heine's affair, about Heine's influence in the church, about legalizing gay marriage. I gathered that, although many priests in New York City loathed Heine, conservatives north of the city considered him one of their own, and Schick was Heine's buddy. Heine had followed the liberal pal of the Kennedys, Bishop Bulla, and now they wanted their say.

I stared out the window and noticed gathering clouds. The trees along the way were blowing in one direction, the way they do before a storm. No one discussed liturgy, issues in dealing with parishioners, or even how hard it was to maintain church buildings. It was just gossipy politics.

Maybe a clap of thunder would help.

We had been assigned a motel near the conference resort hotel, and my room had a bed and that was about it. A phone sat on the floor, but there was a bathroom. For twenty-five a night. Stephen knocked on my door, and we four met back at the car and rode to the large resort hotel.

"They put the old guys and the retired priests in the big hotel," said Stephen. "I'm surprised we didn't get tents."

Men in black and women wearing light colored suits with collars filled the gleaming, too-much-marble lobby. Everyone wore a collar save for a few people plus me. Stephen introduced me to everyone we bumped into, and everyone seemed to stop to talk to him. He was eager, calm, happy.

Women hugged me. "I was so sorry to hear about your terrible experience. I worked with Rick on his hunger program. What a loss."

No one is just "sorry." Everyone is *so* sorry.

Others came to hug me and express their compassion, although one woman said, "He died in a place he loved," or something like that. I wanted to say that he died while crushing his head against centuries-old granite.

One priest stared at me.

"You were at the BACOM."

"Uh huh."

He shook my hand. "You were fine. Heine told us no way. You were upset, acted out. Understandable. Give it another year and try again."

I couldn't respond. Had he voted against me because Heine said no way? And acted out? I thought I had been the soul of restraint. Maybe that's what they were telling themselves, to justify their submission to the big boss.

Luckily, high drama at the door took attention away from the growing crowd around Stephen and me. Father Sully, a big rawboned priest, the rector of a big and formerly wealthy parish on Park Avenue, was yelling, "How dare they put me in a crummy motel! How dare they treat me like some common little priest?"

Sully pounced off, dragging his wife behind him.

We all headed into the convention room. Stephen, like a good boyfriend, found two good seats at the end of a row in the center and pointed people out to me.

It turned out Heine had decided to come after all. Schick introduced him.

Heine welcomed us and droned on for a bit about the diocese's success and problems and launched into an unoriginal theme about Jesus. I started to nod away until he said, "At the crucifixion, all hope ended." Then he went on. "Today, we look around us, trying to assimilate that into our…"

People in the hall started murmuring.

"Did he really say that?" Stephen was delighted. Others were laughing softly. I raised my hand and waved it. So did others. We got Heine's attention.

"I said what? Oh, no." He laughed and said, "I skipped a line. Hope seemed to end at the crucifixion, but…"

Then, like an editorial comment, right above our heads, an angry clap of thunder.

Heine ducked!

The lights went out.

I laughed. Someone ran out into the hall and then came back.

"The power's out all over the hotel!"

"Let's get to the bar," said Stephen.

"Why?"

"That's where everyone's going to go, and I want a good seat."

I followed him, and the mob of priests and deacons and representatives flowed in behind us. Stephen found a table for eight, waved at people, and those seats soon filled up.

"Janene, what do you want to drink?"

"A daiquiri?"

The cash register and credit card verifiers were not working. A few battery-powered lamps provided some light.

A waiter eventually came over. "The whole hotel is out. You wouldn't think that would happen with this crowd." We laughed. "Dinner will be interesting. I'll keep tabs for this table. Someone should sign for it."

I was the only woman at the table, and I listened to the chatter – in Mozartian parts -- about bishops and not-so-secret doings in churches. I wondered if I could venture a question.

"That priest accused of stealing..."

The howls that went up.

"She's Jim Leaf's sister! The actor! This poor kid was going to go quietly, but he was pissed as hell. He started telling the story to the press! She ends up on the *Today* show! Our bishop is in hot water. You'd think he would keep up with Broadway! Bulla may have had a secret sex life, but he was a man of the people..."

"Janene has a grudge against Heine," Stephen said. "For good reason."

"Do tell!" several said.

"Not here," I said.

Stephen said, "He turned her down for postulancy before the BACOM because she's from Saint Philip's. Because of Rick."

"You're kidding."

Stephen was suddenly telling these priests, hungry for gossip and lapping it up, all about my adventures at the BACOM.

"How did you hear all that?" I asked.

"I was talking to Fitz on the phone."

Whoever Fitz was.

I had to live over the story all over again, including all the details about my grades and GOEs, but Stephen had some revelations – that Heine thought the gays were having sex during our services and that Rick had had sex with Meg and ...me!

"Was it a menage e trois?" I heard someone whisper.

I shot my head up. "Not on your life."

Stephen added, "She was the one at Yosemite with Rick and his bride."

People gasped.

"The unnamed friend," said someone.

Stephen was babbling the story for all it was worth. Why was he doing this? He must expect something back from me.

I wiped my face, gulped my daiquiri.

Priests buzzed all around me, white collars, black suits. I had to get out of there. I stood up just as Bishop Schick, microphone in hand, called, "Some power has been restored to the auditorium. We have flashlights available. Please make your way over and we'll finish the meeting."

Thank you, God.

I was quivering and, in my mind, I saw Meg and Rick tumbling down, but I saw myself reach out, grab Meg's hand, and she – with her feet, clasped them around Rick's arm, and he scrambled, got a foothold and Meg grabbed hold of the rail, and they were saved.

But that didn't happen. I hadn't reached for Meg.

Several hands touched my arms. I was trembling. A black woman, a priest, wrapped her arms around me and said, "It's going to be all right. They are in God's hands, and so are you."

I couldn't figure out what was happening.

As we sat down, Stephen muttered to me, "I'm sorry, but we need something to pull us together. You're it."

"Pull you together? What do you mean?"

"We're going to get Heine. And his little dog, too."

What had I plummeted into?

Schick came forward and said a few prayers. I felt caught, confused, but also supported and wanted.

And perhaps used.

A deacon read the Gospel, the story of the woman who washed Jesus' feet with her tears whose sins Jesus forgave.

Heine stepped forward to give the sermon about forgiveness, hypocrisy if there ever was any, and in it, he laid out how the agenda for the meeting would work the next day. The microphone worked, thanks to a generator, and some lights too. I took notes, if only to keep my mind on business.

Then Heine offered a prayer for the meeting. "I ask for your petitions before God."

An arm shot up.

Stephen's arm.

Oh, no you don't.

Heine looked around, as if hoping someone else would volunteer. But someone came with a microphone and started to hand it to Stephen. I stood up and took it.

"No, wait," said Stephen.

I unraveled thoughts as I spoke. "Let us pray for the soul of our blessed late priest Richard Campbell and the Reverend Margaret Madigan, who died in an accident while hiking in Yosemite National Park. Rick, as we knew him, marched from Selma to Montgomery with the Reverend Martin Luther King, Jr, was Director of Banish World Hunger, spoke out against bias against women. He also walked the talk in preaching an inclusive Gospel in opening his church to all God's children, regardless of sexual preference, and in keeping his door open to those whose churches barred them from the last rites and funerals. Or to those whose churches belittled them because they were different."

And oh, what the heck.

"And let us pray for our Bishop Heine, who has let every process in our diocese become political. I know this, for I was told that I would not be approved for postulancy because I was in Rick's parish. Never mind the work I did in seminary or in church. Never mind me. God help Bishop Heine find the way to wisdom and let us pray for the churches who struggle with his guidance. Amen."

I sat down as murmured "Amens" fluttered through the hall.

Stephen said, "You should have let me do that."

Bishop Heine simply bowed his head.

The mic went to another priest who said, "Let us pray that we will not turn away anyone who crosses our threshold looking for Christ and healing. And let us pray that this church will not punish them for seeking Christ."

Several people rose to offer prayers for openness.

Finally, Heine said, "Glory to God, Amen."

He retreated to the wings, followed by Schick.

A few hands clapped me on the shoulder.

I wasn't sure I had done anything.

Well, perhaps declared war.

Walking into darkness. The dining room – we were told it was the dining room! – sheer darkness. Then, a headlight. Another. A table with food loaded on it appeared. It was mounted on generators. Someone handed me a platter.

"Is that roast beef?" It could have been roast dashboard.

When I had a full plate, I stood in a dark void, uncertain. A hand took my arm and a voice said, "You're at our table."

"Who are you?" I asked, hoping to sound as if I were joking. I got steered to a table where three priests and two lay people (judging by their collars, I'm afraid) sat. Someone pulled out a chair for me.

Stephen hopped over to a seat across from me, plopped a plate down, and hurried away again.

People – priests mostly, judging by the collars of course – stopped at our table to speak to…me.

"Welcome to our conference."

"I hear you starred on the GOEs. Nice going!"

"Norman Forrest mentioned you when I called him. He said you were quite the Biblical scholar."

That sounded patronizing, but then she said, "He described your ideas about Joshua and Judges. That would be a good talk at my church."

"Thank you."

Stephen wandered back.

"Hello, Tina darling!"

That dynamic priest swung back her hair, and I saw pearl earrings and one blue eye and one green eye. She winked at me.

"She's a gift!" she crowed, pointing to me. "You should know what she does with the book of Judith."

This was getting too weird.

Stephen said, "Janene, you have plenty of support. I'm telling people that you are giving the sermon at Saint Philip's in three weeks. We'll pack the house."

"And she knows the Resurrection happened," Tina sang out.

"We need to go after Heine in the college of bishops, so we'll need a few bishops to hear her and see what he turned down."

Ah, so that was what was going on. Getting rid of Heine.

Stephen said, "Janene, you're going to get ordained. Heine is going

271

to have to take you. Some of the Commission members are weakening in their support of him. You had sterling qualifications, and we're demonstrating you were a loyal friend, a loyal parishioner."

Stephen's people, I began to see, as I listened to the conversation, wanted Heine out so that a priest sympathetic to the gay community would be chosen. This campaign had many pieces, and I also suspected from what Stephen was saying, that he wanted to be the rector of Saint Philip's and make it the leading Episcopal parish for gay people. And that gay marriage should be approved in the state where he and his lover lived.

I certainly agreed with a more welcoming stand to everyone, and I knew that my refusal from Heine had nothing to do with me. Still, something about all of this made me feel uncomfortable.

I was being used again.

"You were cheated at the BACOM," said a priest I recognized. Oh, yes, the priest wearing the bright red skirt.

"You were one of the cheaters," I said.

She laughed. "Yeah. The idea was to give Heine what he wanted while we figured out a way to pin it against him. You know, pressuring us to vote against liberal candidates for the postulancy. And we'd have proof."

That gave me a headache.

The lights came on.

Everyone applauded.

I grabbed my wine.

Yes, I despised Heine. Yes, I despised how I had been cheated through no fault of mine. Yes, Rick and Meg had done me in, blinded to everything but each other. And they did love me, though they forgot it sometimes. They'd wanted to make amends. That's why they had come to Yosemite. Perhaps if they'd lived, they'd have tried to put us back together. Maybe we'd have parted enemies forever. I'd never know.

I got up for ice cream, and as I passed through the tables, priests and lay people smiled at me. Heine and his pals sat at a table nearest the ice cream.

I smiled at him.

He saw me. He turned away.

But when he talked to Schick, I saw him gesture towards me. He laughed. Schick laughed.

"What do you want?"

"Huh?"

I realized it was the ice cream guy.

"What do you have?"

"Vanilla, chocolate, mint chip…"

"Speak no more. Mint chip."

"There are three more kinds."

"Mint chip."

I realized that I felt more certain about ice cream than about my own future.

Taking my cup, I smiled at others in line and went slowly through the tables. Priests pointed me out. Or some looked at me and then looked away.

They were all using me, the way I had been used before – even loved by my users. Was this what ordination would be – just like the world outside – constant politics, constant juggling in place of who you were and what you believed? This sense of undeserved superiority because of the white collar around your neck? A sense of superiority toward lay people? I thought of the sexual abuses of children that had been uncovered in the Catholic church that always made me cry. It was the collar that had given those men the belief that they could do whatever they pleased to people.

For some reason I thought of the *Star Trek* episode, where Captain Kirk was captured and made a thrall, symbolized by a collar around his neck. And how, once freed, he had pulled that collar off with repugnance.

The priest's collar was supposed to say, I am ready to celebrate the Eucharist, to counsel you, to work in a parish with you, to help you when I can, to know the Bible as a way – a way to salvation as it says in the oath we take, but saving us from ourselves perhaps is a better way to put it than saving us from Hell. The collar was to be a signal to those needing help.

At Saint Philip's, there had been a real attempt at equalizing – Rick giving the liturgy to the people, assisting with his training and his experience. He had lent his pulpit not only to seminarians but to lay people. He had encouraged us to be active, to be thoughtful, and he had divorced us from politics, staying as much out of it as he could and could afford to given his age and reputation.

And, despite all her moods and mine, Meg and I had loved each other as friends. She and Rick had interrupted their lives, and I guess their honeymoon, to come to Yosemite and try to talk through my fears and suspicions. They could have left me alone.

In trying to help me, they had lost their lives.

I could not turn my back on that. Or on me.

CHAPTER 53

Outside, the rain had ended, but the wind was still strong.
"I'm sorry," I murmured to the sky.
I knew I was forgiven even as I forgave. I felt caressed, held, calm even as the wind blew the trees around the courtyard.

As I went back inside, Stephen waved at me. Everyone was going back to the auditorium. I went to join Stephen.

"Heine doesn't want to have a memorial for Rick."

"Poor fellow."

Stephen laughed. "We're going to get a petition to have them both removed. Once that happens, you'll be approved as a postulant. Shearing is the one who'd be selected, and she's on our side."

Whose side was I on?

I only smiled. No use doing anything without giving it some thought.

The assembly that evening was mindless. A few kids put on skits that had no point I could fathom, but we all applauded anyway. Then it was time to get back to our rooms – or the bar. I didn't go. I hitched a ride to the motel with Mother Lisa from the Bronx, who suggested I preach at her church. I muttered something about needing to know the congregation better.

"Sure. You should visit a few times. You can stay at my place."

She wanted to talk over hot chocolate, but I pleaded that I was tired, and she understood.

Sitting cross-legged on my bed, I took the phone and placed a collect call to Father Ben.

He didn't answer. I wasn't sure I wanted him to and hung up, but I did leave my name. I needed to get my thoughts together.

I slept well.

Stephen called in the morning.

To my surprise, a woman wearing a red blazer and a purple clergy shirt and a long black skirt came to me in the breakfast line.

Stephen did the introductions.

"Bishop Shearing, Jan. Janene, Bishop Shearing is the Suffragan Bishop of New York."

"I fear that is my title," the woman said, laughing. "Miss Shannon, would you start our conference off with prayer this morning?"

"Me?" I squeaked.

"You can use the Book of Common Prayer or make up anything you choose. You know, thank God for a good conversation, praise, safe travels, that sort of thing."

"But me?"

She just smiled.

It was politics. It was shoving me in Heine's face. Even as I felt angry at being used, I found myself warming to the idea. Could I show up both sides, pray to God for help for this insane group, and the world, and show my stuff?

I ate my eggs and ham, slurped my coffee, and retired to the empty auditorium where I quickly wrote and then rewrote a prayer on the back of my program. The priests and delegates started flowing in, and Stephen pulled me to the end of the second row. I ripped off my notes and squeezed them into my hand.

Bishop Heine took a seat at center stage and Schick joined him. They were both chuckling at some joke.

Bishop Shearing came to the podium and said, "The delegate from lower Manhattan, Janene Shannon, will lead us in prayer."

I saw Heine stare ahead. Schick found it amusing, it seemed, but he put his face straight quickly, and I could hear a murmur in the audience that quickly quieted as I climbed up to the stage and put my note on the podium.

I looked out at them.

"Good morning. Let us pray. O God of unchangeable power and eternal light: Look favorably upon those who gathered here in these last few days to improve the spiritual lives of your people and to nourish the life of your church. May we continue to work together in love and community. Let the whole world see and know that things which were cast down are being raised up, and things which had grown old are being made new. Forgive us our faults and our sins, as we forgive those who sin against us. May we leave this place and journey safely home and walk in love as Christ loved us and gave himself for us, an offering and sacrifice to God. Amen."

I heard a loud Amen.

I turned and bowed my head to Heine, who did not look at me. I extended my hand, feeling the hush in the audience. Heine still did not look at me but stuck out his hand, and I kissed his ring. Schick kept his hands to himself, but he gave me a noncommittal nod. Bishop Shearing let me kiss her ring, and she winked at me.

After an hour with finances, it was all over, and we were heading to the motel to grab our bags and check out when one of the lay delegates came up to Stephen and me and said, "That priest's lawsuit of Heine just became public. The *Times* has it. Heine's not long for this cathedral."

Stephen and the other priests were jubilant on the ride home. Schick would resign, too, and Shearing would be in charge, at least for a while they were sure, and they were sure, too, of a more positive attitude toward all people, including me as a postulant.

I silently wished for a barf bag.

At home, I found two messages from Father Ben. I called back and described the meeting and my mixed feelings.

"What do you want?" he asked.

As if I should know.

"I'm trying to separate my ego from my desire."

He laughed. "Tell you what. If you can wangle a month a year, we could use your help at Yosemite. Well, all year, to tell you the truth, but right now, just a month until I can beg for more funding. It's summer, and people are pouring in here. The job's whatever you make of it. Talking to people who need help, giving sermons, meditations, maybe a lecture or two on your feminist work..."

"My help? Are you kidding? I'm not ready for that."

"You're never ready until you do it. We're nondenominational, you know. I know you don't think much of us Catholics."

"Certain ones are nice. I don't think much of the Episcopalians lately, and I'm one of them. But I understand."

But could I go back?

Yosemite was the place of tragedy, but it could be the place where I faced down the tragedy and the feelings. Maybe.

"Room and board," he said helpfully. "And twelve dollars a day. It's not much, but it's more than they used to offer. Come out for a few days, and we can talk about it. The Lodge said you can have a week for free while you decide. How's that for impetus?"

"Can I roll it around in my head?"

"I have to know in three days."

Three days. Was that a joke?

"I'll have to check with my job."

"Let me know."

Could I return to Yosemite?

God knows I had to.

CHAPTER 54

Stephen called every night with news about how his and my causes were progressing. I soon became bored with his jubilation over Bishop Heine's now public shame.

Not that I minded Heine's humiliation, but it was not the greatest news to be shouting in newspapers and on television about the church. I also began feeling sorry for Alice Evans.

The little Community Church called me. Ruth!! How nice to hear from her.

"You've been in the news," she said, dryly.

I had to laugh.

Ben (he asked me to call him Ben) called again. He talked about the park, about the troubles people had. I was having second thoughts.

"My feelings are all over the place. I'm not sure."

I composed a short sermon about Judith for the Community Church. Their pews were filled. Afterwards, I led communion. They don't have any rules about who can consecrate, and I lifted up the bread and said, "This is my body."

The earth did not shake.

In two weeks, just two weeks, Heine and Schick resigned.

Bishop Shearing was temporarily in charge.

She immediately called me in after my workday.

"I am approving you for the postulancy," she said.

"I don't wish to be approved because of some knee-jerk political reaction."

"I don't. I base this decision on facts. You have a brilliant record; you wrote wonderful essays on the GOEs. I read them. You are articulate, sensitive, and you know your stuff. I called a few of your teachers. I even called Father Ben Poletti, your chaplain at Yosemite after that terrible tragedy. I am convinced that your gifts will enhance this church."

"Thank you."

I couldn't say anything else. Yes, I could.

"So, this is not just to slap Heine?"

"I'd love to slap him. But of course not. Several Commission members called me and suggested I do this. I consulted with a few others. I probably could get a majority vote for you."

"The same Commission that said no?"

"Not exactly. Several of them resigned. Some who didn't show up stayed on."

"Is that legal?"

Shearing laughed. "Come on, Janene. You're exceptionally well qualified, more so than all of the candidates who appeared at your BACOM. Stop being humble."

I wandered the Cathedral grounds, watched the peacocks, and sat on a bench.

Don't be a fool. Take the gifts coming down to you.

I called Yosemite and made a reservation at the Lodge.

I left a message with Ben. "I'll be there on Thursday."

He left a message saying, "Everything's going to be okay."

Charley let me off at short notice. "I have a feeling you'll be resigning soon. If you don't mind, we'll hire another writer. We'll figure it out."

The press called. I didn't call back.

Just before I left, as I was closing my carryon bag, the phone rang. I wanted it to be my father. I didn't pick up.

"Hi, this is Ellen Truman at Sophia Publishing. I read about you in the *Times* and wondered if you'd like to discuss your story with us as a possible book. Also, I was intrigued by your reference to Judith. Could we talk about that? We're a feminist press, and we publish books on spirituality, but you might want to publish a shorter piece in our journal. We'll talk."

I picked up the phone.

"Hi. I'm almost out the door and catching a plane, but I'd be happy to talk with you soon."

"Wonderful!"

I took her number.

"I didn't want you to think I wasn't interested."

"Come to see me. I'll call your machine and give you the information. Any morning between nine and eleven. Just let me know. We could have breakfast."

Judith. It seemed a long time ago that I had been so excited about her story, which had led to revels in the stacks at General Seminary's library.

Now, thinking about her again, I felt the same excitement. And the excitement caught up with all the things that whirled around me, all the possibilities.

This was who I was. Everything I wanted.

CHAPTER 55

It was June, but the falls in Yosemite were still active thanks to a heavy snowfall – I could hear the waters pouring down while I was on the bus.

The cliffs – the sky – the forests - I had to suppress my sobs. Are you really here, God?

Well, Father Ben and the chaplains were all there. I was embarrassed that I'd forgotten their names. We hugged and hugged. I checked into the lodge and hurried back to them. They were treating me to dinner at the Ahwahnee, the first-class hotel with a stellar restaurant just down the road in the valley. I wanted to kiss the huge fireplace, but Ben grabbed my hand. Possibly because I looked as if I were going to dive into it.

How lovely to meet them when I was feeling on top of the world, with possibilities firing at me. As I spoke with them, I began to calm down. Outside, Yosemite – eons old and patiently living through our times – began to infiltrate my soul.

"All this has been nice," I said, "but with regard to the church business, I'm still a pawn in their schemes."

Ben took my hand. "I'm glad to hear you say that. Your feet are both on the ground."

"They should get rid of him," said Patty, who lifted her fork up at the ceiling as if to stab the stupid bishop.

"I agree," I said. "But the church has not said it will. He's just moved, and they haven't decided where he will go. What does it take to shock the church?"

"It's quick to forgive its bishops and priests," said – what was his name – tall, ragged dark hair – yes, Danny, "but a mere mortal says he or she supports abortion or gay rights or women's rights and they don't want to give you Communion or the last rites. The Episcopals are more understanding in many regions but…still."

"What do you think you'll do?" asked MaryAnn.

"You're going to get ordained, right?" asked the guy from Germany. Fritz.

I shrugged. "I'm in for postulancy. It should be six years, but they are putting me on an accelerated path since I've done seminary and GOEs and field service. I'm just not sure. That conference threw me for a loop. Most of the delegates set me up as a cause. It wasn't me they were championing. I was just something they could use to bash Heine with. A lot of them admired Rick. If I get ordained, I shouldn't stay in New York. But being ordained isn't a goal. It's a way of life and a responsibility."

"You have excellent qualifications that will go anywhere," said Ben.

"And a conscience," said Danny.

"I confess I enjoyed the attention. I'm not happy I did."

"Why not be happy?" asked Ben.

"If I do this work here, the excitement about me will calm down. Heine is pushing back hard. There's no guarantee, even with all he's done – not just about me – he might well outlast this movement against him. The wheel turns. I hope not, but abuse of power is addictive -" I broke off. "Sorry. I almost forgot who I was talking to."

"We're not the church," said Ben. "What are your plans for tomorrow?"

"Wander a bit. Then go up the Mist Trail."

"Are you sure?" they all cried.

"Oh, yes."

"Alone?" cried Patty.

"I'm wrestling with angels."

"What time?" asked Ben.

"I want to be at the top of Vernal Falls by noon. I'll set out about eight thirty. Does that sound right? I might want to sit and watch the Merced."

"You'll have good weather," said Danny.

"The Falls is terribly powerful now. Do you have good shoes?"

"I don't think you should go alone," said Ben.

"There'll be other hikers. I'll just go up the steps. I'll go down on the Trail. There had better be signs."

We toasted with wine, and Ben changed the subject, describing the park in winter. Patty talked about cross country skiing in the Valley.

I thought, why not?

I spent a quiet night reading and joined the others in the night prayers. I didn't mind the prayers.

The birds woke me at dawn, and I helped MaryAnn with the pancakes. After breakfast, I took a walk to the lower Yosemite Falls and stood on the bridge, letting the spray wash over me. I took a deep breath, and I said, "Okay. God, you'll get me through this, won't you?"

Not that I expected an answer.

After collecting my small backpack, I took the shuttle to Happy Isles. It was hard not to remember that last time I had been climbing up to the sky. I had felt lonely then. They had hurt me. They had found love in each other and had used me as a red herring. I wasn't going to forget that. But they'd been sorry. I thought I'd been on the road to forgiving them, but I was still in Limbo.

I didn't stop climbing until I reached the bridge. I stopped briefly to watch the river charge down the Merced, rolling against granite rocks, sending up white spray. I went over to the bank, sat on a rock, and got a bottle of water out of my bag. I checked that the bread, the plastic cup, and the grape juice were intact. I intended to celebrate communion at the top of the falls.

Back up I went.

Being June, and with schools out, there were plenty of people on the walk up. There could have been a million people on that climb, and I would still be alone on this trek.

The morning was cool, just tiny clouds to the west, and the sun was beginning to grow warm. But not too. I still needed my sweater. Up I went, letting others pass me, everyone in pairs or packs.

I would always be alone, I realized. I didn't trust that I could be close to anyone. Church, I thought, was no place for a human being. Why had I wasted so many years of my life there? The parish, a joy, but beyond that…Hypocrisy, deliberate hurting, no mission, just politics. I was being elevated to hurt Heine. Wouldn't I be as bad as them if I let that happen? Or wasn't I being stupid not to grab the brass ring? After all, I was a good person.

The collar deceives us and others.

It should come with a warning sign.

I didn't want to feel bitter, but that's what I was feeling – bitter and alone. I had been happy. But that had been the happiness of the innocent. Still…a part of me felt that I could make some small difference. I could follow my heart. I did, I think, still have one.

I looked around at the simple, sheer, incredible wonder about me of cliffs, some topped with snow, of a terrifying grandeur that called and yet said, be careful. I am dangerous, I am strong, I am here for you, I love you. The cliffs touched the sky, and the waters poured down, touching the earth, giving us all we needed, giving us love, we in her womb.

She is the breath of the power of God, said Scripture.

Alone, more alone as I approached the falls and heard – along with the deafening roaring of the spray– the chatter of laughter of people sitting by the river – snacking, taking pictures, resting before the next climb. I realized I was nervous - my hands trembled as I took out my chicken sandwich. I sat on a rock and looked over at the falls. I winced. I could hear Rick's voice, Meg's laughter.

But you hurt me.

Get over it.

I can't.

If only we'd been able to talk about it, to shed the fury, the anger at selfishness, the sense of abandonment.

I was scared to climb. Judging from the sound of the Vernal Falls, those steps would be…

"Didn't you go up?" some kid was asking.

"Too slick," said a woman's voice. "Let's stop here before we go down."

All right. Too slick. I could reasonably go back and think that I'd tried.

I'd finished my sandwich. I'd eaten it way too fast.

Come on, woman. This is a debt you owe. You'll make it.

I stood up, swung my bag onto my back, and walked toward the steps. My legs trembled. Something called me stupid over and over as I started gasping. I kept walking, kept climbing, but my eyes were filling.

Look how beautiful this world is! Look out at the Valley!

A few teenagers passed me, hurrying to the steps. Following them, I climbed, shivering. The Falls, so beautiful a few moments ago, now showed a brutal face. Mist poured on the sides of the trail. I put on the grip gloves – why hadn't I thought of those before? Would they have helped?

Don't think. Just climb.

Steps. Hello. I remember you. There you are. I looked up and wished I hadn't. They looked more crooked than ever, and they were slick and wet.

Stupid! Go back!

People, laughing, passed me.

Fools.

My foot as Meg laughed.

Rick's howl. Meg's scream.

I climbed. The falls were strong, the steps were saturated, and I placed my foot down, held onto the side of the rock, and stepped up. Slowly. Again. Again. The spray beat against my face. Step up. You're fine. Step up.

Behind me, a man called out, "Everyone go slow. We'll get there."

Step up.

My feet took the steps firmly. Held tight to the damp granite.

Again.

Meg laughing at the idiot in Ministries class who ordered the universe so that women were just above dogs. Meg complaining about the patriarchal tone of the psychiatric exam she had to take as part of the process. Meg calling me up, we quizzing each other on Paul's epistles. Meg messing up when we rehearsed her first Eucharist. Meg and I singing with Marilyn Horne at the top of our lungs as we drove through the desert.

Step. Up. Hold. Again.

Rick laughing when he caught me ironing linens. Putting his hand on his heart after my first sermon. How moved he'd been when I passed my GOEs. His laughter. His energetic slicing of bread during our Lenten suppers. His hugging every parishioner at the end of the service. His circling with joy, arms out wide, at the beginning of the Mist Trail.

Step. Up. Step. Up. I grabbed at a rail. I was panting. I was near the spot, my heart told me. I stopped and leaned against the wall, the falls swooshing over me with a breeze.

Behind me, a woman laughed. "I could have skipped my shower this morning!"

It was wonderful to be caught up in this power. The force could throw me down, but I held the rail and my feet sloshed in little puddles and my gloved hands were cold and I was weeping.

I was coming to where it had happened.

Step. Up. Step. Up.

Meg slipped, struggled to get up. I bent over to help. My foot slipped and she slid into Rick and they both tumbled onto the rocks and were gone.

It was here.

I leaned against the rock. "I'm sorry!" I wailed.

"You okay?" called a woman.

I looked back.

"Are you scared? You're almost there."

She was young. She wore a solid slicker and heavy boots.

"You're almost there!" she yelled.

I shook the tears, wiped my face with my sleeve. My thighs ached.

I turned and looked over at the Falls, the waters pouring down, and I thought of Pharoah galloping through the Red Sea.

"I'm okay," I called.

I love you, Rick. I love you, Meg. I love you, Dad. I love you, Mom. You hurt me. I hurt you. Let's move on.

But could I do that?

I clung to the rock and stepped up. My notorious foot. Step. Up. Go. Move. You'll be fine. They were with me, forgiving me, helping me. Right there. I felt that so strongly that I was not surprised, as the steps turned, to feel the sun warm my body. Oh, guilt still poured through me. But it was mixed with a feeling I could only call gratitude.

How could that be?

"And when they grieved, they went and wandered and searched in the wilderness until it once again bloomed with life."

I had written that. And it was true.

The steps turned, dried out. I grabbed a rope – I had reached the top – just a few more steps.

There – my legs buckled, but there was Ben, and he grabbed my arms.

"Good morning!" he called over the waters.

"What – you're here?"

"We're all here."

CHAPTER 56

"**D**id you climb?"
"We came up the John Muir Trail. You're soaked! Come into the sun!"

He sat me on a bench. I took off my drenched sweater. The chaplains were congratulating me in a babble of voices.

A ranger came over. "Glad to see you, Miss." I recognized his voice. He was the one who had found me on the steps.

I couldn't speak.

I looked out over the mountains, the beautiful, treacherous cliffs. The sun was warm. I took a breath.

"There's something I want to do."

I stood up, tossed my sweater on the granite floor, and opened my bag.

"Communion," I said.

"Yes," said Ben. "I have wine. And cups."

"Well," I said. "How did you know?"

"We saw you snitching the bread!" called Patty.

MaryAnn spread a white cloth on the bench. We sat on the granite of Yosemite.

I looked at Ben.

He gestured toward me.

I nodded, gazed at the swirling, foaming waters and at the blue sky it tried to capture, and I remembered, and I said, "For none of us has life in herself, and none becomes her own master when she dies. For if we have life, we are alive in God, and if we die, we die in God. So, then, whether we live or die, we are God's."

I filled a cup of wine and began.

"On the night he was handed over to suffering and death, our Lord Jesus Christ took bread; and when he had given thanks to you, he broke it, and gave it to his disciples, and said, "'Take, eat: This is my Body, which is given for you. Do this for the remembrance of me.'"

We are bodies. We live to the best of our abilities. We fight to the best of our abilities. We remember. And we commend our spirits.

I set the little roll down.

"After supper he took the cup of wine, and when he had given thanks, he gave it to them, and said, 'Drink this, all of you. This is my Blood of the new Covenant, which is shed for you and for many for the forgiveness of sins. Whenever you drink it, do this for the remembrance of me.'"

We proclaimed, "Christ has died. Christ is risen. Christ will come again."

The sun felt warm, the sky broke – no clouds now.

I held up the bread.

"The body of Christ, the bread of heaven," and passed the plate.

"Amen," they said.

I lifted the plastic cup. "The Blood of Christ, the cup of salvation."

"Amen," they said.

They took a little in their cups.

I looked up. More people had gathered, curious, smiling.

Christ has died. Christ has risen. Christ will come again.

The feast of women and men, the feast welcoming all.

Come to me, and I will give you rest.

I packed up. We went over to the rail, to the powerful waters – nearly white with snow melt pouring down the cliffs, foam and spray flying up.

Somewhere, I thought, the spirits of Meg and Rick, still married, lingered here. Perhaps they whispered in my ear as the waters poured and roared.

Was this my imagination?

I remembered something Rick had said in a sermon. "Nothing becomes real without imagination."

As hokey as it seems, it is true. Creative God, Father and Mother, imagined us. Our bodies, our blood. And despite the pain we will feel, life is the gift of the most extraordinary Imagineer of all. Life – all of it – cannot be denied. We should fight to hold onto it, that in the midst of death, we refuse to give up life.

CHAPTER 57

Down we went on the John Muir trail, mostly down, sometimes cruelly up, but so beautiful among the ponderosas. We sang, we danced a little. The air felt clean.

Ben caught up to me – amazingly I'd been leading, with MaryAnn at my side. She backed away.

"What are you going to do?" he asked.

I shrugged. "I'm graduating in two weeks. Master of Divinity. What does that mean? I don't want to be in their trap."

"The collar doesn't have to trap you."

"I don't think it will, Ben. But I may have to quit a lot of jobs."

"I don't think it would trap you. But - want to work here?"

"You don't need me, and I don't know what I could do."

"I do need you. Patty is leaving in a week, so I have a year-round spot open. It's room and board and a small salary. Not too glamorous. It's services in the pines or somewhere in the Valley. During the summer, it's up in the meadows. We do counseling, some groups. You could do sermons already. But you'd need to learn something about the park so that you could be part of the rangers. As you move up in the process, you can participate in the services more and more."

"The process," I mocked.

"Even without it. Up here, things are a little looser. You have experience and a degree."

"Oh, please. Don't tempt me. I'm a bit of a rebel, you know."

"We have to be rebels up here. It's eight thousand, room and board, and you need to pick something you want to learn."

"Everything!" I laughed. "Oh, but I have so many books and so much stuff."

"We all do. We'll figure it out."

It was silly, impossible, ridiculous.

The pines wafted their breath into my ear.

"You can even get ordained here."

"I'll never wear a collar," I insisted. "Or need to. I'll report to you, not a bishop?"

"I report to a bishop," he laughed. "You don't really report to me. We all consult together. I just make sure things happen. You love this place. The rest? We'll figure it out."

"I don't know. It's all…"

"The bishops leave us alone. I just write a monthly report to them."

"Ben."

"Where will you go? What will you do? It's kinda cold in winter. But people die here, and we're needed for that, too. You could help."

My right foot kicked a pebble down the road.

I looked around – the cliffs, the pines, the rushing waters. *She* showed it all to us here, birth and death, and a place to listen to Her.

"I'd love to work with the rangers. And be able to translate what they teach into what people may need to hear."

"Good. You start next month. Summer is big here, of course."

That made me smile.

It seemed impossible, but the trees whispered, and I heard laughter all around me. Here She whispered and touched us. More than in any other place, I think. But still, the laughter was mixed with pain. With death.

As I looked into the woods, I saw a coyote sitting close to the road, seeming to be watching me.

I stopped.

"Yes," I said. "It's so wild that I have to say yes."

"She said yes!" Ben yelled back to the others. They cheered and surrounded me.

We sauntered down the road toward the valley. The breeze touched my face.

Our walk grew quiet, taking on an inner happiness that seemed tentative but hopeful.

The Valley called to me – its cliffs shining in reflected sunlight, the sky brilliant, the meadows a soft green, the woods and waterfalls singing in the wind. By now, even Vernal Falls seemed gentle as if to say I am really not so awful. Oh, it was, but if it took away, it also cleansed. God, I felt, might be like that, powerful and unknowable, loving and cleansing. Weren't we made in God's image? I would have to think about that.

I will challenge you.

MaryAnn tapped my arm. "I forgot. This was left behind."

She handed me a scarf.

Meg's scarf.

The secret love, the pain of secrecy, the too short happiness.

The river plunged past us, willingly or unwillingly taking from the Vernal's power. You'd be a fool to cross it. I glanced over to the other side. A coyote, again. My coyote? It sat when I looked at it, and she looked back.

I stooped and dipped my hands into the wild current sweeping over boulders, rushing down to the valley where it would become gentle, a caress, but volatile. I let my hand feel its power.

I wrapped Meg's scarf loosely about my neck, but no, it was not mine. It belonged to the love, to the pain, to the desperation of trying to live in a world that fought God tooth and nail.

The coyote was still looking at me. I sensed that she knew where I was going.

I let the scarf drop back into my hand.

"It's a magic scarf. It'll take you to your heart's desire if you take it to a sacred place."

I felt the presence of my new friends, my new life. I felt the spirit of my old friends, my fury, my fears. That was my collar. My mother, my father, my friends.

I lifted my hand, sipped the waters. They tasted cold, yet this was a cold of "come into the warm," a chill that cautioned, a growing warmth inside me before I swallowed and tasted its fresh life.

The coyote walked away, disappearing among boulders and trees.

I let the scarf slip into the water.

Let them be at peace.

I stood up, feeling whole, feeling myself, a child of power.

I watched the waters swirl, I watched the powerful stream wash against boulders, not stopping at the obstacles.

I watched those waters rush on to their destiny.

The Merced.

The river of mercy.

In grateful memory

www.ingramcontent.com/pod-product-compliance
Lightning Source LLC
Chambersburg PA
CBHW030346020726
47493CB00003B/711